Kerry Greenwood

MURDER in MONTPARNASSE

A Phryne Fisher Mystery

Constable • London

CONSTABLE

First published in Australia in 2002 by Allen & Unwin,
83 Alexander Street, Crows Nest, NSW 2065

This edition published in Great Britain in 2017 by Constable

13 5 7 9 10 8 6 4 2

Copyright © Kerry Greenwood, 2002

The moral right of the author has been asserted.

A CIP catalogue record for this book
is available from the British Library.

ISBN: 978-1-47212-669-6

Printed and bound in Great Britain by
CPI Group (UK) Ltd, Croydon CR0 4YY

Papers used by Constable are from well-managed forests
and other responsible sources

Constable
An imprint of
Little, Brown Book Group
Carmelite House
50 Victoria Embankment
London EC4Y 0DZ

An Hachette UK Company
www.hachette.co.uk

www.littlebrown.co.uk

TRANSWORLD PUBLISHERS
61–63 Uxbridge Road, London W5 5SA
www.penguin.co.uk

Transworld is part of the Penguin Random House group of companies
whose addresses can be found at global.penguinrandomhouse.com

Penguin
Random House
UK

First published in Great Britain in 2017 by Bantam Press
an imprint of Transworld Publishers
Corgi edition published 2018

A CIP catalogue record for this book
is available from the British Library.

ISBN 9780552173131

Typeset in 9.79/12.9pt Palatino by Jouve (UK), Milton Keynes.
Printed and bound by Clays Ltd, St Ives plc.

Penguin Random House is committed to a sustainable future
for our business, our readers and our planet. This book is made
from Forest Stewardship Council® certified paper.

MIX
Paper from
responsible sources
FSC® C018179

1 3 5 7 9 10 8 6 4 2

AL-BRITANNIA

A Journey through Muslim Britain

JAMES FERGUSSON

CORGI BOOKS

This book is dedicated to Dr Ruth Campbell, most excellent of historians—this is all your doing, you know . . .

And in loving memory of Cecil Murgatroyd, parfait joculator

With thanks to the cast of usual suspects and Alice B. Toklas, who did all the cooking while Gertrude did the writing. I would also like to thank Mark Pryor (wine expert), the immensely learned Stephen D'Arcy for the bal musette and especially Kay Rowan, local history librarian for the city of Bayside, for her exemplary organisation and patience.

CHAPTER ONE

The sun glared off the shop windows, the wind blew fine sand which stung the eyes. It was both chilly and sunny, a thoroughly uncomfortable combination only found in the less successful ski slopes and in Fitzroy Street, St Kilda on this particular day in 1928.

The Hon. Phryne Fisher blinked, wiped her eyes, wished she had brought sun goggles and wrapped her sables more closely about her thin frame. With her fur coat, fur hat and Russian leather boots she looked like one of the smaller members of the Tsar's guard who was about to lose his temper with a serf and resort to knouts.

She was cold, cross, half-blinded by the wind and just about to decide that she had chosen the wrong day or possibly planet for trying to understand St Kilda's street numbering system when she simultaneously found Café Anatole and a well-dressed male body left it, mainly through the window.

Phryne stood back courteously to allow the man to complete his swallow dive. He hit the pavement with a thud and lay still. Phryne was mentally balancing (1) the duty of every human to go to another's aid when they have been thrown through windows and (2) the danger of getting blood on her sinfully lavish and exceptionally expensive sables when the prostrate one rolled over, groaned a fair bit, then scrambled to his feet and stumbled away. This solved her problem.

And Café Anatole might easily prove more interesting than she had been led to believe. Bits of lettered glass crunched under her stacked leather heels as she opened the door and went in.

The letter had arrived the day before. Written in flawless, formal French, it had invited her to a special lunch at Café Anatole. It had been sent by Anatole Bertrand himself. Phryne had heard that his cuisine was remarkable and since the distance was not great, she had walked from her own house on the Esplanade.

A moment before she had been regretting the journey. Now, as a heavenly aroma stole over her senses, she would have walked twice as far, over a lot more than broken glass.

The scent took her straight back to Paris in 1918. Onion soup. Real French onion soup, made with cognac, with real gruyère cheese melted onto real baguette. As the slim, good-looking person in an apron tripped forward to greet her, she gave him a blissful smile which knocked him back on his heels.

'Miss Fisher,' she said.

'Mam'selle does us great honour,' said the waiter, taking her hat and coat. He saw a small woman with black hair cut in a cap, pale skin, bright green eyes and the most beautiful smile.

He sagged slightly under the weight of the coat, hung it carefully behind the bar, and conducted Phryne to a table set for one at the back of the café.

'The chef will be very sorry that such a scene greeted such a charming lady,' he said. Phryne waved a hand.

'Bring me a pastis,' she said, 'and we will say no more about it. Are other guests expected?'

'No, mam'selle, just yourself,' the waiter told her, beckoning to the girl behind the bar. Two men were already outside, fixing a tarpaulin over the broken window. In the kitchen, someone was roaring. Phryne recognised the voice of the bull chef in rut and nodded to the waiter that he could go. He grinned at her and fled.

The drink came in a moment and Phryne sat sipping and considering Café Anatole. It was as though some gourmet whirlwind had picked up a Parisian bistro and, tired by the journey to the Antipodes, dropped it carelessly in St Kilda, just before it ran out of land. There was the zinc counter with a saucy girl leaning on it. There was the row of stools for the passing trade. There was the mirror and in front of it an array of bottles, from Chartreuse to Armagnac. There were the little tables, each covered with a white cloth and over it white butcher's paper. There were the wrought iron chairs. There was the group of artists drawing on the paper and arguing about Modernism. There was a group of respectable bourgeois, a little affronted by the brouhaha, settling back to their lunch; a meal, it is well known, which must be eaten with a knife and fork. Everyone in the café was speaking French. She might be back in Montparnasse at Au Chien Qui Fume, talking to the trousered girls from the Latin Quarter, drinking pastis and smoking Gauloises.

She sniffed. Someone *was* smoking Gauloises. And someone else was shortly about to provide her with soupe à l'oignon, or something else concocted by a master chef. Bliss. Phryne settled down to enjoy herself.

She wasn't even beginning to be bored when the waiter brought her quenelles of pheasant in a delicate broth and poured her a glass of fragrant white wine.

'Is the chef not dining with me?' she asked in surprise.

'Desolated, mam'selle,' said the waiter. 'An emergency in the kitchen. He will join you for coffee.'

Phryne shrugged. The quenelles, little spoon shaped rissoles poached in broth, were superb. Presently, the waiter brought her poulet royale with French beans and poured her a glass of white wine. She ate slowly. Each mouthful burst upon the taste-buds with fresh savour—tarragon, perhaps, or was it parsley?

She heard a shout of despair from the kitchen, and a cry of 'Plus de crème!' Sauce must have curdled, she thought. The remedy for anything short of an outbreak of cholera in a French kitchen was 'Add more cream!'

Finally the waiter brought Phryne a tiny vanilla soufflé, a glass of cognac, a cup of coffee and M'sieur Anatole.

He was of the thin, stringy and miserable class of chef, weighing in at perhaps ten stone in a wet army greatcoat. His hair, far too glossy and black to be natural, was slicked back from a forehead wrinkled with years of concocting sauces béchamel, royale, crème and suprême. His eyes, of a pale grey, had been blasted by the heat from too many ovens and his hands had constructed far too many roux, garnitures and hors d'oeuvres.

Phryne rather preferred the fat, red-cheeked and jolly form of chef, but her excellent lunch had given her an attack of goodwill to all men, even one who resembled a shabby vulture who had just missed out on the last beakful of dead wildebeest. She held out her hand and M'sieur Anatole kissed it.

'Thank you for my delightful lunch,' she said. 'The quenelles were superb. The poulet royale could have been served to royalty, and your soufflé melted in the mouth.'

Phryne believed in the specific compliment. The vulture face softened.

'It is my pleasure,' he said, 'to please such a beautiful lady. Jean-Paul,' he ordered, 'another cognac.'

The waiter, who had clearly graduated magna cum laude from Cheeky French Waiter School, made a face which suggested that a chef who had dinners to cook ought not to be glugging down cognac at lunch, but he slapped down another glass and the bottle of cognac. He then flounced away, turning an ostentatious back.

'He is my sister's son,' said M'sieur Anatole. Phryne nodded. French cafés were usually family affairs. She wondered what had brought such an obvious Parisian so far from the centre of all civilisation and culture—Paris—and decided not to ask. Besides, she had still to ascertain why she had been invited to lunch.

'We have an acquaintance in common, mam'selle,' said the chef. 'M'sieur le Comte d'Aguillon.'

'Ah, yes,' said Phryne. Count d'Aguillon was an aged, exceptionally respectable member of the Alliance Française. Phryne had met him when helping to find the Spanish Ambassador's son's kitten. She had beguiled an hour discussing . . . now what was it? Modern art? Matisse? Something artistic.

'It was to him that I confided my problem, and he suggested that, for such a delicate matter . . .'

'That a feminine touch might be useful?' asked Phryne.

'Precisely.'

People were concluding their lunch and getting up. Jean-Paul rushed to the door to bow the clientele out. The chef leaned forward. Phryne could hardly hear him and she was unused to speaking this much French. She strained to hear.

'I came here from Paris after the war. It was hard then for a cook, though we rose to the challenge. Nothing to cook! No ingredients! It is said that during the siege of Paris the great Escoffier cooked elephant and even sea-lion as the animals in the zoo were killed. I would have welcomed a sea-lion entrecôte! Grey, sad city, my Paris after the war, and a ruined countryside. And my only son, lost. So I came here, as far as I could get from war. A barbarous country, but strangely innocent. In time the rest of my family followed me. My sister Berthe and her sons and my cousins Louis and Henri.'

M'sieur Anatole swallowed his cognac in one gulp and poured another.

Phryne murmured encouragement. Close to the chef, she could smell such a cocktail of scents, spices and herbs, which had obviously soaked into his very bones, that she was afraid she might sneeze.

'All went well. My little café has been successful with the French people here and with such of the Australians who appreciate fine food. We live well. My cousins found themselves Australian wives—they work hard, those Australian girls! That is my cousin Henri's wife behind the counter. A jolly girl, eh?'

'Very jolly,' agreed Phryne, wondering where this was leading and what, if any, connection this had to the gentleman who had exited so abruptly. The dark-haired young woman behind the counter caught Phryne's eye, winked, and hitched up her considerable bosom. The chef sighed.

'Such breasts! They are fortunate men.'

'M'sieur Anatole,' said Phryne gently, putting one hand on the white sleeve, 'what is this delicate matter? You may confide in me.'

'It began three months ago,' said the chef, looking more like a dispirited vulture than ever. Even his moustache drooped. 'Three men. They came to demand that I pay them, or some accident would happen to my café. Such things are common in the milieu, are they not? But this is not Paris. I was outraged and bade them begone.'

'And then,' Phryne guessed, trying to hurry the conversation along, 'accidents began to happen.'

'Yes. A fire was started in one of the rubbish bins. Jean-Paul found it and put it out before it spread. Then a brick through the window. Then—and this is where I became concerned— a whole block of butter was ruined with paint thinner. In my own kitchen! Someone must have come in to the kitchen when the door was open and . . . well. I called a council. We sat in here after the café was closed; Jean-Paul and Jean-Jacques, my sister's sons, my sister Berthe, my cousins and their wives. What were we to do? The criminals were not asking very much, we could afford to pay it, and that might preserve us from further sabotage. But they were all against this. So we bade them begone. There was peace for a week, then they came back today and we rejected their offer again.'

'Rather forcefully?' asked Phryne. 'And through the window?'

'Yes,' said M'sieur Anatole, gulping another cognac. 'Henri was enraged and he is very strong. Now there will be revenge.'

'Why on earth don't you go to the police?' asked Phryne.

'If we do that,' said the chef, 'they might kill us.'

'This is Australia,' said Phryne. 'We don't do things like that here.'

The chef shrugged. Jean-Paul slammed a pointed cup of coffee down in front of the patron and removed the bottle. This time his flounce would have registered about six on the Richter scale.

'Well, I suppose if you hire a few heavies and make sure that your café is always occupied, you might be all right,' said Phryne. 'But what has this got to do with me? Standover men are resistant to the feminine touch, patron.'

'Oh, no, mam'selle, no, that is not the problem I am asking you to give your consideration to,' said M'sieur Anatole, shocked. 'No. It is a matter of a lady.'

'A lady,' said Phryne.

'After my wife died, I did not wish to marry again. She was a saint, my Marie. But as the years go on, a man becomes lonely. I have a friend here, the first Australian friend I made. A man of taste and wealth, though no culture. His daughter seemed perfect. I discussed it with my family. They had objections. I overcame them. Then I discussed it with him. He was agreeable. Then . . .'

'Did you think of discussing it with the lady? She must have reached the age of discretion,' said Phryne.

'But no, I did not have a chance. The family agreed. The father agreed. I agreed. But the young lady . . .'

'The young lady?'

'Has disappeared,' said M'sieur Anatole, and burst into tears.

Phryne walked back to her own house in possession of all available information about Elizabeth Chambers and her father, company director and racing identity Hector Chambers, a slight headache incurred from drinking two glasses of wine and a glass of cognac at lunch, and considerable bemusement.

She could not forget the picture of poor M'sieur Anatole weeping into his moustache under the scornful gaze of Jean-Paul, who had taken him back into the kitchen to mop him up. It was all very sad. She wondered how Elizabeth Chambers, aged eighteen, had felt about being married off to an elderly Frenchman who dyed his hair. If the girl had fled to Cairns, it was explicable. And which collection of standover men was targeting Café Anatole? Detective Inspector Jack Robinson, her old friend, would know, but she did not feel she could approach him yet. Perhaps Anatole's family could defend their own café without police help.

Phryne walked briskly up her own path and was admitted by her own housekeeper, Mrs Butler. She seemed agitated.

'Oh, Miss Phryne, I'm so glad you're back. Mr Bert and Mr Cec have brought a friend of theirs to see you.'

'Just what I need,' muttered Phryne ungraciously. She shucked the coat and hat and went into the parlour.

There she saw a bright fire, the short dark Bert and the tall blond Cec, wharfies and taxi drivers for hire, and a sad man holding his hat in his hands. He seemed intent on tearing off the brim.

'We got a problem,' said Bert.

'Too right,' echoed Cec.

'Then let's sit down. Mrs Butler will bring us some tea, and you can tell me all about it,' said Phryne, as politely as she could manage. She could not take off her boots without her maid Dot and a shoehorn, and her feet were hurting.

Bert put the sad man into a chair. He had still not raised his eyes from his hat.

'This is our old mate Johnnie Bedlow. Been with us through Gallipoli and then bloody Pozières,' said Bert, not even apologising for swearing in a lady's parlour. He was clearly upset. So, probably, was Cec, but it was always hard to tell with Cec, who preserved the imperturbability of a granite statue in his ordinary dealings with life. Johnnie Bedlow was still mauling his unfortunate hat.

'Hello,' said Phryne. 'I'm Phryne Fisher.'

Johnnie Bedlow raised his eyes for a moment, murmured something, and looked away again.

'There was five of 'em,' said Bert. 'Old mates. Old diggers. Seven with me and Cec. We get together every year about this time to have a yarn and a few drinks.'

'Yes,' said Phryne. What was making Bert so furious?

'Two of 'em are dead,' said Bert.

'Yes,' said Phryne, encouragingly.

'And there's something wrong with the way they died. Come on, Johnnie. You tell the lady.'

'First there was Maccie. He'd gone out to one of them soldier settler schemes. Growing oranges up on the Murray. Found drowned in an irrigation ditch. Coroner said he was drunk. But what about them black bruises on his shoulder blades? What about them, eh? And Maccie never drank much.'

'Too right,' said Cec.

Johnnie Bedlow, once launched on his topic, was shaking with fury, red-faced. The hat tore under his fingers and his voice was loud and ragged.

'Then there was Conger. Supposed to have been fixing his van and it fell on him. But there was nothing wrong with the jack. No one tested it for fingerprints. No one wondered why he ought to be fixing his van in the dark. Inquest said "accident". Accident? Hah!'

'You think that someone's been killing your old mates?' said Phryne. 'Why would they do that?'

'I'd think it might be a coincidence,' said Bert, 'but for the car which knocked old Johnnie right off the pavement and into your front fence. We got a murderer, all right—and you're going to find out who it is. And then,' he added through gritted teeth, 'I'm gonna talk to him about it.'

'Too right,' said Cec.

'Oh,' said Phryne.

CHAPTER TWO

'Mrs Butler!' called Phryne. 'Forget the tea. This calls for beer. Sit down, Bert, do. Now, tell me all.'

She took from her bureau a new, sea-green notebook, found a fountain pen, and sat down, prepared to listen. Ordinarily, nothing discomposed Bert and Cec. They had been through wars, shipwrecks, gang fights and riots without turning a hair. Now they were concerned, even angry. This was serious.

Phryne's parlour furniture was too fragile for outbreaks of insensate rage. This needed to be handled carefully. Beer was distributed and the first schooner went down without touching the sides. Glasses were refilled.

'Names,' suggested Phryne.

'You know Cec and me,' said Bert. 'This is our old mate Johnnie Bedlow. Got a garage in Fitzroy, he's a mechanic.

Tom MacKenzie is dead. So is Alan Eeles—we called him Conger. The others are Billo, William Gavin, and Thommo, Thomas Guilfoyle. Billo's a fisherman, lives down the coast, Queenscliff way, and Thommo's got a building business in Footscray.'

'And you always meet once a year, around this time?'

'Yair,' said Bert. 'It's the anniversary of . . . of a good time we had. When the war finished.'

Phryne raised an eyebrow.

'In Paris,' Bert explained.

Phryne nodded. She understood what sort of a good time seven young men could have had in Paris after the liberation. She had, in fact, been in Paris herself after her ambulance unit had disbanded. The scent of acorn coffee and the sound of the bal musette drifted back into her mind.

'Billo and Thommo will be on their way,' said Bert. 'They'll arrive later today. We'll meet the country train.'

'Good. I'll ask my friend Detective Inspector Robinson to get me the coroner's reports on those two deaths. We need, I think, to all sit down together and go through everything— almost everything—that you seven have done together.'

'Why?' asked Bert.

'Because if you are all in danger, as you think, then the murderer must be trying to eliminate a witness, right? And if he is after all of you, then it must be something you all know or you have all seen.'

'Or that's what he thinks, the bastard,' said Johnnie Bedlow unexpectedly.

'Exactly. Do you want to stay here, Bert? We can put up the shutters and sit a siege.'

'Nah. We're on our guard now. Johnnie's staying with Cec and me. We'll pick up Billo and Thommo as soon as we can and all go back to our place. We'll be all right. But we need to know,' said Bert fiercely.

'Then we shall find out,' said Phryne.

Johnnie Bedlow stared at her for a long moment. Then he sighed.

'All right,' he said.

Phryne saw her visitors out. She shut the door. She sank into a chair.

'Dot,' she called, 'For pity's sake, come and help me take off these boots!'

It took Dot all her strength and the use of a long shoehorn to get the Russian boots to relinquish their suckerlike grasp on Miss Phryne's calves. When they finally came free with an audible 'pop', Dot sat down on the carpet, clutching a boot to her cardiganned bosom. Phryne wriggled her freed toes luxuriously.

'Oh, that is a whole world of improvement,' she said, hauling Dot to her feet. 'Thank you. I've had a very strange afternoon, Dot dear. Have a seat and I'll tell you about it.'

'I saw Mr Bert and Mr Cec,' said Dot. She was a plain young woman with long brown hair, firmly confined in a plait, and a milkmaid complexion. She was wearing her favourite dark brown woollen dress with a terracotta woolly and a worried expression. Dot always worried about Phryne. There had been raised male voices in the refined parlour, and Dot didn't like it one bit. Raised male voices, in Dot's experience, preceded raised male fists. And then Miss Phryne might have to hurt someone.

'They think that someone is murdering a group of their friends,' said Phryne. 'Has already murdered two of them and is intending to collect the whole set. I need to ring Jack

Robinson. I don't know if there is anything in it, Dot dear, but it is never wise to gainsay men who have such a lot of experience with firearms and who appear convinced of the correctness of their theory.'

'No, they might go crook,' agreed Dot.

'And also I have met Monsieur Anatole, a superb French cook—we must dine there, Dot, it is the most wonderful food—and he has lost the girl he was going to marry.'

'How did he lose her?' asked Dot, wincing at the idea of being dragged along to a place full of foreign smells and tricked-up foreign food. There might even be—horrors—garlic. And Miss Phryne would make her eat it. 'Did she die?'

'I hope not, Dot dear. Here's her picture.'

They both considered the postcard sized photograph. It was of a plain young woman. Her mouth was too wide for beauty, her forehead too high, her eyes too small, her nose too beaky, her jaw too determined. She was staring straight at the camera and frowning.

'Bad temper?' asked Phryne.

'More as if she doesn't like having her picture taken,' said Dot. 'She hasn't got the crease between the brows that means bad temper. I reckon she knows she's not beautiful and she doesn't want to be photographed.'

'This is an expensive studio,' said Phryne, looking at the back of the picture. 'Mostly they can coax and flatter a subject into compliance. And they couldn't even get Miss Elizabeth Chambers to smile. That argues a strong will.'

'Yes,' agreed Dot. 'I reckon she's a redhead, Miss. Look at how pale her skin is.'

'You're right. My notes say that she has blue eyes and beautiful auburn hair, feuilles mortes, dead leaves. Her only beauty, apparently.'

'Except for a clear conscience,' said Dot sententiously. She disapproved of this modern cult of the body. It smacked too much of the world, the flesh and the devil. 'And maybe a sense of duty.'

'Yet she has vanished,' said Phryne. 'Just when her father was concluding arrangements for her to marry an excellent French cook of good character and perhaps fifty summers.'

'How old is this girl?' asked Dot.

'Eighteen, almost nineteen,' said Phryne evenly.

'Then she had a reason to run away,' said Dot. 'What sort of man is her father?'

'A company director and prominent racing identity,' said Phryne.

'A crook,' decided Dot.

'Yes, probably. I still don't precisely understand why Monsieur Anatole wished to marry her, or why her father agreed. Something odd there, Dot dear. There are, I should imagine, plenty of women of the right age who would appreciate Monsieur Anatole's heavenly cooking and overlook his age and his moustache.'

'A moustache!' Dot shuddered.

'Yes. One of those droopy ones. This needs looking into, Dot. Nasty things can happen to young women astray in the world without guidance.'

Dot thought of her own distressing career as a housemaid, working her fingers to the bone while fighting off the young men of the household, and sighed in agreement.

While Phryne frequently caused her anxiety, she was no threat to Dot's virtue, only her nerves.

'But you were all right,' said Dot. 'You said you joined an all-women ambulance brigade in France during the Great War when you were only seventeen.'

'So I did, but I was lucky. I grew up in Collingwood. One learns a certain savoir-faire and a lot of ways of surviving with that kind of background. But this young woman went straight from home to boarding school and straight from boarding school to finishing school and then back home and what she knows of the world you could put on a stamp with a lot of room left over. She's always been looked after and she's always been supervised. There has always been someone to tell her what to do and there have always been rewards for obeying the rules. She has, in point of fact, always done what someone told her, and that, in the everyday world, gives her the survival quotient of a snowflake in hell.'

Dot thought about it. She nodded.

'We have to find her,' she said.

'Once we have done that, we don't have to send her back to her father,' Phryne commented. 'We can probably extort a living allowance for her from Daddy.'

'How? He wants her to marry this old Frenchman.'

'Prominent racing identities always have a few secrets, Dot dear,' said Phryne. 'And I bet Elizabeth knows them. On the darker side of this disappearance, Dot, there is the possibility that her father has disposed of her for that very reason. He hasn't made any effort to find her. It is Monsieur Anatole who is concerned about her. I gather that her mother is dead, so there may be no one to wonder where the poor girl is if Daddy has buried her under the stables.'

'Don't say things like that, Miss,' Dot complained, hugging her cardigan closer.

'All right,' said Phryne kindly. 'We'll treat it as a disappearance. Monsieur Anatole is no oil painting, I admit. Now, get out the society papers, Dot dear, and let's see what we can find out about Hector Chambers. If he's that rich and famous, he ought to be in *Society Spice* or *Table Talk*. You can take *Table Talk*.'

Dot hauled a bundle of the well-produced, respectable *Table Talk* out from its box, and Phryne began to flick through the grubby, low-class, frequently closed-down *Society Spice*, in which she herself occasionally figured as 'High Class Girl Dick', to her great delight. The only thing which mitigated against pure enjoyment of *Society Spice* was the bad quality of the paper, which flaked and tore and refused to separate into pages. Perhaps due to its peripatetic existence, the typefaces were rarely the same two issues running, and if it had ever employed a proofreader, he had retired in tears after the first day and could never bring himself to go back. Divorces and maids' evidence flitted under Phryne's regard: thefts and nameless assaults and—aha! Horse racing news.

'I've got something, Dot. From Old Jock, their racing correspondent. "Jaunty Lad, owned by well-known identity Hector C, disqualified from the Ballarat Cup for boring. Jockey states that he was instructed to ride unsafely by the owner . . ." Hmm. This seems to insinuate that other horses in the race were doped. Clearly a wide field for criminal activities. And, yes, here we are, I knew I'd seen something. Here is an accusation of substitution. Jaunty Lad was absent from his stables when Jolly Tom won the sixth . . . Interesting. Not one of our most honest citizens, this Chambers. What have you got in *Table Talk*?'

'Here's a photo,' said Dot, marking another place with a hairpin. Phryne looked over her shoulder.

A smallish man with the lined face of someone who spent a lot of time in the open air; perhaps small enough to be an ex-jockey. He was elaborately dressed in full evening costume, complete with top hat, which almost doubled his height.

He was standing in the midst of a group of society persons at a garden party. 'Mr Hector Chambers shares a glass of wine with Mr and Mrs Thomas Chivers and their daughter Julia at the Garden Party in Aid of Distressed Jockeys.'

'How does he strike you, Dot?'

'Mean as a rat,' said Dot unhesitatingly.

'I have never really trusted appearances, you know, but you are good at faces, Dot dear. Do we know anything about Miss Chambers' mother?'

'Died last year,' said Dot promptly. 'I remember the funeral. Very posh. The young woman wasn't here at the time.'

'Cause of death?'

'Don't know. She wasn't that old.'

'Wheels within wheels. Let's put these back and I'll call Jack Robinson. Where's Mr Butler?'

'Taken the car for a service, Miss, you remember. You said it was running a bit rough.'

'Of course. Well, I am going to occupy myself unexceptionably for the rest of the day. I really shouldn't drink wine at lunch. Break out the aspirin, Dot dear, and sling me the rest of our *Society Spice* collection. I suppose you could call it research.'

Dot did as she was requested and went off to struggle with the telephone. Dot appreciated the usefulness of the instrument, but could never really convince herself that flames and lightning bolts were not going to shoot out of the receiver one day.

The return of Mr Butler coincided with the post, which he brought in on a silver salver. Mr Butler was pleased by subtle nuances and Miss Fisher had bought the salver especially for him. She took the paper knife and cut envelopes.

'Bills, bills, more bills, aha! Invitation to the Lord Mayor's Ball, how nice. And to supper afterwards. I'll think about it. How's the car running now?'

'Purrs like a tiger,' said Mr Butler. He doted on Miss Fisher's Hispano-Suiza and had hung over it as anxiously as a mother while the mechanic had tuned the engine.

'Good. Detective Inspector Robinson will probably join us for dinner, Mr B. Now I'm going to have a little nap. It's been a fatiguing afternoon.'

Mr Butler nodded, mended the fire, and took the mail away. Phryne shut her eyes. Paris, 1918. How had Phryne entered Paris at the end of the Great War?

On the back of an army truck with a lot of convalescent poilus, she recalled. At the end of a dark, tiring, bitterly cold winter's day in early December. Her ambulance unit had been paid off, the girls had gone to other units, and Phryne was going back to Paris, eighteen years old and so tired she could hardly remember her name.

She had left her school in June, hitched a ride on a freighter to Boulogne and joined an all-women ambulance unit attached to the French Army. She had thought herself cool, efficient and proof against shock. She had found out, as the first shell burst, that she was not cool. At the end of the first fifteen-hour day tending the wounded, she had dropped a retractor and been unable to convince her fingers to pick it up—not efficient. And bathed in blood, collecting amputated limbs for burial, she discovered that she was not proof against shock.

But she had persisted. Gradually her frozen horror thawed. She had learned to drive and steered her clumsy, jerky, heavy ambulance over rutted roads and around shell-holes under fire, and thrilled to the danger. Once, dragging the moaning wounded out from half-burial in mud, she had been clipped by a stray shell fragment. Streaming blood from the head wound, she had completed the rescue before she gave gently at the knees.

A week's leave and she was back again, a decorated French heroine. Mademoiselle the Honourable Phryne Fisher, Médaille d'Honneur. The scar did not show under her close-cut black hair. She was as thin as a knife blade, and as sharp, after months of heavy, demanding, dangerous work, stronger than she had ever been, but almost exhausted by the time she took her last load of recovering southern boys into the city and was set down, at her request, outside the Hôtel Magnifique.

She clambered up the steps, shucked her knapsack at the counter and leaned on it, momentarily dizzy.

'Bonjour, m'sieur,' said the clerk, disapproval in every syllable. The Magnifique did not approve of grimy, bone-thin tramps soiling its marble and gold foyer.

The figure raised its head. Cold green eyes, red-rimmed, stared into his. He jumped.

'Madame,' he corrected. The face was female. Now he looked properly, so was the hair, cut in a cap. And the clerk, who had been a stranger to every human emotion through four long years of war, found that he had one left. Fear.

'Mademoiselle Phryne Fisher,' said the woman. She handed over an identity card and passport. 'My father has an account. I want a suite, private bath, some toiletries—let Madame la Concierge attend me. At once.'

The tone of voice suggested that there was no possibility he might demur, and he didn't. He knew the name of mademoiselle's father. Milord was a frequent visitor in times of peace, and the Magnifique wanted him to return, dripping with new crisp pound notes. This must be the eldest daughter . . . by her passport, just eighteen. She looked forty.

'At once,' stammered the clerk. 'We have a nice suite, Mademoiselle Fisher. Has mademoiselle any baggage?'

'Not yet,' said Phryne.

Then it was easy. Phryne fell into the calm pool which was the Magnifique and was carried along. First the lift to the suite on the second floor, the plush carpet and the private bathroom. The attendance of Madame la Concierge, the order for Guerlain soap, perfume, powder and suitable cosmetics.

Madame was concluding her list when she caught sight of the medal pinned to Phryne's ambulance tunic, tossed among her other garments on the floor. 'Mademoiselle was with an ambulance unit?' she asked.

Phryne, sitting on a chair by the window drinking hot chocolate as though it was nectar, nodded.

'La Toupie?' asked Madame la Concierge, naming the eccentric head of her unit. Phryne nodded again. Madame swept the guest into a close embrace. Phryne was beyond surprise. Madame smelt sweetly of orange blossom water and starch.

'You rescued my grandson,' she explained. 'What do you need other than these? I would be of service to you.'

'Some clothes,' said Phryne. 'What was your grandson's name?'

'Pierre Valcluse.'

'I remember him,' said Phryne. 'He was on the truck today. Very soon you should see him.'

And I hope you can cope with it, she thought. He's only got one arm now. Still, he's alive, which is more than one could say for the others in that trench.

'Bon. I will send my friend to you and she will make you some clothes. For tonight I will lend you some. This order will be here as soon as possible.'

'Good,' said Phryne. 'I have been thinking about this bath for six months.'

'It will be memorable,' promised Madame la Concierge, and left.

Phryne stared at the view. Paris looked the same. Dirtier, perhaps, grimy with smoke, noisy with soldiers. But the roofs were the same, all those little lives carried on underneath them, washing still drying on precarious lines between windows. Paris was Paris. She felt comforted.

Madame la Concierge returned with a basket of toiletries and ran Phryne's bath. It *was* memorable. It took considerable scrubbing to remove the patina of grime, gunsmoke, trench miasma and ingrained disinfectant from Miss Fisher's person. Even after the bath had been emptied and refilled, her feet were still giving Madame la Concierge pause and her finger-nails were beyond repair. She was also far too thin. The clerk had shown Madame the passport photo and *that* Phryne Fisher must have weighed a good seven kilos more than this one. Well, the war was over. The young woman could rest, drink chocolate, and regain some female curves. The young were very resilient. This one had mistreated her body and seen far too many horrors. Her eyes were haunted.

On her own responsibility, Madame ordered a strengthening dinner and a whole bottle of good Côte du Rhône. A robust southern wine, full of sunshine.

Phryne had found herself dried, slicked with a variety of unguents, inserted into a voluminous nightdress and tucked into bed. It felt so good to be warm, tended and clean that she burst into tears once Madame had left the room, promising dinner in due course and a dressmaker in the morning.

Phryne Fisher, 1928, looked back on Phryne Fisher, 1918, and marvelled at how young she had been, how tired, how fragile, how unwise. And how lucky. She still had one of the dresses Madame's friend had made for her, and she still remembered how safe she had felt, snug in her flannel nightie in the steam-heated shelter of that hotel, knowing how cold and dangerous the world outside could be.

Phryne shivered and got up. The memory of Paris seemed very close and somehow threatening.

'Dot? How are you going with *Table Talk*?' she called.

'I looked in,' said Dot from the doorway, but you seemed to be asleep. I've found another bit of news. I went back to when the wife died. Suddenly, it says, of a heart attack. She was only thirty-five.'

'And the gossip columnist in *Society Spice*,' replied Phryne, trying to shake off her dream, 'suggests that he is intending to marry again. "Hector C wants Julia C to change her name but not her initial." You don't think that could be Julia Chivers, do you?'

'She doesn't look more than eighteen,' said Dot, scandalised.

'The same age as Elizabeth,' said Phryne. 'There might be more than one explanation for why Elizabeth Chambers ran away, Dot dear. That would be an uncomfortable situation, a stepmother of the same age.'

'But he's practically a dwarf!' objected Dot. 'And fifty if he's a day!'

'He's rich,' said Phryne. 'Wealth can add inches to one's height. And I've known some very civilised dwarves. Perhaps he's a nice man, Dot.'

Dot looked at the picture again. Mr Hector Chambers smirked into the lens, pot-bellied, double-chinned, thin-mouthed and narrow-eyed.

'No,' said Dot. 'I don't think so, Miss Phryne. Not a nice man.'

The prisoner woke and opened her eyes. She was secured to the bedposts by her wrists and ankles. There was matted blood on the side of her head where he had struck her, and it itched as it dried.

She did not scream.

CHAPTER THREE

Mr Butler announced Detective Inspector Robinson at seven, just in time for a pre-dinner cocktail (though he usually preferred sherry), and Phryne watched him sit down in her sea-green parlour with her usual pleasure in his company.

Even Phryne, who had a good memory for faces, found it hard to recall his face if she looked away from him. Mid-brown hair, mid-brown eyes, standard number of features, middle height, middle weight. He might have been anyone, a fact which he had found useful in a career in which not being noticed could save your life, or at least spare you a belting. He stretched his legs and sighed. He knew that he was in for the usual Phryne interrogation, but he also knew that as a reward he would get an excellent Spanish sherry and a superb dinner.

'M'wife's in the country with her sister,' he said, accepting a small glass of Amontillado. 'New baby. So I'm back to my bachelor days and I was never very good at catering. Still, with a tin of beans and some toast you've always got dinner,' he said cheerfully, causing Mr Butler to shudder slightly.

'We can manage something better than that, Jack dear,' said Phryne, sipping her cocktail. 'Now, would you like your interrogation before dinner or after?'

'Before,' he said. 'As soon as I've had this sherry.'

He sat sipping nervously, eyeing Phryne as though he had never seen her before. He exhibited, in short, all the hallmarks of a Man Grappling With An Ethical Dilemma. Phryne decided to sit him out. At last he spoke.

'Got a favour to ask,' said Jack bashfully.

'Ask,' said Phryne.

'My missus . . .'

'Yes?' said Phryne encouragingly. Was the estimable Robinson about to confess to adultery? Surely not.

'She's always wanted to . . .'

He stuck again. Phryne gestured to Mr Butler to refill his glass.

'Well, you see, she knows that I often work with you, and she knows that you're one of the nobs, and she wondered . . .' He was actually writhing. He was, she reflected, an extremely honest policeman and this looked too much like bribery. What was he going to ask for?

'Spit it out, Jack dear. Even unto half my kingdom. What can I do for the worthy and charming Mrs Robinson?'

'I mean, I'd pay for them and all. But you have to be asked. Invited. Tickets to the Lord Mayor's Ball,' said Robinson, very fast.

'And supper afterwards?'

'I don't know,' he confessed. 'Is that usual?'

'If you're a nob,' said Phryne affectionately. 'I'll telephone the Mayor tomorrow. Anything else?'

'No. Rosie will be so pleased. She's always wanted to go to the Lord Mayor's Ball. You're sure you can do this?'

'Oh, yes,' said Phryne, who was sure. The Lord Mayor had been attempting to get her to go to the ball for some time. A couple of extra tickets would be cheap at the price in return for Miss Fisher's presence. She could suffer a few hours of having her toes trodden on by St Kilda's Best and Brightest— a small return for Jack's friendship and help. 'The invitations shall be delivered in the next couple of days. Was that all, Jack?'

'Quite enough,' said Robinson, who felt that he was walking a perilous line on the edge of peculation. 'Now, what can I do for you?'

Phryne told him about the two dead soldiers.

'I can get the inquest reports easy enough, but they probably won't tell us much. Did they get the number of the car that attempted to run them down?'

'No, they were trying to extract their friend from my hedge. I can't judge whether this is a real case or not, but Bert and Cec think it is and they are not prone to panic.'

'No, they ain't.' Robinson did not approve of red-raggers, but Bert and Cec had been in some tight places and seemed stable enough. Besides, they were diggers, and Gallipoli diggers at that. Any small tendency to diffidence or anxiety they may have had would have been burned out of them on those hot cliffs.

'Then there is the disappearance of Elizabeth Chambers.'

She explained again.

'She's over eighteen, still a minor though,' he said, shaking his head. 'Can't do much. Most runaway girls come back after a year or so with a husband . . . or a baby . . . or both, sometimes. I can put out the word to the Vice chaps and make sure she isn't in a "house". Not much I can do about the other states, though. I can ask,' he said dubiously.

'Also, was there any investigation into the death of Miss Chambers' mother?' asked Phryne. 'Died young and unexpectedly.'

'If there was an inquest there'll be a record. Someone must have signed a certificate. I'll look into it.'

'Good.'

'Anything more?' asked Robinson, who could smell savoury scents drifting in from the dining room. He personally never wanted to look a baked bean in its good, nourishing face again.

'A funny thing, possibly nothing. Standover men in Fitzroy Street. Sabotage in the form of a burning rubbish bin and paint thinners in the butter. One was thrown through a window this morning. Anything leap to mind about them?'

'I know a bloke who'd know,' said Robinson, trying not to drool. 'And I used to be on that beat myself when I was a youngster. I'll inquire.'

'Very confidentially,' warned Phryne.

'Of course.'

'Dinner is served,' announced Mr Butler. Jack Robinson leapt out of his chair like his namesake.

Mrs Butler, who had overhead Miss Phryne enthusing about Café Anatole, had decided on an aggressively English dinner, just to demonstrate that not all good cooking resided on the right-hand side of the Channel. The saddle of lamb sat oozing pink juices in the middle of its complement of perfectly baked vegetables: potatoes, onions, parsnips, carrots and turnips. A large bowl of green peas steamed in the middle of the buffet, butter melting into them. A silver gravy boat full of claret-enhanced gravy accompanied it, and Mrs Butler's sister's own home-made mint jelly cast little crystalline flashes from its perfectly faceted surface.

To begin, there was a light vegetable julienne in chicken bouillon. Jack Robinson inhaled it in a trice. When his plate was laden with a little of roast everything and gravy and mint jelly, he stared at it for a moment of perfect silence that was a benediction and a delight to any cook's heart.

Mrs Butler retreated from the kitchen door, satisfied.

The other diners fell on the feast as though they hadn't eaten a good meal for days, though this was only the case for Jack Robinson, whose diet of baked beans and ''Ot pies! Dead 'orse on 'em! Get 'em while I'm 'ere! 'Ot pies!' from the pie cart in Russell Street had not been a satisfactory substitute for even his usual warmed-over meals. Jane and Ruth had childhood starvation to avenge and had still not really come round to the view that there would, infallibly, be dinner every day. This also applied to the ex-stray Ember, tucking in to roast meat scraps in the kitchen. It even applied to Dot, who had a healthy appetite, and Phryne, who had spent a lot of her childhood in a state of semi-famine.

They were a pleasure to cook for, they were, Mrs Butler said to herself, and drew out her apple pies from the oven. The steam rose, smelling of cloves. Perfect. Those French cooks knew a lot about cooking things which no mortal would eat unless they had to—snails, for the Lord's sake!—but they couldn't dish up a good roast to save their lives.

Some five minutes elapsed before anyone at the Fisher dining table said anything but 'May I have some more gravy, please?' and 'Good meat this' and 'If you could pass the bread?' but gradually the fever eased and they began to converse.

'Miss Dot says that you've got a new case,' said Jane. 'About a missing girl.'

'Yes. However, she may have just run away,' said Phryne.

'Was she badly treated?' Jane wanted to know. This was the thought which would instantly occur to both girls, of course, thought Phryne. They had been badly treated, so badly treated that they had not even dared to run away.

'I don't know,' she answered. 'If so, it's recent. She just came back to Australia from a finishing school outside Paris. Her father wants her to marry a fifty year old man with a moustache, so she might have run.'

'She might have a boyfriend,' said Dot. 'From France.'

'And she's eloped!' said Ruth.

'Possibly. I don't know enough about her yet. I didn't go to a finishing school.'

'Where did you go after you left school, then?' asked Jane.

'To a war,' said Phryne. 'Have some more lamb, Mr Butler?'

She waved her glass at him and he refilled it with a light hock. Phryne found herself violently unwilling to consider that war. She wondered at her own reaction and decided to think about it later.

'She fell in love with him in Paris,' said Ruth dreamily. 'A dark southerner, full of passion. She was torn away from him by her stern father and sailed off in tears. Then he took a job as a deck hand and climbed up to her window one night and . . .'

There was a short silence as Ruth's voice trailed off.

'Ruth, what have you been reading?' asked Phryne.

'Romances,' replied Jane, scornfully. 'There's a whole shelf of them in the library and she's read them all.'

'I'm sure she hasn't taken any harm, Miss,' said Dot. 'They're just books.'

Phryne was about to say that a lot of harm was wrapped up in inoffensive covers with embossed flowers on them, caught sight of her expression in the mirror over the mantle and laughed.

'I'm in no position to censor your reading,' she told Ruth. 'You may bathe in romances if you like. Just don't act on them yet.'

Ruth blushed and took more potato. At least indulgence in railway reading hadn't ruined her appetite. At this delicate juncture Jack Robinson exclaimed, 'Of course! Billy the Match!'

'Sorry?' asked Phryne.

'The burning rubbish bin, Miss Fisher, and the thinners on the butter. When I was a young constable there was a rash of house fires. Each one the same: started with thinners on something in the kitchen. Took us weeks to find him, too. He was my first real good collar.'

'Tell us about it,' breathed Ruth, and the subject of romance faded.

'I was told to watch out for smoke while patrolling along the Esplanade—in fact, Miss Fisher, I walked along outside this house every night for almost a year. I'd heard about arsonists from this bloke who'd been on the Force for donkey's years, seen everything, he had. Taught me a lot, Sergeant Patterson did. He said that arsonists got a real charge out of the fire, and he'd likely be among the crowd, watching. Look for the gleam in his eyes, the old Sarge said. So when I smelt smoke just along here, I blew my whistle and got the fire brigade, and then instead of continuing on my beat I hung around in the shadows, watching the mob.

'Well, everyone was there. The house was burning like a torch. The people had got out all right and the lady of the house was standing on the pavement in her nightie going crook—I saw her point, of course—and most people were looking sad or sympathetic except this one bloke, towards the back. His eyes were gleaming, all right, and he was excited. My word, he gave a jump when I came up and put the arm on him. I arrested him for being knowingly concerned and took him back to the station. He stank of thinners and told us all about it, casual as you like. He liked fires, he said, they made him feel alive, and when no fires happened natural like, he had to start them himself. Billy the Match, they called him. I don't remember his real name, but that was his style—thinners every time.'

'Did he go to jail?' asked Jane.

'My word he did, despite his lawyer telling the judge that he was insane. Ten years, he got. Which would mean, now I think about it, that he'd be out. I'd better see what's happened to our Billy,' said Robinson grimly. 'It was only luck that he didn't kill anyone. He didn't care if there were people in the house or not. And if he's up to his old tricks in Fitzroy Street, I want to know about it.'

'He might be in league with someone else,' said Phryne. 'The gentleman who left Café Anatole through the window, perhaps?'

'Yeah, well, you meet a mixed group of people in jail,' said Robinson, 'not select company, Miss Fisher.'

'Hardly.'

'And you never know, someone in quod might have found a use for Billy the Match. Sorry, Miss Fisher. I interrupted you. What were you saying?'

'Nothing of any importance, Jack dear. Just wondering if Miss Chambers had met a lover in Paris who might have followed her here.'

'If you can't meet a lover in Paris, where can you meet one?' asked Robinson, as if this was a silly comment. 'But I can tell you which French people came through customs at the docks, anyway, if you want.'

'Thank you,' said Phryne. 'Now, what's for dessert? Oh, wonderful. Apple pies.'

Jack Robinson sighed happily and surreptitiously undid a bottom waistcoat button.

Phryne slept the night without dreams and woke in the early morning, thinking about Paris in a warm, sleepy trance. What was it she didn't want to remember? Her time in Paris had been fascinating. She had mixed with artists and poets, had been to one of Miss Stein's Sunday Afternoons, eaten bread and cheese and drunk vin so absolutely ordinaire that it stained the teeth and eroded the palate; vin du table made of real table . . . and all because Daddy had sent a fierce telegram ordering her to stay at the Magnifique until he could send someone to get her and escort her home in time for the County Ball. And Phryne wasn't going to go to that ball . . .

No. She was not going to think about what happened next. She dragged herself brutally awake, took a punitive shower and dressed soberly.

Lin Chung looked up from his toast, marmalade and coffee and stood as she came into the room. Paler than the moon, with the Manchu red mouth, the silky black hair and those strange, disturbing green eyes.

'Silver Lady,' he said gravely, taking her hand.

'Lin dear,' she said, sitting down firmly and taking up a napkin and a cup of coffee in that order. Lin Chung looked as immaculate as ever; a smooth, cultivated young man, of surpassing amatory skill and extensive education. He was wearing a silk suit which might have been woven in China but was definitely cut in Savile Row, and a four in hand tie with a pearl pin. Phryne found him altogether a charming sight for so early in the morning.

'Today I must go to Station Pier to meet a person,' he said. 'Would it please you to come with me?'

'If you don't mind a detour or three,' said Phryne. 'Who are you meeting?'

'My new wife,' said Lin smoothly.

Mr Butler, laying some poached eggs in the bain-marie, jerked a little and just saved his egg as it tried to leap off the spoon. Miss Fisher, however, did not turn a hair.

'Would it be suitable for me to be there?' asked Phryne. She was closer to Chinese culture than most Australians, but she was still unsure about the finer points—for instance, whether it was proper for a young man to take his mistress to greet his new wife as she got off the ship.

'Perfectly,' said Lin.

'But it would not be suitable to take the poor girl on trips to offices and police stations, which is where I am going, and then to visit a racing man who is probably, as Dot so accurately puts it, a crook. The young woman will want to find a wash and a meal and a place to lie down until the ground stops moving. I know those passenger ships. A long voyage. Has she come from China?'

'Indirectly. She has been staying with my cousins in Hong Kong until we could get the necessary permits. Australia does not want to be overrun with the heathen Chinee and it takes time to get permission for a young woman to travel here. I must marry her within three months or she will be deported.'

'Who is she?'

'Her name is Camellia. She is not very familiar with western ways and speaks little English. The cousins funded her voyage from the Four Counties and I understand it was more like an escape. Her family has traditionally been allied with mine.'

'How old is she?'

'Seventeen,' said Lin Chung evenly, taking more marmalade.

'Ah,' said Phryne. 'And she understands our . . . arrangement?'

'Yes. I made sure of that.'

'Good. No, I don't think I should come with you. She will be afraid and she doesn't need a strange face—I mean a strange occidental face—to disconcert her further. I'm sure that you will introduce us in due course.'

Phryne found that she had lost her appetite. She gulped her coffee and a shaken Mr Butler refilled her cup. He was proud of the fact that he did not spill a drop. Drat, he was thinking. I liked this one. He was charming and conversable and Miss Fisher really liked him, and now Mr Butler would have to laboriously train the next lover in the ways of the house. The girls liked Mr Lin, too. Bringing them shawls and teaching them that Chinese satin stitch. Perfectly proper that he should marry a suitable girl, of course, bound to happen some time, but Mr Butler was going to miss Mr Lin. It was most regrettable.

Miss Fisher's next comment made him flick a drop of coffee onto his own immaculate white apron.

'So will I see you tonight?' she asked.

'Of course,' said Mr Lin.

Lin took his leave and Mr Butler offered Miss Fisher more coffee, perhaps an egg, and his resignation.

'What?' asked Phryne, passing a hand over her eyes.

'Our notice, Miss Fisher.'

'Why?' she asked, blankly.

'Mrs Butler and I have never been concerned about your . . . company, Miss Fisher. We can take the rough with the smooth. But adultery, no. Old-fashioned we may be, but that is our principle.'

'Adultery?' repeated Phryne.

'Run a house with adultery in it, Miss Fisher, and sooner or later you find yourself standing up in a court giving evidence and breaking all oaths of confidentiality so that no one will ever employ you again, or refusing to answer and getting locked up for contempt. Happened to a friend of mine. His name was all over *Society Spice*. It ruined him. So if you are continuing with Mr Lin, and he is getting married, then I'm afraid that we must regretfully . . .'

'Oh no, you don't,' said Phryne. 'Not regretfully. Not with the greatest respect, either.' She stood up. Her Paris memories, in which something lurked which she would not face, fired her temper. 'If that is your view, Mr Butler, then you may take your leave as you wish. I will not have my morals the subject of adverse comment by my servants!'

'As you wish,' said Mr Butler, and withdrew.

Phryne gave herself a mark for good conduct. She didn't throw the epergne at his retreating, stubborn, righteous back.

Her fingers itched to box someone's ears. She took her coat and hat from Dot, who was troubled but bit back any comment. Then she ignited the Hispano-Suiza with one vengeful twist of the starting handle, leapt in, and roared down the street, scattering small boys, delivery bicycles and startled pigeons in her magnificent wake.

By the time she had reached the city, she had slowed down. However irascible the driver, it did not pay to try conclusions with the nine tons of unstoppable steel which was a tram in its own right of way. Adultery! Did people really think that way? How dare they! Courts, indeed. And yet, there was the excellent cooking of Mrs Butler and the unobtrusive, imperturbable service of Mr Butler, who also mixed the best cocktails in Victoria. Damn! And there was Lin Chung, whom she had personally rescued from durance vile, risking her life and her virtue in the process, and the memory of his silky, sure touch made her shiver. No. There had to be some way to keep the Butlers and Lin Chung, and she would think of it as soon as she had time.

Now for the records of French travellers, the strange fiery passion of Billy the Match, and the unexpected silence of a prominent racing identity.

She flicked the car around a baker's van and set off for Russell Street.

CHAPTER FOUR

Jack Robinson in his little cubbyhole in Russell Street Police Station looked just as subfusc as Jack Robinson in Phryne's dining room. He fitted perfectly into any surroundings, like a chameleon, if one could imagine a chameleon with no colour except, probably, mid-brown.

'Here's the list of Frenchies for the last two months. Not too many to cope with. And the inquest reports ought to be somewhere here—yes, both of them. I've had a look through. They don't help much if this really is murder. In fact, if this is the work of one murderer, he's a clever chap and I hope he doesn't continue murdering. They both look like pure and simple accidents to me.'

'They would,' Phryne pointed out, 'if they were successful murders.'

Jack Robinson nodded. 'You'll have to look at them here,' he said regretfully. 'But you can have the next office if you want to make notes. Old Smithy's on leave. Getting married! Smithy! Strewth, you could have knocked me down with a feather. Smithy's a confirmed bachelor, that's what we all thought. Then he ups and sweeps this young typist off her feet. Nice girl, of course. Seems devoted to Smithy. But I would have given good money . . .'

Robinson gradually became aware that his cheerful patter was not going over well with Miss Fisher. The glare of her green eyes finally penetrated his amusement. He coughed.

'Yes, well, as I said, the office is empty. Here's the gen on our old mate Billy the Match, too. He's out. Been out a good three months. Supposed to be living with his old mother in a boarding house in Fraser Street, St Kilda—he's a neighbour of yours, Miss Fisher.'

'Oh, good,' murmured Phryne.

'Here's his photo,' said Robinson.

She looked at a smallish, dullish face, scant as to chin and forehead, with a big nose and a wide mouth. He had beetling eyebrows, the only sign of character. The notes said that he was mousy, with blue eyes.

'Face you could pass in a crowd,' said Phryne.

'Not as anonymous as he once was. He got on the wrong side of some people in jail and he's got a scar on his face now. Right across it, apparently. Slashed with a bottle. He was weeks in the infirmary, but he wouldn't tell who did it.'

'Honour among thieves?' asked Phryne, with conscious irony.

'No, I reckon it was just fear of what they'd do to him if he told. His associates are unknown. He doesn't seem to have had any friends inside. Now, I can't haul him in for a little chat unless you tell me more about these fires and we get an official complaint.'

'I'll talk to the owner,' promised Phryne. 'If he agrees, I'll tell you all about it and you can take action. I'm sorry I glared at you, Jack dear. Mr Butler has just given me notice.'

'Mr Butler?' gasped Robinson. 'I thought he was set for life.'

'So did I, but . . . well, he's decided he can't stay in a house where . . .' she struggled for a euphemism, 'he risks getting a headline in *Society Spice*, if I can put it that way.'

Jack Robinson was very fast on the uptake. And, it seemed, a confirmed reader of *Society Spice*.

'Who's the married bloke?' he asked.

'Lin Chung.'

'Miss Fisher,' Jack Robinson took Phryne's hand and patted it. 'That's awful. I suppose Mrs Butler goes too?'

'Of course.'

'Real awful,' he repeated.

Phryne had to agree.

Safely ensconced in the absent Smithy's office, she examined the account of the death of Alan 'Conger' Eeles. The coroner certainly hadn't extended himself on the subject. Mr Eeles was twenty-nine years old, married with two small children, and made his living as a delivery man. Three weeks ago he had been found dead, with the front wheel of a truck crushing his chest. Massive internal injuries, heart crushed, ribs broken, huge internal bleeding, death by exsanguination . . . Evidence had been given that the jack had slipped, though no one had asked what he was trying to fix in that position and why, if there was something amiss, he had been trying to do it in the dark. His two-ton truck was examined by a mechanic and found to be in sound condition. So was the jack. The conclusion that it had been placed on an unstable surface seemed optimistic in explanation of his death. Good mechanics do not take any chances with jacks, knowing that their lives depend on them not slipping.

Odd, thought Phryne. She had mended a fair number of cars herself, in her ambulance days—was everything conspiring to remind her of France?—and offhand she couldn't think of any part of the engine easily reached by lying under the front wheel. He could have been interested in the suspension, of course, or the axle, but that would not entail him reposing under a wheel. Someone should have noticed this. But the coroner took only formal evidence of identity from the prostrate widow, clearly not wanting to upset her further. Mr Eeles had left her a small sum in insurance, and the house. From the comments in the 'remarks' section of the badly typed form, Phryne read that the police had no doubt that this was an accident. The coroner's jury brought in a verdict of death by misadventure and they had added a rider expressing their sympathy for the widow and suggesting that all buyers of jacks should be instructed as to their use. Oh, very helpful. Date of death—three weeks ago, almost to the day.

Mr MacKenzie got even shorter shrift from the Crown's judicial officer. Cause of death: drowning. Alcohol content of blood .38. Very drunk, Phryne thought. Evidence given: identity Thomas MacKenzie, aged twenty-nine, farmer, unmarried. Had attended a birthday party at the pub that evening for his employee Richard Trewes. Ordinarily abstemious, he had drunk two beers and eaten a meat pie. He had left the pub at ten p.m., saying that he had a lot of work to do on the morrow. No one had seen him again until his employee had found him, face down in the water-filled ditch, at nine in the morning of the next day. By then he had been dead for about eight hours.

Two beers would not produce a blood alcohol content of damn near dead, said Phryne to herself. How had he got that load on between the pub and home? Someone must have either spiked his two abstemious beers or met him outside and filled him as full as a boot with something like whisky. What did the autopsy say about that? Stomach almost empty except for a yeasty fluid—that was the beer—and acidic fluid—apparently he was a confirmed orange juice drinker—and some pastry and meat—that was the pie he ate at the pub. Therefore he was killed shortly after someone had filled him full of the old familiar juice and laid him gently in a ditch to drown. Hadn't Bert said something about marks on the body? She flicked over the page. Aha! Yes. Rounded bruises on the shoulder blades of unknown but unconnected origin. How did the medical officer know that? What sort of marks would be produced by someone standing on—no, rounded edges—kneeling on a prostrate victim to hold him down in the water until he stopped struggling? How much struggling would he be able to do anyway, when even a vampire feasting on the deceased would be locked up for drunk and disorderly? Also bruises to the back of the head. Did someone tip his head back and make him drink? Coroner's jury verdict—accident. The fatheads. The jury added a rider that people coming home drunk should be careful where they walk. Helpful.

And the murderer had got away with it, if murderer there was. A clever person, to use two different methods. How would you get someone to lie down under a wheel? Simple. Feed them a Micky Finn—chloral hydrate was not hard to obtain—and arrange them suitably, then kick the jack away and let yourself out the back, unobtrusively. So the murderer was physically strong. There were no drag marks on poor Conger's back, nor were his clothes disarranged. He must have been carried, not hauled. No one would check for fingerprints or bother too much about why a respectable tradesman in possession of his senses lays himself out on the cold ground in the middle of the night under a wheel. Voilà! No more Mr Eeles, and whatever inconvenient knowledge he had had died with him. The chloral scent would escape through the destroyed organs—and in any case they hadn't even tested for it.

Or, if that was too difficult, he could be belted over the head with a handy spanner and laid out for execution. The same for the farmer. Someone lurks in the pub as the birthday party goes on and slips some high proof spirit into the beer or walks along with Mr MacKenzie as he leaves and offers him— what? A sip from a flask? The farmer had not been drugged. Chloral hydrate was very easy to find at an autopsy on an intact body, because of its peculiar and very unpleasant smell. Someone must have spiked the drinks or had a sure-fire way of making someone take a drink from him.

But in any case, both deaths were highly suspicious. Each singly could have been an accident, but together they looked extremely worrying.

Billy the Match's unedifying record lay before her. A petty criminal as a child—two years in a boys' training school, she noticed, that should have perfected his skills—and then the usual run of handbag thefts, minor assaults, the victims always other children or old people who wouldn't or couldn't fight back. A nasty little person, but not dangerous, until Billy the Match found out about fire. A note from the informant suggested that William Joseph Bland had been responsible for hundreds of small fires in rubbish bins. His favourite method was to tie several matches around a cigarette, light it, and toss it into a bin where, as the cigarette burned down, it would produce a burst of flame and ignite whatever was in the bin. Then he had graduated to houses and discovered the glories of turpentine.

A medical report, attached, said that he was not insane, he just liked fires, and could not be prevented from lighting them. The fact that he was good at not being caught suggested that he knew that what he was doing was wrong, which proved sanity. The physician also suggested a Freudian analysis; fire was a cleansing element, and Billy felt dirty. His background was dire. His mother was a whore and his father a toss-up between a selection of ten men, mostly sailors, among her clientele. She drank too much, took drugs, and locked the child out of the house, often in the rain, while she was working. He was malnourished and lacked nurture. He had been an early truant and still could not read or write. If the ratbag hadn't taken to trying to burn down Melbourne, Phryne would have felt sorry for Billy the Match.

Phryne scanned the list of passengers with French passports who had entered Australia in the last two months. Not many names. Usual selections of Duponts and Duponds. Then one name leapt straight off the paper and struck Phryne between the eyes.

Oh, no. Not now! Not when she was already feeling destabilised, uncertain, and angry! What was he doing here? What cruel, Phryne-hating fate could have brought René Dubois to Australia?

She put her hands over her face. René Dubois. René of the scented nights in the Bois de Boulogne. René of the wicked smile. René of the compelling, shrill, intricate music. René wrapped around her in his ill-clothed bed under the eaves of the Montparnasse atelier in which he lived.

It was all because of that telegram . . .

'Mademoiselle will await the escort from London?' asked Madame la Concierge.

'Non,' said Phryne, furious at the unmitigated gall of her father, expecting her to wait and be called for like a parcel. 'Mademoiselle will not wait.'

'And may we say where mademoiselle is going?'

'You may not,' said Phryne, folding her new clothes into her knapsack. 'I will write a letter for my father. Where is the nearest postal office?'

'I will carry mademoiselle's letter, if she will trust it to me,' said Madame, stiffly.

'Of course.' Phryne sat down and wrote furiously.

'Send it as soon as you can,' she said. Then, out of the francs which the hotel had advanced her, she stuffed some money into Madame's hand. 'You have been very kind,' she said. 'I could not have had a better welcome back to the real world. Thank you.'

Then she was gone down the stairs. Moving well, Madame saw, refreshed by her rest and the good southern wine. But Paris was no place for an unaccompanied young woman of English background, and Madame worried about her as she watched her walk away. Out of the Hôtel Magnifique and into the grey Rue de St Honoré.

'The young will no longer be advised by the old,' she said to the hall porter.

'That is because we advised them to die,' said the hall porter.

Paris was cold. An icy wind sprang up, ruffling Phryne's hair and chilling her bones. She stopped at a boutique where her father had an account and ordered a stout leather coat, then walked on. Where to go? Toupie had a lot of friends in Paris and it was time Phryne found some of them. Left bank—

so she needed to cross the Seine. Now, where had Toupie told her to go if she found herself at a loose end? Aha. The tea shop of Sybaris at the end of the Rue du Chat qui Pêche.

Strange to just be walking again, with nowhere to be, no hurry, no shells bursting. No wounded men crying. Paris was crowded. Well-dressed women in fur coats gathered around the few open food shops, shrieking at the proprietors. Not much to eat in the shops. People looked thin. Paris had been besieged, more or less, for four years. Most people carried a bag of some sort, in case they came upon an open shop with some chance-arrived stock.

Phryne skirted two city gentlemen almost coming to blows over half a kilo of sugar. She heard one woman say, 'The farmers' market is tomorrow. Not that many will dare to come in, now that the Spanish influenza has arrived.'

Phryne winced. The Spanish 'flu had romped through the weary soldiery in May, and again in late September, when Phryne had caught it. She had been delirious for three days but assumed that she was now immune. It was very infectious and she wondered what it would do to an unprotected, malnourished population who had to be out and about if they wanted to eat. Would M. Poincaré, the President, be able to rule a city as hungry and downtrodden as this one if another plague came upon them?

She came to the Pont Neuf and put down her knapsack. There she was, Notre Dame, bone-coloured towers still lacy and perfect against the hurrying grey clouds. The river slid away beneath her, boats were hauled, men shouted. She caught sight of a red and white striped fisherman's jersey and a voice shouted to her from a barge, offering various delights.

Standing and staring was always perilous, she knew. So was looking vulnerable, scared, or obviously a stranger. Time to pace along the Pont Neuf, walk quickly along the Quai des Grands Augustins and find the Place St Michel and Thé Sybaris. She was beginning to notice the number of eyes upon her, cold eyes, summing her up; female, fragile looking, alone. She began to feel like a target.

She lifted her chin, deliberately slowed her pace so that she would not be tempted to run, and resolved to fling her first attacker into the river. That ought to discourage the others. She might look frail, but Phryne could woman-handle a full-sized unconscious soldier onto a stretcher. One learned that most weights were all a matter of points d'appui—leverage. Her attacker would have time to say 'Merde alors!' as he fell, but not much else. The change in stance registered with her prospective assailants. Maybe not such an easy mark after all. Catch her on the way back, perhaps. Probably not carrying anything worth having.

She was conscious of malicious attention moving away from her. She reached the end of the bridge, patted the last knob for luck, and turned along the Quai des Grands Augustins, where hundreds of small craft were moored. From the Quai, one looked down into the boats. They were bringing into Paris late spinach in bitter, dark green bunches, apples from Normandy and cheeses in golden rounds. Sheep bleated on one barge, milling about in the nervous manner of sheep and controlled by one old, intelligent, experienced black and white dog. Phryne watched him with delight. He did not even rise, but lifted his grey muzzle from his wayworn paws and gave a small, imperative bark, and the sheep moved as he required. Even this late in the year, a few bookstalls were open under the leafless trees. Phryne went into a small tabac and bought a packet of Gauloises and a box of Matelot matches. The scratch and fume of the match and the suck of scented smoke soothed her soul. Free of war. Free of Daddy. One hundred francs in hand and all Paris before me, she thought. What could be better? Who is as fortunate as I?

Well, those who know where they are going to sleep tonight probably have something of an edge, she considered. The bare-limbed chestnuts all along the Quai dripped gently on her as she walked along. The knapsack was not heavy. Phryne owned less at this moment than she had ever owned in her life.

Down the tiny Rue du Chat qui Pêche. She walked, with one hand on either wall, wary of things falling from above, squashing through mud in which all-too-nameable substances were mixed. Paris drainage had not joined the twentieth century, not in the Quartier Latin. She came out into a tiny square, with a small fountain on which some mythological figure struggled with a dragon—St George?—and she saw the white tablecloths, brass fittings and lettered window of Thé Sybaris. Phryne scraped her boots carefully. The floor inside was of polished wood and she did not want to mar it. A woman in trousers looked up as she walked in and let her knapsack slide to the floor.

'Bonjour, madame,' said Phryne. 'Thé, s'il vous plaît, et un pastis. La Toupie, est-elle ici?'

The woman, who had not seemed welcoming, smiled suddenly. 'Oui, mam'selle,' she said. 'Il est là.' And on that sexually ambiguous note, she opened an inner door. A gush of steam, scented with garlicky roasting, rushed out. Phryne swallowed saliva and went in.

There was Toupie. There was Madeleine, known as La Petite because she was as tall as a man and built like a wrestler. There were several women dressed in full male costume and there, sitting at a side table, were the American Sylvia Beach and nun-clad Adrienne Monnier, who owned the bookshop. They were correcting proofs and arguing fiercely. The poet Djuna Barnes was scowling impartially at both of them. Romaine Brooks was sketching the group in charcoal on white butcher's paper.

'Phryne!' called Toupie. 'Take the weight off. Have a drink. Lunch in a moment—it's horse. Lucky to get it, too. Poor thing died in the Rue Jacob and they had the devil's own job trying to get the cart out. So you got back all right, then?'

That was Toupie. Barbara Lowther. The Hon. As long as you were alive and on your feet, she considered that all was well. She was a solid, jolly woman with cropped salt and pepper hair and big, capable hands. Freed from uniform, she was wearing a sombrely magnificent gentleman's smoking jacket, a fez, velvet trousers and a soft silk shirt.

'You look gorgeous,' said Phryne, sinking down into a Turkish cosy corner and finding a cushion. 'Toupie, I need a place to stay. Not too expensive. My father has ordered me back to London.'

'Kismet,' said Toupie. 'La Petite was just saying that she needed someone to share her apartment. Two bedrooms. Very cheap. In the Rue de Gaîtés in Montparnasse. Suit you?'

'If it suits Madeleine.'

Madeleine nodded. 'And if you want some spare cash, why not come with me to Rue d'Odessa? Artists' model. Easy. All you have to do is lie still and try not to freeze to death. They'd like you,' she commented dispassionately. 'Nice. Thin. They want 'em thin, the Moderne. You can go there now if you like. Or, wait. Come home with me tonight? It's Friday. We're going to Madame Barney's. She's having a late soiree. Miss Stein's in Belgium with the War Relief, but Madame Natalie doesn't admit wars in her salon.'

'Lovely,' said Phryne, and sank down into her cushion again. Paris was beginning to feel like home.

And that's how it started, thought Phryne, wondering how long she had been staring at a list of French passports. And what was she going to do if she saw René Dubois again?

Because the last time she had seen him, she had sworn to kill him.

Onward, she told herself. Now for a prominent racing identity and his lost daughter. She got out the Hispano-Suiza, which had been attracting general attention in the police garage, and drove to Flemington.

It was a large house, she noticed as she stopped her car at the huge iron barrier. Someone with a lot of iron and their very own pair of pincers had gone to a lot of trouble to do a Palace of Würzberg on the gates. In the middle of each collection of tortured metal was a panel enamelled with a racehorse galloping at full stretch. The jockey's silks were purple, green and white.

'I wonder if he knows that he is racing under suffragette colours,' Phryne said aloud. She honked the horn. 'Come along,' she added, 'I haven't got all day.'

Three large men, wearing the kind of suits which are only bought to impress a magistrate, surrounded the car. Phryne noted a suspicious bulge under each ill-tailored arm and put her own hand on her bag, in which reposed her own pearl-handled pistol. Mr Chambers had some heavy muscle on the staff. What was he afraid of?

'My name is Phryne Fisher,' she said, smiling sunnily at the nearest thug. 'Here is my card. I would like to see Mr Chambers.'

'Mr Chambers don't want to see no one,' grunted Thug One.

'Oh, he'll want to see me. Your education in grammar didn't extend as far as the double negative, did it?' she smiled again. 'Take in my card and ask,' she prompted. 'And get a wriggle on, there's a good chap. It's cold out here.'

Thug One examined the card. Engraved, not printed. 'The Hon. Phryne Fisher. Investigations.' 'Did Mr Chambers call you?'

'No,' said Phryne patiently. 'Tell him it's about his daughter.'

At this, the men were galvanised. The gates swung open. Phryne was joined by Thug One in the front seat of her car, much to her annoyance. She drove up to the house along a carriage drive which had been both asphalted and swept. Green lawns sloped away on either side, bordered with flowerbeds and old elm trees. Phryne stopped the car by the front door and got out.

'Well?' she asked.

'This way, Miss,' grunted Thug One. Clearly Mr Chambers had given orders that anyone who came inquiring about his daughter must be instantly admitted. Maybe he was concerned about her, after all. Thug One opened the front door, which was magnificent, and handed Phryne over to the indoor Thug Two. Phryne wondered whether there was a factory somewhere which turned out big, solid men with no necks and muscles like bags of walnuts.

The hall was carpeted and there was a general air of plush and chestnut furniture in the grand salon through which she was conducted. Then a door was opened, Phryne was almost pushed through, and the door slammed and locked behind her.

This was unusual behaviour, even for a racing identity. A small, red-faced man was sitting at the desk, surrounded by papers and refreshing himself at intervals from a large decanter of ruby port.

'Yes?' he growled.

'I'm Phryne Fisher,' said Phryne, sitting down composedly on a near-Morris chair. 'I've come to talk to you about your daughter's disappearance.'

She had looked away for a moment. When she looked back she was staring down the barrel of a large handgun, backed by a steady hand and a scowl.

'Where is she?' demanded Hector Chambers. 'Where's my little Lizzie?'

The prisoner was drinking cold tea. It tasted vile. There were deep rings around her wrists and ankles and she was far too afraid to complain. If she did, he would come back and hit her again. The memory made her cringe and whimper.

CHAPTER FIVE

'Let's not be hasty, Mr Chambers,' said Phryne.

She had looked down her fair share of gun barrels in her time, and the experience had not improved with repetition. Mr Chambers' hands were steady, the gun was a large one and the barrel appeared to be quite as deep as a well and twice as wide as a church door.

'Lizzie! Where is she? If you've hurt her, I'll—'

'Let's take this one point at a time,' said Phryne very gently and clearly. 'One, I don't have Elizabeth. Two, I don't know where she is. Three, I'm trying to find her. Four, put down the gun, Mr Chambers. I know how distraught you must be, but killing me won't help.'

'Why are you looking for her? No one knows she's missing!' snarled Mr Chambers, not lowering the gun.

'M'sieur Anatole is concerned about her,' answered Phryne. 'He asked me to investigate quietly, so as not to produce a scandal. If you still have my card, you will see what it says.'

Mr Chambers allowed the barrel to slide away from Phryne. She opened her purse. The barrel moved back.

'You really are in a state, aren't you?' she asked in a friendly tone. 'How about pouring me a glass of that red ink and sitting down for a chat? And do you have a light?'

Of all the various responses to being menaced with a firearm which Mr Chambers had met, a request for a drink and a light for a cigarette was unique. Finely honed hospitality reflexes were already snapping the cigar lighter before he realised what was happening. His visitor breathed in, blew a perfect smoke-ring, accepted a glass of port and smiled.

Mr Chambers emptied his glass at a gulp, sloshed himself another, and said, 'Lizzie is all right. She's on a holiday with friends she met in Paris.'

'Nonsense,' said his visitor composedly. 'You wouldn't have been doing that startling impression of the Gunfight at the O.K. Corrall if Lizzie was all right and holidaying with friends. Wouldn't it help if you told me about it?'

'How can you help? You're a sheila,' diagnosed Mr Chambers, zoology expert.

'Yes, true, well done, I can see you are an acute observer. Tell me, what was it that gave me away? The hair? The lack of Adam's apple? The intelligence? Let me ask you a question. With all your big men and big guns, all your bullying and sticking people up, has it produced any clue to Lizzie's whereabouts? Hmm?'

Mr Chambers had to shake his head.

'Then perhaps we can try it another way,' said Phryne.

'Well, you're cool enough, Miss . . . er . . . Fisher,' said Mr Chambers. 'But I can't tell you anything about Lizzie. They say they'll . . .'

'Ah. Kidnapped. Now you don't need to say anything. Just nod or shake your head. For ransom?'

Nod.

'Money?'

A nod.

'Five hundred pounds?'

'If you're guessing, you're a real good guesser,' snarled Mr Chambers, his suspicions back at full-bore. His pistol had replaced itself in his hand as if by magic.

'A five year old child could have guessed that much,' responded Phryne. 'You're rich, but that doesn't mean you have the stuff lying around in sackfuls. Five hundred is about as much as anyone could raise in a couple of weeks without selling real estate or—a horse, perhaps. Now put away that cannon and talk to me. There's a time limit to this, isn't there?'

'Two weeks from Sat'day,' muttered Mr Chambers. 'I got to wait until they tell me how to deliver it. Personal column in the *Argus*. Under the name of Jaunty Lad. The name of my best horse, dammit.'

'And what do they say they will do to Elizabeth if you don't pay?'

Mr Chambers stared at Phryne, face blank with despair, and did not need to answer.

'And you don't know who these people are? I ask,' explained Phryne hastily, 'because you look like you have some reasonably expert help with the rough work and they should have been able to track down any known extortionists.'

'No idea. No one's heard anything. Not a whisper round

the pubs, like you'd expect. I've had blokes in every dive, in every sly-grog shop and SP pub, and not a clue.'

'How about enemies?' asked Phryne. 'Other racehorse owners?'

'I thought of that,' groaned Mr Chambers. 'Most of 'em are straight—straight as a die. Nothing iffy about most of 'em. And I ain't done nothing to the ones who ain't straight. Can't see any of 'em pulling a stunt like this anyway. I mean, we compete all right, but we buy each other a drink in the Members' after the races. We're all in the same business.'

'No owner with whom you might have had a quarrel? Someone to whom you sold a horse with re-done teeth, or a vicious brute warranteed free from vice? Such things happen,' she said soothingly, as Mr Chambers' fingers twitched towards his gun again. 'Horses occasionally develop bad habits after they have been sold.'

'I've known that to happen, yeah,' admitted Mr Chambers. 'No, I haven't sold anything in the last six months. Not so much as a donkey. And I ain't done no one in the game no bad turns that I can remember.'

'Think about it,' urged Phryne. 'I don't imagine Elizabeth has had time to make any really strong-minded enemies. You hold the key. Now, when did Elizabeth disappear?'

Mr Chambers had given up his resistance. 'She was only back four days. Then she went out to a dance with a friend of mine—a girl. At a private house. She didn't go out to dances much but I reckon she wanted to show off her Paris clothes. She and Miss Chivers went off in the car about eight. Dance went on and on and the driver got bored and slipped out for a drink. I've already skinned him for that, the lazy idle hound. When he came back the car was gone and this was pinned to a lamppost.'

He rummaged in a drawer and produced a letter. Pinholes in each corner, Phryne noticed. It was written in a bold backhand in very black ink: 'If you want Liz back in one piece collect five hundred in 14 days and watch the personal columns in the *Argus* under Jaunty Lad. No cops, no snoopers, or no daughter.'

'No signature either,' murmured Phryne. 'Good bank paper, expensive. The backhand probably disguises the person's real handwriting. Have you checked all the handwriting? Especially of—as it were—employees who feel that you haven't treated them as well as they deserve?'

'I treat my men as they deserve,' grunted Mr Chambers.

'Yes, I expect that you do. Which of them might have resented your judgment of their deserts?'

'What?' Mr Chambers blinked.

'Let me put it more clearly. Who have you flung out of your stable or household lately, neck and crop, without wages, and told them that you'd set the dogs on them if they ever returned?'

Mr Chambers blinked. His hand was reaching yet again for the gun. Phryne had wearied of this autonomic reaction. She reached over and grabbed the revolver, rotated the chambers to unload it, clicked the mechanism together and offered it, butt first, to the startled man.

'How many times do you have to be told? I'm not a kidnapper and I'm not reading your mind. You, my dear sir, are a Type, and one can usually predict Types. Now, who did you sack?'

Mr Chambers huffed, turned pink, then replied, 'Three or four. One stable boy, a rider, and my butler.'

'And did you throw them out in the manner described?'

'Yes, well, yes, I did my block. The boy left a horse without water—a valuable horse—should have known that he always kicks over his bucket. The rider disobeyed me and gave me backchat about it, and the butler, well, I sacked the butler.'

'Did you? Because?'

'He told me that he would have to give his notice if I got married again. He don't like married households or children, and I told him to boil his head and he tried to quit before I could sack him. But I sacked him first. Without a character. The cheek of these servants!'

'Indeed,' agreed Phryne, warming to Mr Chambers for the first time. 'I do understand. Do you have his address?'

Hector Chambers bellowed 'Jenkins!' and a small rabbity man scuttled in. If he had pulled out a gold watch and exclaimed, 'Oh, my paws and whiskers!', he could not have resembled the white rabbit more without surgically enhanced ears.

'Mr Chambers?' he said nervously.

'Give this lady all the information she wants. All right, Miss Fisher. Do what you can. You're so good at second-guessing, perhaps you can second-guess this. Here's your retainer,' said Mr Chambers, peeling notes off a roll the size of which could have choked a racehorse. Phryne waved a dismissive hand.

'No money. I'm in this for another reason. I'm not working for you, Mr Chambers, but M'sieur Anatole.'

'He wants to marry her,' said Mr Chambers. 'Dunno what she wants. But I want her back,' he said fiercely. 'She's *my* daughter.'

'Quite,' said Phryne. 'I'll let you know what I find out. Oh,' she said as she turned from accompanying White Rabbit Jenkins to the door, 'these are yours, I believe.'

She poured into his hand the bullets from his revolver, and closed the door quietly behind her.

Mr Chambers stared at the closed door for a bit, then swore. 'Bloody women!'

Mr Jenkins wrinkled his pink nose and asked, 'What do you need to know, miss?'

'I would like you to show me Elizabeth's room,' said Phryne.

'Oh!' he gasped. 'I don't know if Mr Chambers would—'

'He told you to give me all the information I needed,' Phryne reminded him. 'You wouldn't want to disobey him, would you?'

'No!' squeaked Mr Jenkins. 'He gets very nasty when he's crossed. Sometimes when he isn't crossed, as well.'

This sounded promising. Mr Jenkins had a sense of humour.

'Have you been with him long?'

'All my life. My father worked for his father and it made sense that I should work for him in my turn. I started out as a stable boy but I wasn't strong enough and I didn't like the horses, so old Mr Chambers sent me to business school.'

'So you do all the accounts, investments, that sort of thing?'

'Yes. Ever since I graduated.'

'Are his business affairs in good order?' asked Phryne, following the White Rabbit up a set of richly carpeted stairs and along a gallery hung with indifferent oils of horses; horses with jockeys, horse races, more horses and, just for a change, horses. All by himself, Phryne reflected, Mr Chambers was keeping the horse painting, framing and picture hanging industry in business. Mr Jenkins glanced at the decor.

'He is very proud of his horses,' he commented. 'And his business is in excellent order. Any enterprise involving livestock and'—he raised a finger—'the element of chance is risky, but with sale of bloodstock and some good returns, he is doing quite well. We also have great hopes of Jaunty Lad. Possible Cup winner there, so they say. He's a stallion and his stud fees, should he win . . .' He allowed the sentence to trail off, lingeringly. The stud fees for a Melbourne Cup winner were obviously beyond the dreams of accountants.

He tried the handle of the third door on the right and found it locked.

'Odd,' he murmured.

'This door wasn't locked before?' asked Phryne.

'Well, no, I don't believe so . . . but possibly I never checked. No matter, I have all the keys here.'

He dragged out a large ring of keys and tutted over them until Phryne took them out of his hand, separated off the large outer door keys and found one marked '3', which was the number on the lock. The door opened easily. The household was well maintained. The lock had been oiled recently.

'Wait out here,' she instructed him.

'Oh! Er . . . well . . . if you say so, Miss Fisher,' he stammered, stepping away.

Phryne did not know what she was going to find when she entered Elizabeth's room. A body, possibly. Therefore she was relieved when all she saw was a young woman's room, richly appointed, which had evidently suffered either hasty preparations for a dance or sack by a major Viking invasion. Clothes were tossed everywhere, most of the drawers in the large tallboy were pulled out, and a disembowelled shipping trunk spilled silky undergarments into shameless public view.

'Has Miss Elizabeth a maid?' asked Phryne, coming to the door.

'Oh . . . well, yes, so to speak, one of the housemaids helped her with her clothes, but she . . .'

'. . . has been dismissed by Mr Chambers?' guessed Phryne.

'Quit,' said Mr Jenkins. 'Yesterday. Said she wasn't going to stay where her character was called into question every five minutes. Went off this morning with her wages and—why?'

'I wondered if this is how Miss Elizabeth usually leaves her room,' said Phryne, allowing Mr Jenkins to edge past her into the boudoir. He let his glasses drop to the end of their tape in surprise.

'No, well, I don't think so, she was a very neat child. I remember her lining up her dolls on the windowsill, every fold in place. And she liked the pretty clothes she bought in Paris. She wouldn't leave them all strewn about like this.'

He picked up a blue silk nightdress, cobwebbed with exquisite embroidery, as though he had never seen such a garment before, then blushed and dropped it onto a chair.

'Girls get careless,' Phryne told him, 'as they get older.'

'I suppose so,' sighed Mr Jenkins. 'But really—it looks like the room has been ransacked.'

'Yes, it does, doesn't it?' agreed Phryne. 'And no one to tell me if anything is missing since the maid is so conveniently gone. Well, I should know what constitutes a Parisian wardrobe. You can help me, Mr Jenkins. Stand that trunk up and we'll put everything back into it.'

Mr Jenkins blushed pink again and temporised. 'Really, Miss Fisher, shouldn't I go and get one of the maids?'

'No, you're here and you'll do and the fewer people in here the better. Get on with it,' she advised, kindly.

Mr Jenkins, inured to long obedience of insane orders, obeyed. Phryne sorted clothes and piled them into his shrinking arms.

'Ten pairs of camiknickers, nine present, six petticoats, six nightdresses, should be ten pairs of silk stockings, no, eight and a half, there's a stocking missing.'

'Three stockings,' ventured Mr Jenkins. It might have been the first time he had ever said the word, but he was an accountant and figures were important to him.

'She was wearing one pair when she vanished. Likewise one pair of camiknickers, saving your presence, Mr Jenkins. But the dress must have had its own underthings, because all six petticoats are here. Dinner dresses, two. Ball dress, one. Shawls and stoles, six. Pairs of shoes—nine. Dressing gowns, one warm, one light. Day dresses—the girl must have had such fun choosing these, they're definitely made in one of the better studios. How tall is she, Mr Jenkins?'

'Smaller than you, Miss Fisher. Five feet tall.'

Mr Jenkins received a load of frilly garments and deposited them in the shipping trunk. The sweet, clean scent of the clothes was making him a little giddy.

'Is that a French scent?' he asked, greatly daring. Phryne paused and sniffed. 'Lavande de Provence,' she answered. 'Very suitable. Trés jeune fille. Right. That's the clothes. Let's do the drawers next. I wish I had my maid here! She'd know what to make of all this. Toiletries—soap, washing things—all Lavande de Provence. Such a clean smell, is it not? Hmm. Nothing unusual here.'

Phryne felt around the back of each drawer before she shut it.

'What are you looking for?' asked Mr Jenkins, emboldened. He had endured a quarter-hour in a lady's bedroom and was feeling no end of the devil of a fellow.

'Anything she might have hidden. And under or at the back of a drawer is a good place. No, nothing here.' She shut the last drawer.

'Purses,' she said. She opened a small pouchy evening bag, a leather satchel, a Russian leather purse and a large silk drawstring bag. All contained nothing but lost handkerchiefs, metro tickets, stray francs and one cough sweet glued to the lining.

'Books?'

A small cedar bookcase under the window revealed Elizabeth's taste had largely run to books on French grammar and vocabulary, a few novels of the modern persuasion, possibly unread, a lot of detective stories and a comprehensive collection of cookbooks in both French and English. They were well used and opened easily. Phryne took each one and shook it over the bedspread, releasing a sheaf of bits of paper, metro tickets, chocolate wrappers, a postcard of Notre Dame and a few letters.

Phryne sat down to examine them all. Nothing to be learned from the chocolate wrappers except that Elizabeth liked hard centres. One metro ticket was much like another. The letters were a disappointment. She read through each one carefully, looking for codes or underlinings, but they were so innocent that she grew suspicious and read them again. To no avail.

'Two schoolfriends, female, and one from her father enclosing her pocket money. The postcard is from her chère amie, Adeline. Oh, well. Push that chair over to the wardrobe, Mr Jenkins, if you please.'

'Why?' asked Mr Jenkins, doing as he was bid.

'Well, unless she has a cache under a floorboard or something of that sort, which is unlikely given how little time she has spent here recently, the best bet is the wardrobe. People often hide things on wardrobes. Give me a hand.'

Mr Jenkins, breath held, watched Phryne climb nimbly onto the chair and sweep the top of the cedar wardrobe with her hands. He averted his eyes from her knees, which were on shameless display.

'Nothing up here but dust,' she said. 'I'd have a word with the maids, if I were you, Mr Jenkins.'

She hopped down.

'The desk,' she said.

This was a slender-legged escritoire meant only for the production of little notes of condolence or very small thank you letters. The tiny desk space would have constrained any writer to be brief, if not minuscule. Phryne extracted sheets of scented notepaper, visiting cards, a few leftover ribbons and one spray of artificial baby's breath, a packet of nibs and a bottle of royal blue Williams Superfine Ink. Elizabeth had written out several favourite recipes on square white filing cards in a small, very neat hand. Someone who wrote like that did seem an unlikely candidate for such wholesale, almost deliberate, untidiness.

'I see what you mean,' she commented. 'She seems to be a tidy wench.' Mr Jenkins winced at the word. 'No sign of a lover, no passionate letters, no contraceptive devices— oh, Mr Jenkins, I am sorry, forget I said that.'

'Miss Elizabeth,' quavered Mr Jenkins, 'is a good girl. She wouldn't even have heard of . . . such things.'

'If she has been to school in Paris she would have heard of them, but I agree that there is no sign of her having taken such measures. She likes hard centres, which argues good teeth and a good digestion. She likes cooking, ditto. Her favourite perfume is the unexceptionable lavender of Provence, not the scarlet passion of Jicky. Her clothes are very modest, considering her age and her position and the persuasive talents of French dressmakers. She is a young woman of decided tastes and strong character. She might have inherited that from her father.'

'But she has sweetness of disposition from her mother,' said Mr Jenkins, sounding much more certain. 'She was a saint, that woman. When she died Elizabeth was shuttled off to Paris. Almost as though her father couldn't bear to see her. Of course, she is not beautiful,' said Mr Jenkins sadly. 'That might have made a difference to him. But she is a good girl,' he said firmly.

'My opinion exactly. Now, Mr Jenkins, there are two matters to which I would draw your attention, and one question.'

'Ask,' said Mr Jenkins, squaring his rounded shoulders.

'Did Elizabeth have any jewellery or money?'

'Her mother's. But it is all in the safe in Mr Chambers' office. She had a small gold cross she always wore. Otherwise, no. Money? She would have had her month's allowance. I paid it myself. Five pounds in one pound notes.'

'That's a reasonable sum.' Phryne seemed to be examining the window. Mr Jenkins coughed to attract her notice.

'And you were going to draw my attention to . . .?'

'Oh, yes. One, her passport is missing. And two, someone has forced the lock of this window. Just here, see? With a screwdriver, I'd hazard.'

'But the dogs . . .' whispered Mr Jenkins. 'What about the dogs? And the guards?'

'What about them indeed,' said Phryne.

The prisoner tried to guess what time it might be. Getting on for afternoon, perhaps. All morning she had lain and watched the sunlight move from right to left, which argued that the house was aligned east–west. She was so frightened that fear had become part of her world, a black cloud, settling on her eyes, dimming her senses.

Then she heard the door open, and writhed as a bolt of terror shot through her.

CHAPTER SIX

Something was gnawing at Phryne all the way home. Something was missing from Elizabeth's room. Her passport, of course. But she might have had that in her purse when she was kidnapped. She had been living in France for a long time and one always carried a carte d'identité in France. And she might easily have had her allowance in her purse. Things accumulated in purses. Unless they were deliberately unloaded and all contents examined for utility occasionally, one could find oneself transporting around in one's daily life three lipstick cases each with just a crumb of lipstick left, an old eyebrow pencil sharpener without a blade, pieces of defunct watch, odd earrings, handkerchiefs (three crumpled, one uncrumpled), two grubby powder puffs, bent hairpins, patterns of ribbon to be matched, a cigarette lighter without fuel (and two with fuel), a spark plug, some papers of Bex and a sprinkling of loose white aspirin, eleven train tickets (the return half of which had not been given up), four tram tickets, cinema and theatre stubs, seven`pence three farthings in loose change and the mandatory throat lozenge stuck to the lining. At least, those had been the extra contents of Phryne's bag the last time Dot had turned it out.

The thought refused to coalesce into anything useful. Phryne allowed her mind to drift. Someone had broken into the room, evading guards and dogs. They had gone to the trouble of bringing their own screwdriver to prise open the snib and had flung all those expensive garments to the wind. What had they been looking for? And had they found it?

She needed more information. But right now, she needed a cup of coffee and another look at Café Anatole. Fitzroy Street beckoned. For the first time, Phryne did not want to go home to her bijou residence. The Butlers had given notice, Lin Chung was getting married, and she was troubled by memories of Paris and the thought of René Dubois . . .

She turned the big car into the Strand. Coffee. Real coffee. French conversation. And at least one cheeky French waiter. Things could, she considered, be a lot worse.

Coffee was instantly forthcoming as soon as she walked in the door. The glass window had already been replaced, and a sign painter was standing on a ladder outside, blocking in the curly script of Café Anatole, ready for the gilt leaf on the morrow. The air smelt of impatience and painter's size.

Inside, the air smelt of freshly baked pastries—almond, if she was any judge—and coffee. Made in a coffee pot, with ground beans which had not been through the bleaching process which was evidently specially designed to remove all trace of unpalatable coffee flavour from the bottled product. Phryne shucked her coat into the ready hands of Jean-Jacques, or possibly Jean-Paul, and sat down at a small table. There sat M'sieur Anatole, scowling over a menu, his sister Berthe, and a Jean of some denomination who brought a tall coffee pot on a tray with cups, scalded milk and loaf sugar.

'Non, non, non!' protested Anatole. 'It is insupportable! How may I make my renowned quails with white grapes if there are no quails!'

'There are also no white grapes. They are out of season, and you have forgotten that you are on the other side of the world,' said Madame composedly, settling her bosom on her crossed arms. 'It is time for spring dishes, mon brave.'

'You could consider lobster,' offered Phryne hungrily. 'Homard à la Newburg? or maybe Thermidor? What's wrong with lobster in the French manner, à la Française? Plenty of fishermen just down the road, m'sieur.'

'Homard Victoria,' decided the chef. 'With sauce Normandy—yes. We still have some truffles. And we will need also scallops. A good idea, madame.'

Madame Phryne inclined her head. 'What else are you thinking of, chef?' she asked. 'I'd be delighted to try anything you are experimenting with.'

'For the other fish course, I have found the most delicious local fish—flathead. Good for bait, these barbarians say. It is as full flavoured as sole or whiting and twice as fine. Flatheads aux fines herbes, I think. Of course, I call them merlans, but they are flatheads just the same. Then since these Australians insist on steak, we could have a Parisian dish—tournedos Béarnaise, that should satisfy the carnivores. And perhaps a duckling with cherries—sweeter, to my mind, than orange and delicate of savour. Of course, one must have a game pie—rabbits here are the equal of anything in Europe and I'm sure that we can find a few pigeons.'

'Just ask a small boy with a slingshot,' said Phryne, sipping. Ah, coffee. She had never liked living pigeons. No mere bird ought to be able to grumble like that. They seemed to view the human race with a beady, almost reptilian and always jaundiced eye. Besides, when Ember caught one he had a tendency to tear it wing from wing all over the house and it was amazing how many feathers there were on one small pigeon. But cooked— that was another matter, as the cannibal said to the missionary. M'sieur Anatole was continuing.

'For soups—a printaniere, of course, a vegetable soup, and also a consommé Mireille . . . then perhaps ices for dessert. Mandarins glacés and something lush—I have it! Fraises Romanoff. Will you have more coffee?'

'I will,' said Phryne, and did. 'What are fraises Romanoff?'

'Strawberries, the large ones. Soaked in orange juice— freshly squeezed orange juice, you understand—and Curaçao. Served with crème Chantilly. Truly seasonal . . .' The chef's moustache whiffled in ecstasy. 'I would make them au Petit Trianon—La Reine Marie Antoinette loved strawberries like that—but I cannot get fraises du bois in Australia—they just do not taste the same, these tended fruits.'

'Never mind,' said Phryne, patting his hand.

'True, it is of no importance. Ma soeur, will that suffice?' he asked. The elder lady nodded and got to her feet.

'No soufflés?' she asked delicately.

'Non,' said M'sieur Anatole. 'One needs a light heart for soufflés and my heart is not light.'

He poured another cup of the fine, fragrant coffee and sighed. He looked at Phryne.

'Have you found my Elizabeth? No, don't tell me, I can see that you have not.'

'No, but I have been investigating,' said Phryne. 'I met her father today. He drew a gun on me.'

'Ah, that Hector, what a quick temper he has! Truly, it will get him into trouble one of these weeks.'

'Truly,' agreed Phryne. 'I convinced him not to shoot me, which is always an advantage. And I am working on the matter and I will find Elizabeth, I assure you. Also, I have mentioned to a little bird that this end of Fitzroy Street might bear a little more policing. Now I need to know more about you and yours. Would you show me your establishment, m'sieur? I have not even met all your people.'

'There are few outside the family,' said M'sieur Anatole. 'But come in. The kitchen is quiet now, just between lunch being cleared away and dinner preparations starting.'

He led the way through a swinging shutter beside the zinc counter into a large room which seemed to be entirely full of white coats, tall hats, steam and a reek of boiling washing-up water and soap; sour as old milk. Phryne's nose wrinkled involuntarily.

'This is Jean-Paul,' said M'sieur Anatole.

'Madame,' Jean-Paul bent and kissed her hand, holding it a little too long. He had clearly also graduated from Charming Rich Ladies School.

'This is Henri, my cousin.'

Stocky, dark Henri took her hand in a grasp greased lightly with chicken fat and kissed it.

'And this?'

'Oh, that is just Sam. He is our washer-up.'

A straw-polled boy ducked his head and grunted something. He was dressed in a flannel shirt which had evidently belonged to an older relative, and a pair of washed-white moleskins. When Phryne bent to look into his face he turned away. Not before she had seen a livid scar puckering his face, as though someone had tried to gouge out his eye with something curved—say, a bottle. The face was young but mutilated, the lip drawn up into a permanent sneer.

Not by one word or surprised declaration did Phryne let it be known that she was fairly sure that Billy the Match was working in the kitchen at Café Anatole.

Still, he was doing a good job with the washing up. Those plates were being scoured to within an inch of their patterns under the steel wool held in goose-skin wrinkled hands, red with heat and suds.

'Sam doesn't talk much, does he?' she asked.

'Il est un sourd-muet,' explained Henri. 'Deaf-mute. But a good industrious boy, nonetheless. Works hard. And sometimes you'd swear he could understand every word. But he can't, of course.'

'Of course,' echoed Phryne. 'How long have you had him?'

'He came here looking for work a few days ago. He had a little sign, all written out. And we shall keep him—eh, my brave boy?' Henri patted the shoulder under the checked shirt.

'Hello,' Phryne signed, holding her hands under the boy's downcast face. He lifted his hands out of the water long enough to return the greeting, clumsily. Billy had picked up some skills in prison, then.

She followed the chef back into the shiny bright bistro and allowed him to pour her more coffee.

'I want to ask your advice, now,' she said. 'I want you to remember Paris for me, at the end of the Great War.'

'That is a sad place to send me,' he objected.

'But it is where I must go,' she answered.

'What I really remember,' he said slowly, 'is the funerals. I was living in Montparnasse in the Avenue du Maine and they went past all day, a dark parade, a sad procession, and the bell tolled—oh, all the day.'

'The influenza epidemic,' agreed Phryne. 'When they were still having funerals, in November, I walked after the coffin of my dear friend Adelie, out from the Rue de Gaîté and into the Avenue, so slowly, so sad. And the cemetery like a city of the dead, all those little stone houses for the families. I had not thought that death had undone so many . . .'

It was very cold. The wind cut through Phryne's new leather coat and did not bother slowing in its course through her for minor matters like bones. Rain dripped off her only hat and ran down her face, colder than tears. Just near Professeur Larousse they were burying Adelie, who had survived the Great War, ambulance crashes, a near-direct hit with a shell and the armistice celebrations in Brussels, where the triumphant soldiery had brewed a victory cocktail made of rubbing alcohol and absinthe. But the 'flu had made an end of her.

Phryne sniffed. Standing at her elbow a young man with a clever, brown, shrewd face groped in his pocket and gave her a handkerchief. She mopped and blew. Poor Adelie. Phryne had caught la grippe early in May and thought herself immune to this 'flu. She was not feeling endangered, just hollow and sad, although so many had died in her sight, even under her hands, that she had thought that she had no feeling left.

'She gave me her last piece of chocolate once,' she sobbed.

'She was a generous person,' he agreed.

'You don't understand. She gave me her last piece of chocolate when we were starving hungry, filthy, trying to dig out a bogged ambulance full of shell-shocked men under fire. The stretcher cases were all screaming. I couldn't stand it any longer. And she gave me her last piece of chocolate.'

'Not just generous, then,' murmured the man. 'Heroic generosity.'

If there had been any trace of irony in his voice, Phryne would never have spoken to him again. There was not. The priest concluded his address. Earth landed on Adelie's coffin not with a rustle but a terribly final, soggy thud.

'Come,' he said to her, laying one hand on her shoulder. 'The friends of Adelie are going to drink to her. Will you come?'

'Where are you going?'

'La Closerie de Lilas. It is quiet. Also the girls from Au Chien Qui Fume will cross the road for this once.'

'What is your name?' she asked, slipping an ungloved hand into the crook of his arm. He smelt of Gauloises and cognac, a male scent.

'You are Lady Phryne Fisher,' he said in his almost comic sibilant Auvergne accent. 'And I am René Dubois. A musician.'

Phryne blew her nose again and looked into his brown eyes and fell desperately, completely and all at once in love.

'I fell in love at a funeral in that cemetery,' she said to M'sieur Anatole.

'They say it is Life, struggling against death. I myself was once violently seduced by a widow when her husband's grave was just covered. I was strangely surprised, but what would you? A grieving woman should not be refused. But it was grey, my Paris, in 1918. That was a long winter, colder than the grave.'

Not cold in René's bed, where he had taught her many new

and interesting skills, huddled under all of their combined blankets and her leather coat. Not cold, though frost caked the panes of the tall wood-framed windows of the atelier in Impasse d'Enfer. Not cold even though milk froze in bowls and water in taps and even the goatherd's pipe, as he led his nannies up the cobbled streets, sounded wavery and distant in the icy air.

She recalled the taste of goat's milk, drunk blood-warm from the bowl, when the street was so cold that the milk appeared to be smoking. Cold? No. The only cold thing in Paris that year had been René Dubois' heart, and it took her a long time to find that out.

'And nothing to eat,' the chef went on. 'Turnips, potatoes. Some dry legumes, haricots, lentilles. Nothing to cook but a pot-au-feu with whatever ingredients we could find. No sugar, no cream, no honey, no game, no chickens. Not even mushrooms. It was when I had to pay five francs—five francs!—for a piece of pig which would have been thrown out in disgust at a beggars' banquet that I decided to leave. Challenges, yes, a good cook needs challenges, but one must have ingredients.'

'Eels,' said Phryne. 'I remember eels, mussels, once even a turbot. Bread made out of pease flour. But there was a lot of army surplus tinned food. We used to feast on sardines and sop up the oil with that crumbly bread. We even made rissoles out of bully beef.'

M'sieur Anatole shuddered. 'Madame was very young.' He strove to find an excuse for Phryne. 'And madame was in love.'

'Yes, I was. But there was a scandal late that year,' she said, trying to jog the old man's memory. 'Something—I can't recall—was it about a train?'

'But of course,' he said. 'Jean-Jacques! Bring me the cognac! I cannot remember the sorrows of the past on coffee! The train, yes, you were there, madame, you must remember.'

Jean-Jacques plunked down the bottle and two glasses.

'Why do you need cognac to bear the past?' he demanded, filling two grudging measures of fine golden spirit.

'You wait until you have some sorrows of your own, my boy,' M'sieur Anatole chided him. 'You'll start getting them just after the little mouse has taken your last baby tooth.'

Jean-Jacques demonstrated Sulky French Waiter and flounced away. The swinging doors banged behind him. Phryne smiled. There was somehow no real malice in the young man. His uncle clearly felt the same.

'He will be a good restaurateur, that one,' he said comfortably. 'He has the élan. And his twin brother Jean-Paul. Some have it and some don't. You were asking me about the scandal. It was a year of scandals, indeed. Food riots. Women were shot outside the Presidential Palace, demanding bread for their children. But the one you are thinking of was the scandale fou about the painter, Sarcelle.'

'Of course,' said Phryne. 'He was just beginning to sell . . .'

'And he ended his days under a train at the Gare du Nord,' said M'sieur Anatole. 'The picture dealer Dupont was arrested, you recall?'

'And freed for want of evidence.' It was coming back to Phryne. 'And there was something about his wife . . .'

'Could not have been in the Gare du Nord,' said M'sieur Anatole. 'Was in a Paris office, trying to get a travel exemption to visit her sister in Toulouse before her baby was born. Went there, I believe, in the end. Did you know her?'

'Oh yes,' said Phryne, as it all came flooding back. 'I knew her. Véronique, that was her name. She was very fond of Pierre Sarcelle. I never believed that she had anything to do with his death.'

'But several persons suggested that he might have been

pushed,' M'sieur Anatole said, relishing this safely dead scandal. 'Sarcelle owed the picture dealer Dupont un mille. Dupont had been heard to say that Sarcelle would only be able to pay him back if he had the good taste to be deceased—thus his pictures would be more valuable.'

'A pleasantry, perhaps,' said Phryne.

'The examining magistrate was not convinced, but he had no proof. A good artist, that Sarcelle. Something of the school of Cézanne, but his colour—I thought his colour was better.'

'So did I,' said Phryne. 'I have some paintings of his. Nudes and landscapes. I sat for him. You must come and see them. Now I must be getting along. Thank you for your coffee and your company,' she said, and Jean-Jacques bowed her out.

'That one—she has some sorrow on her mind,' he commented, watching her start the great car and pull out into the traffic.

'Ask me again,' said M'sieur Anatole, 'when la petite souris has called for the last time.'

Annoyed at this reference to his baby teeth, Jean-Jacques didn't reply.

Phryne rang her own front door bell, wondering if anyone would answer. Her house was destabilised and she did not like the feeling. However, she had the address of the sacked Chambers butler and she would call him and arrange an appointment. She was not going to give way on this point. Lin Chung stayed.

Mr Butler admitted her without a flicker of an I-have-just-given-notice eyelash.

'Miss Fisher,' he said. 'The post is on your desk, the young ladies have arrived home from school and are in the kitchen, Miss Dot is in the smaller parlour and Detective Inspector

Robinson has called and says he will call again tonight. There are, otherwise, several messages.'

'Yes?'

'The Mayor was so good as to return your telephone call and assures you that you should find all the invitations you requested in your hands tomorrow,' he told her.

'Good,' said Phryne, not to be drawn. She shrugged off her coat and Mr Butler took it carefully.

'Mr Lin left a message that he would bring his . . . young lady to dinner tomorrow night, if you please.'

'I please,' said Phryne stonily. 'Please call him and tell him so.'

'And Mrs Butler and I are wondering if you might have . . . softened your firm line in this matter.'

'No,' responded Phryne. 'Is that all?'

'Yes, Miss Fisher,' Mr Butler said, with just the suspicion of a sigh.

Phryne went to find Dot, who was sitting in front of a small bright fire, knitting. The thread looked like fine silk and the small needles were moving with unthinking efficiency.

'Miss Phryne! You look cold! Come and sit down here. Can I get you some tea?'

'No thanks, Dot. I'm full of coffee. It's been a busy day. I've been threatened by a racing identity with a gun at least ten times the calibre of his brain and then I was reminiscing about Paris with M'sieur Anatole.'

'That would have been nice,' said Dot.

'No, no it wasn't. Dot, do the Butlers really mean to leave?'

'Yes, miss. Mr Butler's got a real bee in his bonnet about appearing in a divorce case. Mrs Butler's very upset. It doesn't worry her, and she keeps telling him he's a fool. They've been quarrelling all day, the milk's curdled, and the hens have stopped laying. It's been murder in the chookhouse all day. I've been hiding in here. They only stopped fighting when the girls came home, and I don't know how long that's going to last.'

'Are you worried about a divorce case, Dot?' asked Phryne, staring into the fire.

'Don't you think it, miss,' said Dot stoutly. 'I'm staying with you. I never heard such nonsense. But that's men for you.'

'Yes,' said Phryne, suddenly feeling much more comfortable. 'So it is.'

She was diverted from dark thoughts of death and war by the entry of her two adoptive daughters, Ember the cat and Molly the dog. Molly was sporting a fine new red scratch across her sensitive nose.

'It's her own fault,' said Jane. 'She wanted to play with Ember and Ember wanted to sleep. So she stuck her silly nose right under Ember and you can't do that to a cat.'

'Not if you want to preserve your nose intact,' agreed Phryne. 'Cats have strong opinions on dignity.'

'There was a sort of blur and Ember was out the door and poor old Molly had a scratched nose. It all happened so fast that I don't think she really knew what hit her.'

'How are you, young ladies?' asked Phryne. Both girls were glossy with health and shiny with good food and expensive soap. When she thought of herself at the same age, immured in that freezing cold school in the more depressing wilds of Norfolk, she could have laughed at the contrast. 'And how was school?'

'All right,' said Ruth. 'Chemistry was mercury reactions. Amazing. One moment it's a red powder, the next it's a silver liquid. And all the time it's a metal.'

Molly, who was not generally allowed into this parlour, sniffed suspiciously at the hearthrug before throwing herself down on it and waving all four paws in the air. The girls joined her there. Ember scaled Phryne's chair and perched on the arm, all four paws together and tail wrapped around, black as ink and poised like Loie Fuller.

Jane had a question.

'Miss Phryne, is Mr Lin getting married?'

'Yes, to a Chinese girl.'

'And yet he's still . . . seeing you?'

'Yes. That was the arrangement,' said Phryne coolly.

Jane thought about it. 'That's why Mr Butler is so upset?'

'It is,' said Phryne. Dot leaned forward and touched Jane's arm and the girl fell silent.

'It's all right,' Phryne told Jane. 'You can ask me any question. I just don't guarantee a reply.'

Jane wrinkled her brow and bit the end of her plait. 'So he'll have a wife and—'

'Got it,' announced Ruth, looking up from tickling Molly's tummy.

'What have you got?' asked Jane.

'Miss Phryne's a concubine,' said Ruth. 'Like King Solomon and the Queen of Sheba.'

'Ruth!' said Dot and Jane in one shocked exclamation.

'Got it in one,' said Phryne. 'Break out the clever chocolates.'

'And one for Jane,' bargained Ruth. 'She thought of the question.'

'Done,' said Phryne.

Jane and Ruth brought from the cupboard the large box of Haigh's Superfine Assorted Chocolates, awarded by Phryne for clever answers. Ruth got two and Jane one, and Phryne gave a peanut brittle to Dot because she looked so distressed.

She almost managed not to think of who she had been when another person had pressed on her one last piece of crumbly wartime chocolate, and smiled on her very own family, who were well fed, and warm, and safe.

CHAPTER SEVEN

Phryne woke in fright. It was black dark. The wind had picked up, a northerly which would probably bring scorching heat tomorrow, Melbourne weather being what it was. You could look on it as changeable or you could look on it as unreliable, depending on personal preference. If you don't like the weather, her mother had told her, go inside, turn around three times, and when you come out, it will have changed. And remember to take an umbrella wherever you go, she had added.

Phryne disliked the north wind with all the fervour of a Provençal whose opinion of the mistral has been requested or a Persian asked for a few favourable comments on the khamsin.

It scraped at her nerves. She turned over and Lin Chung awoke. She snuggled into his silky shoulder, resting her cheek on the pad of his muscular chest. He smelt of saffron: they had been unloading spices all day at his import/export business in Little Bourke Street. She breathed in, deeply. A most exotic scent for an exotic man.

'You are awake,' she murmured.

'So are you. The wind has changed. Listen to it claw at the house! In China this would be called dragon's breath.'

'Here, too. No one has a suitably diabolic name for that north wind. It's tormented me since I was a child. Damn.'

'What must you do tomorrow?' he asked gently, feeling the tension sing through her body.

'I have to try and find Elizabeth Chambers, so I am going to see her friend Miss Chivers, I am continuing to worry about Bert and Cec, Jack Robinson is coming back to talk to me and I must remember to tell him that I think his Billy the Match is working in Café Anatole, I have a fitting for my ball dress, you are coming to dinner with Camellia and . . . well, nothing else, really. A lot of things depend on things which depend, which makes me very uneasy. I like to be up and doing, even if it's nasty, strange, or dangerous.'

'I know. But there is something else, isn't there? By my actions, I have disrupted your house.'

'The Butlers? They will either change their mind or I will find someone else. A lot of people are looking for work. I have the name of a butler sacked by Mr Chambers, and I would be a better employer than that old grump even if he does get interviewed by the Hawklet about my scandalous household.'

'There is something more,' insisted Lin Chung.

Phryne hauled herself up on one elbow, found the switch, and put on her rose-shaded bedside light. Lying back on her moss-green pillows was a young man of unsurpassed beauty. His skin was golden, his hair as black as patent leather, brushed straight back. His slim, strong body was as smooth as amber and as electric. His unfathomable black eyes were regarding her with concern. If Rudolf Valentino had been born in Shanghai, he would have looked just so and another generation of women would have swooned over him.

'I have been remembering the first time that I fell in love,' said Phryne.

'Ah,' said Lin. He did not reach for her but sat up with his back against the pillows, prepared to listen intelligently. Phryne found this so seductive that she had to fight down a wave of pure lust.

'His name was René Dubois,' she said slowly. 'Damn, where did I put my cigarettes? Pour us a glass of champagne, Lin, there's some left.'

Lin obeyed. The champagne still held a little fizz and Phryne found her cigarette case and lit one, dragging the smoke in deep.

'He broke my heart,' she said, quickly.

'Of course,' said Lin Chung. 'One's first love always breaks one's heart. That is what it is for.'

'But Paris—Paris taught me something very valuable.'

'And what was that?'

'Paris taught me that I was beautiful,' said Phryne.

She was lying prone on a blue satin shawl while three painters argued over her pose, and she was getting very bored, which was bad, and cold, which was worse. Even the presence of Kiki, Sarcelle's wolfhound, did not help. He was sleeping under his blanket and was a lot warmer than the model.

The Atelier de Montparnasse was an impasse, a dead-end

cobbled lane. On either side were continuous three-storey buildings, all composed mostly of wood-framed glass windows to let in the maximum amount of light. Washing was usually strung between them, done by a shifting population of mistresses and models and even, occasionally, wives.

In accordance with ancient custom, sculptors lived on the ground floor, due to the weight of their work. No one wanted to wake up in the shattered remains of their studio surrounded by lumps of marble which had once been called 'Endeavour' or 'Spirit of Flight'. On the second floor were the painters and the workers in small crafts, clay and wood. On the top floor, reached by a precipitous creaking stair, were the poorest inhabitants, who were usually art students, prostitutes and people who had begged or stolen fifteen centimes and thus could avoid sleeping in the Bois.

Because of this and what Edouard l'Anglais called 'drains'— or lack of them—the Impasse de Montparnasse smelt of hasty, squalid cooking, unwashed humans, clay, paint, poverty and a local spirit sold at the Luxe Café known as Laissez-le Tombez, because more than one bottle and anyone was down for the night, or possibly the foreseeable, very short, future.

Madame la Concierge, a large figure indistinguishable among greatcoats and shawls, occupied a small kennel outside her own apartment at the entrance to the Impasse. She demanded Danegeld from any who might try to come in; lately she had been harvesting a fortune from the quarrel between Dupont and Sardou, two picture dealers who were convinced that they were onto something in the work of Sarcelle, the Modernist. Sarcelle thought so too.

Enough was enough. Phryne sat up, dragged Kiki's blanket around her (to his grave displeasure) and shouted, 'Ça me suffit!' into the argument.

There was a silence. Artists' models were not supposed to speak.

'Make up your minds,' she begged. 'I'm dying of cold. I give you one minute, then I'm putting on my clothes and I'm going home.'

This was not an idle threat. She might be proof against influenza, but she wasn't immune to pneumonia.

'No,' said Sarcelle, ruffling a worried beard. 'Don't leave us. See what beautiful things we have made of you? See how beautiful you are!'

Phryne stuffed her freezing feet into slippers and draped Kiki's blanket around her naked body. She shuffled along behind the easels and looked.

From Anton: one set of pinkish cubes which might have been anyone, including Madame Raphael, the concierge, who had a body like a box. From Edouard l'Anglais, one slight, delicate watercolour, a nymph with short hair staring into a pool, very airy and shadowless. That was she? So slim, so graceful? Sarcelle signalled to Véronique, his wife, and she flicked the cloth off the oil painting. Phryne gasped.

A naked woman, lying in a landscape composed of coloured blocks, blurred at the edges. Purples and blues faded into a dim distance. The body of the woman was perfect, pale as a pearl, her nipples lipstick pink, her hair and pubic hair black as pitch, redeemed from doll-like prettiness by the direct gaze of the eyes, which stared straight at the viewer, challenging, intelligent and bright spring green.

'Had you never known how beautiful you are?' asked Véronique, hugging Phryne. Véronique was a plump, pretty, comfortable woman, much tried by her highly strung husband. Sarcelle had been caricatured in the newspaper as all hair, beard, bones and high-collared Russian shirt. Everyone had instantly recognised him. His fellows were good artists in their way. Picasso had been kind about Anton's cubism and Miss Stein had bought two of English Edouard's delicate decorative nymphs. But Sarcelle, while he liked Phryne and his co-tenants and probably loved the devoted Véronique, adored Art with his whole passion, and seldom thought of anything else. He left the bargaining between Sardou and Dupont to his wife, who was from Burgundy and could squeeze a sou until it squeaked.

'I will finish the painting and lay on the gold leaf tomorrow,' said Sarcelle. 'But you must not leave me. You are the most beautiful model in Paris, it is well known.'

'I have a contract with DeBain, downstairs. He is doing a water nymph fountain,' said Phryne, still astounded. No one had ever told her she was beautiful. First she had been a street Arab with scabbed knees, then a sulky schoolgirl (too thin and too disagreeable) and then an ambulance driver, valued for her strong wrists and good sense of direction under fire. But the woman in the painting was undeniably beautiful.

'You are a great success,' Véronique told her. 'They all want you to pose for them, ever since Sarcelle discovered you. You are the body of the future; they dote upon you. Triple your fees,' the Burgundian woman advised. 'Except for Atelier Sarcelle,' she added, for even artists must eat.

'Madame,' said Phryne from the depths of her dog-smelling blanket, 'I will do as you say.'

'I am not surprised that you were a success,' commented Lin Chung. 'But I am surprised that you had to discover your beauty. Although, come to think of it, it came upon me as a great shock, that night in Little Bourke Street, when I first saw you. Grandmother thought that you might be a deity of some kind, and I thought so too. A silver lady, with perfect Manchu colouring except for those strange, compelling eyes. Beautiful and strange.'

'Precisely what I thought about you,' returned Phryne, taking a deep gulp of the champagne. 'Strange and beautiful, like and unlike.'

'Paris taught you that you were beautiful,' prompted Lin Chung. Phryne lit another cigarette.

René poured her another glass of thin colourless liquid.

'It will make you warm,' he urged. 'Drink it in one gulp, or it will burn your mouth. And it is such a beautiful mouth,' he added, tilting his head in a bird-like gesture to absorb her countenance. Phryne gulped, gasped, and sat down on René's knee.

All around the friends of Adelie were getting rapidly drunk and talking and crying. Phryne had cried herself out on the walk back from the cemetery. The drink mounted rapidly to her head. All she could taste was aniseed.

'Raki,' said Toupie, reclining massively on two chairs by the wall. The café was packed. Outside it was beginning to snow. Inside the brass glittered and the palm trees swayed their fronds in the hot air. Phryne took off her coat and unbuttoned her shirt. René grinned and helped her with the buttons as her fingers had unaccountably turned clumsy. 'That is firewater, my dear. And that young man is going to seduce you if you don't watch out.'

'Indeed,' agreed Phryne, who had made up her mind on this point.

'Well, you know your own mind,' said Toupie. 'Dolly!' she called. 'You know how you like seductions. Here's one happening right before my eyes.'

Phryne reflected that she ought to be embarrassed. She wasn't. From the first moment she had seen him, René was her destined lover, forever and forever amen. She had known that he would come along if she didn't think about it. She hadn't, and here he was.

A dark-haired young woman in the ambulance uniform perched on the arm of Toupie's chair. She was the image of her Uncle Oscar, even down to the beautiful Wilde hands and the sparkling, seductive eyes. She folded the long, sensitive fingers on her knee and said, 'How thrilling! Ah, René, when you pursued me for so long and so unavailingly! My chevalier is faithless at last!'

'As you say,' said René.

'I like your taste,' said Dolly, examining Phryne from several angles, fingers poised as if she were holding a quizzing glass. 'Oh, yes, she has points.'

'I believe so,' said René, holding Phryne tighter. She felt heat rising in his lap, matched by her own ascending temperature. How long was this wake going to last?

'You are aware,' Dolly leaned close to Phryne, almost whispering in her ear, 'that René is a rampant, a self-confessed . . .' she leaned even closer, her lips touching Phryne's neck '. . . heterosexual?'

Phryne laughed and kissed the red mouth, held out in a pretty pout.

'I shall just have to accept it,' she said sadly.

The women watched as she left with René, bundling out into the snow. As she shut the door Phryne heard Toupie say, 'Another one lost!' and then she was running in snow, pulled along by René's clutch on her hand. They dared roads, skidded on ice, found the Impasse d'Enfer almost by instinct and ran inside, shaking off snow, laughing, shivering.

René lit his kerosene heater and completed the unbuttoning of Phryne's shirt. He kissed each nipple as it was exposed, hard in the cold air. Phryne moaned. He laid her down in his tumbled bed, stripped in haste and threw himself after her, dragging blankets over both of them.

He was not the first naked man Phryne had ever seen, but he was the first she had ever wanted. She handled his body in wonder, so different from her own, the skin rougher, the hair wiry, the touch of his hardened fingers so exciting. And this jigsaw piece, she knew, was meant to fit . . . there.

It felt strange. Not painful. Not pleasurable, either, though it was pleasing René. His swollen lips kissed and sucked, his hips moved in a convulsive, effortful slide inside the cocoon of coverings.

Then a small light lit itself inside Phryne, growing hotter with friction, until it exploded in a burst of such strong sensation that she found herself crying into a sweating man's neck, her arms around him, collapsed on top of her.

'Death and love,' gasped René. 'Such is life.'

'I wanted to move in with him,' she told Lin Chung. 'But he would not allow it. So I stayed in the Rue de Gaîté with La Petite and kept on being an artist's model. René was a musician. I used to go to the bal musette to hear him play. In the Rue des Trois Colonnes.'

'And he broke your heart?'

'Oh yes, but enough of this. What about your first love?'

'She was an English girl, when I was at Oxford. Her name was Jonquil—don't laugh—she was a dancer in the chorus at the Gaiety Theatre and I thought she was wonderful. She had a rope of red hair down to her waist and she could dance like an angel.'

'I'm not laughing.' Phryne lounged down into her bed again and took his hand. 'How did your romance proceed?'

'I went to every show,' said Lin Chung. 'I watched her every night. Then I waited at the stage door. Once I had managed to gather the courage to talk to her, she would sometimes allow me to take her out for supper. It's hard to recall how much I adored her. I could just sit and watch her eat lobster—she was fond of lobster—and I even loved the way she banged the claws to get at the meat.'

'I know,' said Phryne, reminded of René Dubois and roasted chicken.

'I spent my whole allowance on her,' said Lin Chung. 'Grandmother was displeased. Someone told her that I had contracted an unwise relationship with a non-Chinese.'

'And you are still doing it,' said Phryne.

'So I am,' said Lin Chung softly. 'So I received instructions to break off this friendship at once. What do you think I did?'

'You defied her,' said Phryne. 'At that age and in that situation, I would have gone to the stake for René Dubois. Singing the whole time they were lighting the fire, too.'

'Yes,' said Lin. 'I had written the letter to Grandmother. I went out to post it. And there I saw my Jonquil, kissing a man. Kissing him as I would have wished to kiss her. I stood there with my defiance in my hand and watched as she caressed him, standing in a corner of the theatre doorway.'

'Poor Lin,' said Phryne.

'Then she walked past me with him—and I knew where they were going—and she saw me and waved a hand, carelessly. And I heard her say as they walked away, "Nice little Chink." I was devastated. I tore up the letter and went home to my digs and for six months I seriously contemplated suicide.'

'Oh, Lin dear,' said Phryne.

She drew him into her arms and his mouth came down on hers. Phryne knew about sex, now. As the clever fingers slid down her spine, seeking the pressure point which would light her response, she considered that, perhaps, after all, things had improved.

Breakfast was late and served by Mrs Butler. Mr Butler was, it appeared, absent on some errand. Phryne expected that he was at the employment office, seeking a new position. Mrs Butler slid a perfectly poached egg onto a warmed plate and Phryne ate with pleasure.

'Have the hens started laying again, Mrs B?' she asked. Surely hens were a safe topic.

'Seven this morning, Miss Fisher. Are you likely to be in for lunch?'

'I have to go and visit a young woman, but I will be home for most of the day. Mr Bert and Mr Cec are coming, as is Detective Inspector Robinson, and Madame Fleuri, probably not in that order. So, a light lunch, possibly for all of them. Bert and Cec always need feeding.'

'Pies, perhaps?' offered Mrs Butler. 'I've got three cooked and they can be reheated easily.'

'Sounds wonderful. Thank you.'

'Another egg, Mr Lin?' asked Mrs Butler, to show that there were no hard feelings and this wasn't her stupid idea. Lin accepted.

'What do you have to do today, beautiful man?' asked Phryne.

'We must sort and package the spices. I will bring you some saffron and some of our curry powder, ready to be ground. It is the best in Melbourne.'

'I'm sure it is,' Mrs Butler beamed on Lin Chung and bustled away.

'And you?'

'You heard. I wish I had some clue about that poor girl. I'm a firm believer in direct action when there is some action to take but I don't have a clue as to who snatched her or what they are likely to do. I mean, Lin dear, those Chinese pirates had kidnapping as a cottage industry. They had to hand over the subject or their credit would be shot. Westerners do not handle these things as well.'

'I believe there has been an epidemic of kidnappings in America,' said Lin. 'The Mafia make a good living out of kidnapping.'

'They've got the organisation for it,' said Phryne. 'This sounds like someone who is making it up as they go along . . . now why should I think that? The actual grab was well arranged. And how did they know she was going to be at a private party? She seldom went to parties. It smacks of an inside job. Mr Chambers is so notably unpleasant to work for that he must have scattered enemies all over the Melbourne metropolitan area.'

'Why would they keep the car?' asked Lin. 'If Mr Chambers is as described, it would be a big, showy car. Much harder to hide than a small frightened girl.'

'Good point. I'll tell Jack about it. But modern car thieves are pretty good at car-faking. Change the colour, alter the engine number, new headlights, Bob's your uncle and Fanny's your aunt.'

'No,' said Lin. 'I meant, if they are aiming for a five hundred pound profit, isn't it an odd thing that they should keep the car, too, when that might lead to their being detected?'

'Greed? There's a lot of it about. I could say something

withering about the idiocy of the typical criminal mind. Or maybe this is a frolic of some subordinate. Told to take the car and dump it outside Flinders Street Station where it would be readily found, he decided that he just had to keep it. Might be a crack in the case, Lin dear, thank you.'

'My pleasure. Camellia and I will be here tonight—about seven?'

'About seven,' said Phryne. She kissed him goodbye in a lingering fashion, and let him go.

Ember floated up onto Phryne's knee, indicating politely that a piece of bacon rind a day was a dietary supplement which all cats needed. She supplied it and considered her day.

An hour later, dressed in a dark blue suit made of fine crepe de chine and a white blouse, which seemed businesslike enough for what was indeed going to be a hot day, she set off for Kew and the home of Miss Julia Chivers, whose name had been publicly coupled as a prospective bride with that of the well-known racing identity and grump, Hector Chambers.

Darkness flowed over the prisoner. Today he had allowed her to wash. The water was half cold and the bath was filthy but it felt very good to scour some of the dirt off her skin with yellow soap. Then, knowing how cowed she was, he had allowed her to remain unsecured. She lay rubbing her wrists, contemplating a hopeless escape.

CHAPTER EIGHT

Phryne left the car in the street because she could see that she would need both hands to get to the door, if she ever made it alive. What she really needed was a solar topee, tropical kit, a native guide, a team of bearers, and something rather tasty in the guise of a Great White Hunter. Whole tribes of pygmies, probably with blow darts tipped with some strange untraceable South American poison, were doubtless lurking in the wisteria. The jasmine had twined itself through the iron lace on the verandah, falling down into heavy veils of green shadow. Rhododendrons rose like a black wall. Phryne wished she had brought a machete. Or a tank.

A narrow path had been beaten through the jungle to the front door, doubtless trodden down by the feet of the postman and the bailiff. This house was not even shabby genteel.

It was something in a new category . . . ruined genteel? Phryne searched for a definition. This might, she decided, be that Distressed Circumstance about which she had always wondered.

She rang the doorbell, which came off in her hand. The iron wires had rusted through. Placing it on a windowsill, she knocked at a door from which the paint was peeling.

Through the stained glass panels she could dimly see someone moving. Reminded of her own poverty-stricken past, she called, 'It's Phryne Fisher. I'm not a sheriff, a bill collector or a cop. Do let me in, I'm sure I can hear war drums in the undergrowth.'

She was answered by a faint giggle and the opening of the massive door, just wide enough for her to slip in.

'Hello,' said Phryne. 'Are you Julia?'

'Yes,' said a slight, golden-haired girl. 'Come into the kitchen. It's the only furnished part of the house that's halfway comfortable.'

Miss Julia Chivers, Phryne thought as she followed the girl's straight back down the dark hall, was beautiful. She had spun-gold hair like a princess from a fairy-tale, china-blue eyes, a mouth like a pink rosebud and a slim body, emphasised by the short and skimpy house dress she was wearing. It was made of cheap cotton cloth with cornflowers printed on it and was washed white in some places.

The girl walked like a deer, not in an elegant or studied manner, but as a product of being young and strong and given to, Phryne guessed, long walks and five sets of tennis before breakfast. She shone with health.

The kitchen was huge. Feasts for fifty guests (plus coachmen and lady's maids) had been cooked in these cavernous ovens. Thousands of elaborate desserts had been concocted on this long scrubbed table. On one end of it, directly opposite the large window, lay an ivory crepe gown with a heavily beaded hem. Boxes of beads and fine needles indicated someone's occupation.

A small portion of the room contained Julia's family's remaining comforts; two easy chairs, a shelf of tinned and packaged food, a basket of eggs and some fruit. There was a tea tray on the table, two cups and saucers, both unwashed. Julia lit the primus under the kettle. It sputtered and went out. The fuel bottle was empty. Julia let the match burn down before she dropped it. Phryne could not see her face.

'I'm so sorry,' she said mechanically. 'I can't offer you a cup of tea. Do sit down, Miss Fisher. What brings you here?'

'Come out,' said Phryne. 'Let's go and get a proper tea. This place must be getting on your nerves.'

'Can't, I haven't anything to wear. My only good dress is on the line.'

'Wear my coat,' said Phryne. 'It's nice and voluminous and you won't need to take it off.'

'The girl looked longingly at Phryne's crepe de Chine coat, a poem in dark blue with faint damasking patterns, and was lost.

'Good,' said Phryne, flinging it briskly round the slim shoulders. 'Wrap it around you and tie it on the hip and your secret is safe. Is there any other way out?' she asked, not wanting to contend with Darkest Africa again.

Without a word Julia led the way out of the back door and through a yard in which someone had, without much success, tried to grow vegetables. Depressed silver beet drooped in rows and sad pumpkin vines failed to clamber over the broken fences. The couch grass crop, however, was going to be abundant.

Julia didn't speak until she was seated beside Phryne and the car had pulled away from the kerb. Then she drew a deep breath and said, 'Oh, lovely to be out.'

'Cinderella, Cinderella, what is your pleasure?' murmured Phryne, quoting the fairy-tale, turning the big car towards the city.

'Tea,' said Julia. 'With cakes. Lots of cakes. What did you want with me, anyway?' she demanded, suddenly aware that she had been lured out of her house.

'I wanted to talk about your friend, Elizabeth. I'm trying to find her.' Phryne handed over one of her cards.

Julia read it and faltered, 'Her father . . . has her father hired you?'

'No,' said Phryne, wondering what had elicited that note of fear. 'The chef of Café Anatole, he is concerned about her. I gather he was expecting to marry her—is that true?'

Julia giggled again. 'He went to her father and asked for her hand. So sweet! And he is such a good cook. His rillettes de veau—delicious.'

'Shall we go to Café Anatole, then?' asked Phryne.

The girl shivered a little. 'No. I want tea and cakes.'

'The Windsor, then,' said Phryne.

'But I can't go to the Windsor without stockings!' wailed Julia.

'My dear girl,' said Phryne, 'you can go anywhere you want to go. The management of the Windsor wish you to come into their establishment and buy a sumptuous tea, and I shall personally reprove anyone I catch looking at your legs. They should be attending to their business, which is to make you comfortable. Now stop worrying and talk to me. Are you not concerned about your friend? Can you tell me what happened on that night when she vanished?'

'Not much to tell,' said Julia. 'We went to my cousin Raoul's birthday party. There was going to be dancing and Elizabeth loved to dance. She doesn't like clothes much and she's death on gossip. She is really only interested in cooking but she does—did—love dancing. And charades. Raoul always has charades. I wasn't going to go because I didn't have a dress which everyone hadn't seen twenty times before. Mother was saving for another dress. Madame Fleuri's prices are wicked. But Lizzie gave me an armload of her French clothes and told me to take whichever I wanted. Beautiful things, silk underwear and day dresses and ball dresses. Her school had taken them all into Paris to be properly equipped and Lizzie's father had paid up without a murmur. When I was there, I couldn't do that. I do love beautiful things.'

'Yes,' said Phryne. She was thinking, you are a nice young woman. She also remembered how she had gone through the rest of those clothes, and most of them had still been there. Julia could only have taken one day dress and one dance dress. That was restrained, since Lizzie wouldn't have cared if she'd taken them all, and the temptation must have been severe.

'How did you pay your way through finishing school, then?' she asked.

Julia flushed as pink as a paeony. 'I taught English and fine needlework,' she said. 'I do the beading for a fashion house in Collins Street. My mother cleans houses. My father sells cough medicine. Now you know!' she declared.

'Yes, now I know,' said Phryne. 'Now I am in a position to ruin you socially. Such secrets as you care to tell me will never be disclosed, and I consider that society needs me a lot more than I need it. I'm notorious, haven't you heard?'

'Oh, well, yes, Miss Fisher, I have . . .' Julia dissolved in confusion.

'Well, then. I can guess a little. Your family could be quite comfortable if they sold that great big house, sending in a few missionaries first to deal with the tribes living in the undergrowth. Then you could buy a small house in Footscray and live quite well. But instead you are all camping in that Good Address and scrimping to buy you one good dress so that you can go to the right ball and catch the right husband. Such as Mr Chambers, the well-known sporting identity? You have to repair the family fortunes, eh?'

She had stopped the car outside the Windsor. Julia was hovering on the verge of tears.

'Yes,' she whispered. 'That's what I have to do.'

'Ah,' said Phryne, allowing the doorman to help her out. 'And I thought that Bride Sacrifice had died out with the Chaldeans. Come along,' she said imperiously, and Julia followed her, intensely conscious of her bare legs, wrapping her concealing coat about her in a frantic swathe.

To her relief, Miss Fisher was right. No one stared at her. They were conducted to a table by the window and immediately supplied with a silver pot of tea, a silver service, and a trolley piled with delicious cakes. Phryne took a selection of petits fours and poured tea liberally.

She waited, watching Julia's hand hover over the rich, cream-filled dainties, until she selected one.

'Have two,' said Phryne. 'Or three.'

Julia blushed again and loaded her plate like a greedy child.

Phryne allowed her ten minutes to stuff as many cakes as she could into that rosebud mouth—it was charming to watch a girl eat with such frank enjoyment. Then she said gently, 'So you went to Cousin Raoul's party in the big car with Elizabeth. Then what happened?'

'It was a nice party,' said Julia, her pink tongue discreetly licking the last smear of cream from her lip. 'Raoul's parties are always good. We did charades. We had a nice buffet supper and Lizzie danced every dance.'

'With one person in particular?' asked Phryne, watching the girl closely.

'No, with whoever was free. I don't think Lizzie is interested in boys much. She danced with Raoul—he's devastating, all the girls are after him—but she said he was only a fair dancer and she wanted Tim Purcell next, and everyone knows he's a weed. Good dancer, though. He can foxtrot like a dream. But all he can talk about is his medical studies and how he is going to do good to the poor and no one made money out of that.'

'Anyone there that you are interested in? Cousin Raoul, perhaps?'

'No,' said Julia sadly. 'He hasn't a bean. He has to marry money, too. Anyway, I don't want to marry anyone. Look at Father and Mother! They work hard, all to help me find someone I can sell myself to, so that they can fix up the house and get some more servants and go back to how they used to be before the war. I don't think we can go back to what things were like before the war.'

'No,' said Phryne, 'we can't. It's a new world and we have to get used to it. So you and Lizzie were at the party . . .'

'And I was thinking it was time to get going, it was getting late and some of the hearties were getting a bit rowdy. I don't like that sort of thing. They were all ragging Tim about his doing good and he was blushing and I thought it was time to go home. I went looking for Lizzie and I couldn't find her. I didn't want to cause any talk, so I searched the house. The maid in the ladies' room said she'd been there about eleven.

The maid had repaired her hem. I looked through the window and the black car had gone, but I saw Mr Chamber's man on the doorstep, shouting at the butler. So I got my coat and slipped down. Mr Chambers' man said that he'd just been away for a minute and where was the car, and I didn't know, and where was Lizzie, and I didn't know that either. So he telephoned Mr Chambers and he sent another car to take me home. The next day Mr Chambers came to see me and I told him all I could and since then I haven't heard a thing. Where is Lizzie? Has something happened to her?'

'I don't know where she is, but Mr Chambers has had a ransom demand.'

Julia's hand flew to her mouth and her eyes widened. It was a pretty gesture.

'Oh! Poor Lizzie!'

'Indeed,' said Phryne. 'You haven't heard from her since that night? I was wondering if you might have had a phone call, a postcard—anything.'

'No, nothing,' gasped Julia.

'Might she have run away?' asked Phryne.

'She might,' said Julia. 'Her father didn't know her very well. He really didn't know how to talk to her. He gave her lots of pretty things and expected her to be a good girl. And she is a good girl,' declared Julia. 'She isn't interested in all those things—fripperies, she calls them. She wants to be a cook.'

'Did she know that her father was intending to marry you?'

'Yes,' confessed Julia, blushing again. 'But she said she didn't mind, as long as I didn't try to mother her, and I couldn't, really I couldn't, it would be absurd.'

'Has it occurred to your parents,' said Phryne deliberately, 'that Mr Chambers is a terrible grump and something of a miser? Mean as a rat, my companion says. He may have spent freely on his daughter, but what leads your father to imagine that he would spend freely on his in-laws?'

'Oh, there's to be a marriage settlement,' said Julia. 'Mr Chambers will agree to settle an amount of money on my parents.'

'In payment for you?' asked Phryne.

'Yes,' said Julia, her blonde head drooping on its stalk like a snowdrop.

'And you'll go along with this . . . arrangement?'

'I don't see,' said Julia, 'that I have a lot of choices. I can continue to bead garments for rich women until my eyesight goes, living in that dank house and hiding when the bailiff comes, nagged all the time about how much money my parents spent on my education and how I have wasted it. Or I can undertake a marriage which will give me pretty clothes, unlimited food, lots of dances and nice places to stay. Holidays. Champagne.'

'And Mr Chambers in your bed,' said Phryne coarsely.

Julia shuddered, but squared her shoulders. 'It's a price,' she admitted. 'But I can pay it.'

'So you can,' said Phryne. 'And it might be a bargain, at that. Now, I had better be getting you home. You have my card. Call me if anything occurs to you.'

'Miss Fisher,' asked Julia, as they were handed back into the car by an attentive doorman whose disposition had been sweetened with silver, 'can I ask you a question?'

'Of course,' said Phryne.

'Do you think he'll pay the ransom?'

'Mr Chambers? If he can't avoid it,' said Phryne. 'He hasn't called the police, and none of his underworld chums have discovered which gang has carried this out. This means that they are amateurs and might panic.'

'Oh,' Julia seemed distressed. 'Oh, poor Lizzie! I hope she isn't too frightened.'

'So do I,' said Phryne.

She arrived back in her own house still deep in thought. Devil's bargains all around. Threats from every quarter. The only consolation she had was that Lizzie sounded like an intelligent, determined young woman. The character of the victim was an important component in a successful rescue. Even now, Lizzie might be rescuing herself.

But Phryne must tell Robinson about that car. An interesting thing, that car theft. Just another chance of extra loot, or an oversight?

While being fitted for a dress in which she expected to astonish the Lord Mayor's Ball, Phryne asked Madame Fleuri if she knew the Chivers family.

'Ah, yes,' said Madame in French, speaking in that dressmaker's dialect which does not disturb the pins in the mouth. 'Poor as church mice and terribly keen to sell their daughter to the highest bidder. What would you? The girl is beautiful. But not a brain in her head. She beads like a professional and could make a living that way—or she could be a teacher, to be sure, she is well educated—but she has not as much courage as would inflame a mouse. She might as well have a husband.'

'You are very severe,' said Phryne, amused.

'Young women ought to have a profession,' said Madame. 'Husbands—they can vanish, pouf! Here one day and gone the next. That is the nature of men. Then what will she do?

For such a one the fall can be sudden. She only knows of one thing which she can sell, and once she is on the streets it is a long way back to the world she has known.'

'So it is,' agreed Phryne. She was observing herself in the long mirror. The dress was an Egyptian design, which was daring. It was made of cotton, which was very bold indeed. No one wore cotton in the evening, but it promised to be hot, and Phryne saw no reason why she should sweat in silk when she could be cool in cotton.

'There,' Madame grunted as she came up off her knees. 'A sensation. We will put on this collar, so,' she laid the jewelled collar over Phryne's shoulders. The Basht pendant hung between her breasts. The body of the dress was made of fine, pale ochre-coloured Egyptian glazed cotton. Almost as expensive as silk but much, much cooler. It hung as straight as a column to Phryne's ankles and was slit behind to her knees, so that when she walked she looked like she was wearing an Ancient Greek tunic, and when she stood the dress fell uninterrupted in one fine, long sweep. With it she had sandals made of pale kid's leather, soft as skin. Madame slid the heavy beaded bracelet up to Phryne's upper arm and put the circlet on her head. The silver cobra head was raised and alert. It was a modified form of the costume of Isis which she had worn to the Artists' Ball, scandalising Sydney.

Ember, who had been catching fifty winks on Phryne's bed, woke, yawned, stretched, and came to sit at her feet, gazing upward with slitted eyes as though she shone. Madame clasped her hands.

'Yes,' she said. 'Le petit chaton is correct. It is marvellous.'

If Ember objected to being called a little kitten, he did not even flick a whisker. He laid a paw on Phryne's foot and she bent carefully to caress him. He batted at the hanging image of the cat-goddess. Madame Fleuri chuckled.

'That one, he is devout,' she observed, sticking her remaining pins into the emery pincushion on her wrist. 'I must go. Between ourselves, madame,' she said to Phryne as she swept her equipment into her bag, 'can you tell me whether the Chivers are likely to pay their account? They owe me still for the last dress I made for their daughter.'

'Young Miss Chivers is about to make a very wealthy marriage with old Mr Chambers,' said Phryne. 'I have been speaking with her this very morning. She seems determined to go through with it and she knows you are the best dressmaker in Melbourne. I would be inclined to risk one more dress. She is likely to be a good customer once she gets her hands on some real money.'

'So. It is worth the chance that the alliance may fall through,' said Madame. 'And my accountant says that such bad debts would be an advantage this year with that wicked income tax. Very well. Thank you, madame.'

Phryne allowed Dot to undress her. When she laid the collar on her bed, Ember immediately curled himself around it and went firmly back to sleep, defying anyone to remove it.

'Odd,' Phryne observed. 'Leave it for the moment, Dot, he can't hurt it. Has Jack Robinson come?'

'Downstairs waiting for you,' said Dot. 'Hugh is with him.'

Dot would never call an unrelated man by his first name if she didn't intend to marry him. She had every intention of doing so, when the right time came. The right time wasn't yet and Hugh seemed content to wait, escorting Dot and the girls to the cinema and snatching an occasional kiss when Dot would let him get close enough. She was entirely pleased with him and regarded the strange feeling of hot jam running down her back when she kissed him as an excellent omen for future happiness.

Robinson and Hugh Collins were eying a cold buffet lunch with barely concealed expressions of extreme greed when Phryne and Dot came down the stairs and greeted them.

'Take a plate, Jack dear, and help yourself,' said Phryne. 'Your wife still away?'

'Coming back tomorrow,' said Robinson, making a beeline for three raised pies. One would be pork, if he knew his Mrs Butler. He could already taste the savoury jelly which she would have poured in through a funnel after the pie was cooked. There had been an armed robbery late last night and he was short of sleep. And all he had had to eat had been a couple of limp ham sandwiches and a boiled egg which had been left too long on the stove and had apparently vulcanised.

Hugh Collins, who had not got home to his supper at all, and then had to listen to his mother complaining about good food left to dry in the oven (and why hadn't he been an engine driver like his father, who worked reasonable hours and always came home in time for dinner?) was starving. Dot cut him large slices of cold steak and kidney pie, his favourite, and watched him polish off a plateful without putting down his fork. She supplied him again, smiling, before she collected some egg-and-bacon pie for herself. Phryne took some salade russe and a slice of cold ham. All those cakes had ruined her appetite, but she always enjoyed watching people eat.

'I've been over those two reports,' said Robinson, agreeably conscious of the probability of second helpings. 'I concur. They need investigation. So I'm sending Collins here to Mildura this afternoon to have a look around and talk to the local police. Shocking oversight, but you know how they are in the country. I'm looking into the Richmond accident myself. Talked to the widow this morning. She said she knew there was something wrong. Said her husband was very careful. Also said that there was a knock at the door, someone was there, her husband went out, saying he had to see a man about a dog. He didn't come back all night and she sat up waiting for him—seems he didn't make a habit of staying out. Then she went to let the coal man in and found her husband dead under the van. The back gate was unlocked.

'She says she told all this to the coroner's officer and they said it wasn't relevant. I'll have that bloke hauled over some coals, I can tell you. Poor woman is real cut up. Seems he had some insurance and she won't have to leave the house. Got two nice little kids. Cruel,' said Robinson. His sympathy for the bereaved had not destroyed his enjoyment of simple pleasures, however, Phryne observed, as Jack cut himself another slice of pork pie. This made sense. If policemen went into a decline every time they met tragedy, the entire force would rapidly starve to death.

Mrs Butler had really done them well, Phryne thought, wondering if this excellent cook had managed to change her righteous husband's mind. Phryne would really hate to lose both of them. But a principle was a principle and a lover was a lover.

When the clatter of cutlery had died down a little, Hugh excused himself.

'Got to catch the afternoon train,' he explained. He brushed crumbs off his shirt, collected his bag and coat from Mr Butler, and had Phryne heard the smack of a chaste kiss in the hall? By the way Dot was blushing when she came back, she had.

'What about that other matter you weren't telling me about when I saw you last?' asked Jack Robinson.

'Well, I suggest you might have a little look for a big black Bentley,' said Phryne, handing over a slip of paper with the number. 'I would really like to know if it has been sold, or whether it is just standing idly by, waiting to be stolen.'

'Can be done,' said Robinson. 'Not that many Bentleys in the city. Nice cars.'

'Also, I would like you to lunch with me at Café Anatole tomorrow and tell me whether you recognise anyone,' said Phryne. 'There's a kitchen boy there with a scarred face. He's supposed to be a deaf-mute and he's employed as a dish washer.'

'You reckon it might be our Billy? I had someone call at his house. His mum ain't seen him and doesn't want to, she says. She says that she runs a respectable boarding house—and that's a lie—and she doesn't want Billy home. I also had a chat with the blokes in the know about who's standing over Fitzroy Street. I reckon your café won't have no further trouble.'

'Why?' asked Phryne.

'We got 'em,' said Jack Robinson, glowing with triumph. 'We've had our eye on them for years and just yesterday they bit off more than they could chew and we've got 'em, every one of the Fitzroy Boys. They reckoned they'd pick a soft target— the Chinese laundry. They put the hard word on them. Then they all went down for a meeting with the Chinese. And when they had all sat down, Poulton giving the beat policeman a greasy smile as he went past, suddenly the Chinese were out with these big steel kitchen choppers and it was on for young and old. By the time the man on the beat could whistle up some help, the Fitzroy Boys were out for the count, bleeding all over the pavement, and there wasn't a Chinese in sight. When questioned, they all said that they had been busy in their laundry and hadn't seen a thing, officer. However, they would be delighted to help the police and give evidence in court that these men had tried to extort money from them.

'Oh, it was pretty,' said Robinson, chuckling. 'We've got 'em cold. The rest of the 'Roy Boys ain't going to dare attack the Chinese now, not with their mates lying there with missing bits. The Consorting Squad were out there all afternoon, picking up ears. So your Café Anatole is safe from the 'Roy Boys. But Billy the Match wasn't with them, and they say they haven't seen him. I'll have a look at this boy tomorrow.'

'Thanks, Jack dear. Congratulations. What a coup! Can I interest you in some of Mrs Butler's orange jelly? It's very good.'

'I'm full,' said Robinson regretfully. 'Couldn't eat another crumb. And I've got to go,' he added, getting up with some difficulty. 'I've got to talk to those coroner's men. There'll be more ears to pick up. And get someone to look at the jack again, and ask the neighbours about anyone hanging around. They're small houses, close together. Someone must have seen something.'

'Well, Jack, thank you. You'll let me know what happens? And as soon as I can, I'll tell you about the other matter.'

'Good-o,' said Robinson. He met Bert and Cec at the door, and was so full of lunch and triumph that he gave them a cordial 'G'day'.

''Day,' muttered Bert, who did not like cops. Cec, acting as rearguard, ushered three other men before him and smiled at the Detective Inspector.

The front door closed behind him. The five men stood still in the hall.

'Well, we're here,' said Bert, heavily.

'So you are,' said Phryne. 'Come in.'

The prisoner moaned. He had beaten her again. She felt the soggy patch below her breastbone. Was it a broken bone? Every breath felt like a stabbing wound. He had gone out, locking the door.

Soon he would be back.

CHAPTER NINE

Phryne gave her guests plates, supervised the collection of food and the allocation of beer. Mr Butler snapped bottle tops as though he had been a barman all his life. Phryne watched as five ex-soldiers slaked what appeared by the evidence to have been a noble hunger. Mrs Butler had made extra pies and concocted a large bowl of salad and it all went, to the last crumb: boiled eggs, roast chickens, galantine of veal and all.

Bert belched politely behind his hand, allowed Mr Butler to refill his glass, and said, 'That was a bonzer meal. Don't know when I've had better. Tell Mrs B thanks. Now, miss, what are we doin' here?'

'We're trying to find out why someone wants you all dead,'

said Phryne. 'And remembering is hungry work. If you would like to bring your drinks into the parlour . . .' She led them into the next room.

'Here is a map of Paris,' she said. 'I want to know how you got there and everything you did once you'd arrived.'

Bert leaned over, pinning down one corner with his glass. 'We come by train,' he observed. 'There's the station. Gare du Nord. We come in there at about ten in the morning, tired out, still pretty dirty, still a bit deaf.'

'Deaf?' asked Phryne.

'Them big guns,' said Johnnie Bedlow, who had relinquished his grip on his hat. 'Takes a long time to get your hearing back. I'm still a bit Mutt and Jeff.'

'Cec, too,' said Bert. 'Let's see. We come in to this Gare at about ten. Nice day, sun shining through that glass roof. We got off the train, kitbags and all, and they said—what did they say?'

'Train to Boulogne,' said William 'Billo' Gavin. He wore a fisherman's jersey and old moleskins, and had a not disagreeable waft of salt and fish about him. 'They told us to get on the train to Boulogne. To the left. Well, you know how it is in them dark stations, a man can get lost,' he grinned with a flash of white teeth.

'We were country blokes,' said Johnnie. 'Not used to them big cities. A man could get confused if he's only used to the outback.'

'And we'd been eleven months on the front line,' said Thomas 'Thommo' Guilfoyle, stabbing down on the map with a finger rendered hard as stone by brick and mortar. 'So we thought, we reckon the army owes us a bit of a spree.'

'So we went right,' said Bert. 'Right and down, into the underground, and got a train to Montparnasse.'

'Why Montparnasse?' asked Phryne.

'Blokes comin' back from Paris said that Montparnasse was the place for girls and music and buckets of booze,' replied Billo. 'Our kind of place, we thought.'

'So when we got off the metro train and went up the stairs the guards let us through,' said Bert. 'Even though we didn't have any tickets. Then we went to a bank and changed all our money into francs. Except Cec.'

'Except Cec?' asked Phryne. She had not imagined Cec to be exceptionally virtuous.

'Cec had to see us all back on the train,' explained Bert. 'He drew the short straw. He kept the English money and he wasn't allowed to get really drunk and he had to get us back. The army didn't court-martial you if you were missing for less than twenty-four hours,' Bert explained. 'We reckoned we could pack a lot of spree into twenty-three hours and fifty-nine minutes and still catch the morning train out of the Gare du Nord. The war was over. Even the British Army was getting lax. And our blokes knew that they didn't have much of a hold over us any more.'

'So you went to the bank—where did you come up?'

'I reckon it was here, in the Boulevard Montparnasse,' said Bert slowly. 'The bank was on the corner of that big road. Credit National. They give us a good rate, too. Then we went . . .' he considered, casting his mind back. Phryne was suddenly aware that she was slipping back in time. 'We went to a bathhouse . . .'

'There,' said Phryne. 'The public bathhouse was there. Corner of the Rue d'Odessa. I used to bathe there. Five francs for as much soap and water as you could use.'

'Threadbare towels, but,' said Bert. The waft of carbolic steam came back to Phryne, a strong, clean smell. 'We shucked our gear and washed ourselves as clean as little lambs. I remember saying to Billo, I didn't know you had fair hair.'

'You did,' Billo chuckled. 'And I never knew that Maccie had red hair, neither. They gave us this lice-killing soap, the carbolic just oozed out of it. I reckon we were a couple of stone lighter when we finally rinsed it all off. Took an hour before the water ran clean off Conger.'

'Seemed strange, too,' said Thommo. 'All that lovely hot soapy water goin' to waste. I kept thinking we ought to be washin' our clothes but the others wouldn't let me.'

'Then we changed into our Sunday-go-to-church clean clothes and out we came into the street. We let Billo do the talking 'cos he can parlez-vous like nobody's business.'

'Sort of,' said Billo. 'Enough. I can still remember a bit of the lingo. "Voulez-vous coucher avec moi, mademoiselle?" and "Combien?" and "J'ai faim" and "J'ai soif" and "Où sont les soldats Australiens?" See, we learned a lot from the Frenchies. Like "Gaz!" and "Faites attention!' and "Prenez garde!" and "Mettez-vous à l'abri!" Things like that.'

Phryne's stomach turned over as she heard the words that Billo had learned from the French soldiers. Gas! Beware! Look out! and Take cover!

'And "bonjour" and "bonsoir", of course,' Billo went on, unaware of the effect his words were having on his hostess. 'And "Bonne chance". They said that a lot.'

'I bet they did,' said Phryne. She allowed Mr Butler to pour her another glass of wine and took a deep gulp.

'So we walked along the Boulevard du Montparnasse like kings,' said Bert. 'Clean as a hospital floor and as rich as Croesus.'

'Who is this Croesus you're always goin' on about, anyway?' asked Johnnie.

'One of them rich blokes,' said Bert airily. 'War had been over a month but they was still bringing in the wounded and the place was full of the maimed and the halt and the blind. And a whole lot of sheilas who had missed out, like, on things while all the men was away. They reckon in the last year, Paris was a city of lonely women.'

'It was,' said Phryne, remembering. 'But they weren't all lonely . . .'

Friday evening and Madame Natalie Barney's soiree was always well attended. Phryne, in a costume improvised from a bedsheet, was posed in the temple of amitié in the garden of 20 Rue Jacob. It was cold and she was hoping that she could stop impersonating a nymph fairly soon and taste the supper which was definitely preparing behind the scenes. Natalie herself, naked except for a wisp of fabric, was declaiming a Renée Vivien poem, based on a line by Sappho.

Attis, today you grow pale, and I pass by
Like an exile whose desire to return is lost.
You, fireless, and I, my soul wearying
Retreat from love.
Behold, as it heaves and climbs with the flame
And the song's rising and the lilies' perfume
The innermost voice of the heart of my soul
I loved you, Attis.

Phryne twitched, attempting to dislodge an ant from her ankle. She leaned a little against one of the three Greek columns of the temple. How dare the beautiful but completely faithless Natalie recite a poem from a woman whose heart she had broken! The tale of her remorseless pursuit of Renée Vivien was gossip in Paris even now. Priestess, siren, goddess, arch-seducer. Phryne wondered if it was true that Natalie Barney's female ancestor had been Mélusine, who turned into a snake from the waist down. In this scented darkness, hearing the beautiful voice chant sorrows, she could believe it. Romaine Brookes, the only person whom Natalie was popularly supposed to really love, sat sketching in the gloom, her pencil flying over the paper.

Natalie Barney was of fabulous age—forty-two! And as beautiful as she had ever been, white and dangerous under the moon. Behind her, Phryne heard an entirely unexpected René whisper, 'You are as silver as a statue, Selene, as entrancing as an angel. Descend to me, your suppliant!'

He dropped to his knees, out of sight of the audience, and his clever hands slid up her thighs.

'I can't move,' she whispered. 'Not until the reading is over.'

'I know,' he said, and his fingers continued to search. Natalie began another poem, Sappho's 'Ode to Aphrodite'.

> *Then, blessed one, smiling your immortal smile*
> *You asked, what ailed me now?*
> *What made me call on you again?*
> *What was it that my distracted heart*
> *Most wanted? Who, Sappho, is*
> *Unkind to you? Far let her*
> *Run, she will soon run after:*
> *If she won't accept gifts, she*
> *Will one day give them: and if*
> *She won't love you—soon she will*
> *Love—although unwillingly . . .*

The sigh of appreciation which greeted this verse mingled with Phryne's sigh as René's caresses achieved their aim. She sagged slightly. Natalie came to her and took her hand, smiling, perfectly aware of what had taken place, and said, 'Ah, Sera-phita—but where is Seraphitus?'

The twins of the Balzac novel. Phryne retrieved her hand. René would have gone back over the wall. He knew that a mere musician who played the debased musette with the even cruder cabrette would not be welcome in this exalted atmosphere.

'Back to heaven,' she replied. Natalie Barney laughed. Phryne was immensely relieved. Miss Barney, if crossed, could expel Phryne from the artistic life of Paris and, apart from everything else, she was relying on these soirees for a reason-able meal. Phryne then felt a burning sensation and saw Dolly Wilde glaring at her. Of course. Dolly was head over heels in love with Madame. Time to find some supper and discuss the end of the war with some nice, safe revolutionaries. With her fee from this night's appearance, she could go to the Rue d'Odessa tomorrow, buy Breton pancakes for lunch then go to the bathhouse and wash her hair . . .

Phryne snapped back to the present. Her reverie had not taken more than a moment. The ex-soldiers were arguing over where they had gone next.

'It was here,' insisted Johnnie. 'That was the first estaminet. That's where we got that raki.'

'Nah,' said Billo. 'Next one along. It had dead geraniums in the window box—I remember because they grow in my mum's garden. Café Luxe, that was it. Like the soap. Lux.'

'That's too far along the street,' said Phryne. 'Café Luxe was a brothel. Much further along, in Rue de Vaugirard. The café on that corner was Café Luxembourg.'

'Yair, that's right, Café Luxembourg. The old chook was called Tante Martine.'

'So she was,' said Phryne. 'Madame Dumas. She had three sons.'

'You knew her?'

'I pulled one of her sons out from under a lot of mud, so she used to give me a free dinner once a week,' said Phryne.

The soldiers looked at her. She felt each gaze sharpen.

'What were you doing in France in the war?' asked Billo. 'We thought you were a lady.'

'I was an ambulance driver,' said Phryne.

'Was yer?' demanded Thommo, voice thick with suspicion.

Phryne excused herself and went out. She came back with a khaki kitbag which she had not opened for ten years. She emptied it onto the table, on the map of Paris. Bert sorted through the contents. French identity card. Scatter of French coins, sous and centimes. British army tunic with all rank badges removed. Leather belt. Certificate of completion of a driving course. Box containing her Médaille d'Honneur. Cake of dark amber scented soap. Driver's cap. Letter of discharge from a military hospital. Pocket watch. Address book with attached pencil (broken). Five photographs. He spread them out.

The first was a group of uniformed girls, squinting in the sun. The central woman, a massive, masculine figure, held a board which said 'Third Ambulance Drivers'.

'That's Toupie,' said Phryne. 'That's Dolly Wilde. That's me.' Bert nodded. Despite the cap and the youth of the face, it was definitely Phryne.

'I heard about her,' said Billo. 'They say she went across the Itie border in trousers and they picked her up for being a woman impersonating a man. Then she went back over the border in a skirt and they picked her up for being a man impersonating a woman. Good old Toupie! So you were one of Toupie's girls! Them Frenchies were very fond of Toupie. Called her Lieutenant Toupie.'

'The next picture,' said Phryne, 'is me and my ambulance.'

'Blanky big brute of a thing,' observed Johnnie. 'How did you steer it with them thin little wrists? Beg pardon,' he added, conscious of making a personal remark.

'It's leverage, not strength,' Phryne explained. They nodded.

'This is Paris,' said Bert, looking at the next photograph. 'That's a music hall, isn't it? One of them bal musette. We went to one of them. Who's the bloke?'

There stood René, hat cocked over one eye, button accordion in his hands. A rush of feeling swept over Phryne: regret, loss, fury. The photo could not show his dark skin, his snapping bright black eyes, his smooth red lips over the white teeth . . .

'No one of consequence. This is a soiree at Madame Barney's.' She shuffled the picture of semi-naked nymphs past them and tucked it under another photo. 'Here are some artists I knew. That is Sarcelle, his wife, some other people.'

'You were wounded,' said Cec. It was the first time he had spoken. 'Is that why they gave you the medal?'

'I suppose so. It was Madame Dumas' son I was dragging out when the shell hit us. Then it was nothing but blood and mud and noise—you know.'

They all nodded. They knew.

The attitude of her visitors had changed. Until they had seen those reminders of Phryne's war, they had treated her as a nice lady: a stranger, an alien. Now they began to slide towards treating her as a comrade. Phryne preferred being a comrade. It was simpler. She folded her tunic and shoved the leftovers into the kitbag. On impulse, she retained the photographs. Something about the Sarcelle picture was itching at her subconscious. And she stole another look at the Barney photo. She had been very beautiful then, the toast of Paris. Now she was a stone heavier. The pictured Phryne was ethereal, impassioned and very hungry. She much preferred her present body. That Phryne was clinging on to the very edge of starvation, and even Vogue did not want women to be as thin as that.

'All right,' she collected her audience again. 'Now, you were saying. You got the raki at Café Luxembourg? Madame Dumas', Tante Martine's place? She was fond of soldiers.'

'Yair.' Billo grinned a reminiscent grin. 'So were all them sheilas at the café. So we had a few belts of that raki and then things started to get a bit mixed. Cec only had two drinks, poor bastard. He'd remember.'

'I only had two drinks,' said Cec. 'But they were water glasses. Then there was that nice little Marie making eyes at me. At all of us. And her friend Yvette. And Yvette's friend Renée. And that Antoinette as well. We were being smothered in girls and it kind of went to our heads.'

'I can imagine,' murmured Phryne.

'And they said to us, come along to a place where we have even more girls, so we went along,' said Billo. 'Along the Boulevard and down through this maze of little side streets until we ended up at a place called—what was it called?'

Heads shook all around. 'There was a big red brick building on the corner,' recalled Cec, 'and the street was a dogleg which led back to the Avenue du Maine.'

'Oh, Lord,' said Phryne. 'You didn't end up in the Rue Falchon, did you? At Madame Printemps?'

'Don't that mean spring?' guessed Billo, language expert. 'Yair. That was the place. Lots of girls. Lots and lots of girls. They swarmed all over us and filled us up with more of that raki and . . . I don't remember a lot more about it,' confessed Billo.

'I never been kissed that much in all my life,' said Johnnie.

'Nor me,' said the builder. 'We were good-looking young blokes then, of course, and we had money. Paris likes young men with money.'

'Until they are young men with nothing to recommend them but their youth,' said Phryne drily. 'Cec, you were supposed to stay sober. What happened to them all?'

'Well, miss, it was a brothel,' said Cec. 'What would you expect?'

'Precisely,' said Phryne. 'I wasn't asking for details. What happened after you were dragged upstairs by all those girls, ravished out of your wits and deprived of all your money and personal jewellery?'

'Dunno,' said Johnnie. 'I woke up with the sort of hangover which makes you wish you'd died on the train going to Boulogne.'

'Cec?'

'It's a bit blurry,' confessed Cec. 'The Madam woke me up downstairs and told me to go and get them all, so I did, and she chucked us out. Then we sort of wavered along that dogleg alley until Billo surfaced and asked the way to the station. A nice lady led us along and gave me two francs to buy some coffee. None of us had a skin to our name and my money was all in English pounds. I only just got them up the steps. Johnnie kept sitting down and falling asleep on me.'

'I don't remember any of this,' said Johnnie.

'Better than Thommo—he kept sitting down and telling me he was dying and I should leave him to his fate. And Bert was seeing things. I don't know what was in that booze . . .'

'Pure metho,' said Phryne. 'Madame Printemps was notorious. She would only have mixed it with raki because raki was cheaper. So, you dragged them all along into the Gare Montparnasse . . .'

'And loaded us on a metro train. Then loaded us off the train in the Gare du Nord. Nearly left Maccie behind, he was so floppy. Then we went left instead of right and found the train for Boulogne. Lucky the girls hadn't half-inched the travel warrants and we still had our paybooks and all. We sagged down onto the platform and waited for the train to come in and wanted to die. Jeez, we was crook.'

'I can imagine,' murmured Phryne.

'Then the train started to come in, the people shoved forward, there was a carriage for soldiers towards the front and we started stumbling towards it, then this bloke went flying straight under the train.'

'The date, Cec, what was the date?' demanded Phryne.

'December 13th,' said Cec.

'The dead man was a painter called Sarcelle,' said Phryne.

'If you say so. He was a scraggy-looking bloke with a beard. He was right next to us. And he was pushed.'

'Cec!' exclaimed Phryne. 'Why didn't you tell anyone?'

'Tried to,' said Cec. 'They stopped the train and backed it up to get the poor bloke out from under, and then the cops came and took the names of all of us. The other blokes were out for the count. I tried to tell them that I saw it all, but they looked at my mates and noticed that we were a day late on our travel warrants and sorta lost interest in my story. Couldn't blame 'em. We was a sight. In the end they loaded us all up and sent us off to catch a boat to Blighty. No one ever asked about it again. We were that sick and sorry the next day, what with the boat and all, that instead of locking us up the MO in London sent us all to hospital. But it was a great time,' said Cec. 'It was worth it.'

'All right,' said Phryne, pushing the map of Paris aside. 'Does anything else occur to you? Was there a fight in the brothel? A girl hurt, perhaps? Did you punch a nose that needed to be punched?'

'No,' said Cec. 'No fights. Lots of giggling. Lots of dancing and drinking. No fights. As long as our money held out they were real glad to see us and when it ran out, they chucked us into the street. We were far too sick and sorry to argue about that. And before we got to Madame Printemps, we were too happy.'

'Well,' said Phryne, 'if that's absolutely all you can remember, then the only odd thing that happened was the death of Sarcelle at the station. You didn't surprise any burglars, catch sight of any prominent politicians in your brothel?'

'How would we know if they were prominent politicians?' asked Billo. 'And anyway, that was ten years ago. Why go crook about it now?'

'Then we can assume it was Sarcelle's murder,' said Phryne. 'And I want to know everything you can recall about the person who pushed him.'

'Don't ask me,' said Johnnie. 'I wasn't among those present. Neither was Thommo. He was leaning on me and I was leaning on him. Maccie and Billo were doing the same. Bert had curled up like a bug in a rug and gone byes like a baby. I don't reckon anyone saw anything except Cec.'

'Then why is this person trying to kill you all?' asked Phryne.

'Well, we looked all right,' explained Bert. 'Apart from me, they was all standing up straight. Could have saluted, too, if an officer went past. Maccie was an expert at that. I've seen him stand like a flagpole when only a little breeze would have felled him like a tree . . . poor old Maccie,' said Bert.

'In that case,' said Phryne, 'I want to know everything about the man who pushed Sarcelle under the train.'

'Who said it was a man?' asked Cec.

CHAPTER TEN

'Sorry?' asked Phryne.

'It was a woman,' said Cec. 'In one of them long coats with a fur collar. Black. And one of them little black hats that fit round the head. With a red feather in it. Lots of make-up like a . . . like one of Madame Printemps' girls.'

'Are you sure?' demanded Phryne.

'Course I'm sure. Can see her as plain as plain. And she was, too. Plain, I mean. Beaky sort of nose, thick eyebrows, as far as I could tell under the paint. Got both hands square on the poor bloke's back and shoved hard, then vanished into the crowd. Lot of people screaming by then, pushing us, and I had all these blokes to mind.'

'Lord,' said Phryne. She racked her memory, trying to find

anyone who resembled the woman in black. Eva, Picasso's wife? No, too tall and statuesque. The clothes were too common. She herself had owned, at that time, a long black coat with a dyed rabbit collar and a small black cloche with a red feather. There must have been thousands of women loose in Paris wearing that combination of clothes on any November or December day in 1918. Black didn't show the dirt as much and the red feather cheered up the sombreness of the dark garments. Who could it have been? Not Madame Sarcelle. She was short and stout and wore bright colours. Her only outer garment was a hand-woven cloak of a penetrating teal blue with green braid edgings. Not her. She was, Phryne knew, devoted to Sarcelle. In any case she had been in the railways building at the time, trying to get permission to go to the south to care for her sister and the new baby. The examining magistrate had established that.

In any case, who would have wanted to kill him? He was a harmless person, interested only in his art. Would an artistic rival, jealous of his success, really have shoved Sarcelle under an actual train? They might talk loudly of his failure of line and his feeble drawing, scoff at his cubism and call his portraits 'pretty-pretty', but would they really have killed him?

It sounded unlikely. Paris, however, at that time, was a strained, anxious city, and when the influenza epidemic hit, a panicky one as well. Odd things happened in times of plague. Phryne remembered that she would never see Guillaume Apollinaire again. He had died of the Spanish 'flu on November the 9th, 1918, and when Blaise Condrass had gone to his funeral on the 11th, armistice day, the crowds were rejoicing and dancing in the street, singing the anti-war song 'You don't have to go, Guillaume', and Blaise had sworn that he had heard Guillaume Apollinaire's characteristic chuckle as his cortége moved off, a perfectly absurd ending for an absurdist.

People had thrown their servants, even their relatives, out to die in the gutter. The artists' colony had not been badly hit, possibly due to the immunity conferred by the earlier 'la grippe'. In any case, despite rivalries, the Montparnasse crowd clung together. Fear was bourgeois, death was ever present, and what was the threat of dying of the 'flu to someone who lived on judicious doses of morphine washed down with absinthe? 'Bah,' they said. 'Vive la mort!'

Some of the parties had been in the worst of all possible taste. Parties at which Influenza, the Spanish Lady, had appeared in her frilly flamenco dress, snapping her fan, flirting, her painted mask snatched away to reveal the skull underneath. The world had always been good at bad taste, ever since English ladies tied a thin red ribbon round their throats and dressed their hair à la guillotine for daring French Revolution balls. But Paris in 1918 knew that the world was absurd, dangerous and randomly fatal. Paris danced on the edge of a volcano, and she danced the tango, a dance that was modern and barbarous and scandalous.

And Phryne had danced the Auvergne waltz to the tune of cabrette and button accordion in the Rue des Trois Colonnes among the smell of varnish and wood-shavings from the vernissagiers upstairs. The room was so small that one had to invent steps which did not take one careering into a wall or the small tables; one, two-three and round in a tight circle, to the heavily accented, ornamented music, a sprinkle, a twinkle of shrill grace notes embroidering 'Rue de Fauborg' or 'Wood Carver's Lament' and round and round again, until the room swung round too. In René's arms, one could dance forever . . .

Back to the real world, she ordered herself. What woman hated Sarcelle enough to kill him, or what man? One who had a female accomplice ready to kill for him? That would have to be uncommon. She might have died for René, but she would not have killed for him.

Bert set down his glass. 'Now we've told you all we can,' he said, 'what do you think?'

'The situation is very confused,' said Phryne. 'Unless there's something you've all forgotten about completely, in which case I can't imagine why someone is pursuing you, then it has to be the death of Sarcelle, and I'll have to think about it and ask around. Meanwhile, my dears, keep up your hearts, stay on guard, and I'll find something, even if I have to go to France. I could get there in a plane in a week, allowing for emergencies. But with any luck I won't have to do that. The murderer is here.'

'And if I get my hands on the bastard,' growled Johnnie Bedlow, 'he won't be here much longer.'

'Quite,' said Phryne.

Mr Butler saw them out. Ember strolled in, followed by Molly. In defiance of all biology, Ember appeared to consider that Molly was his kitten, and Molly had enthusiastically adopted this identification, having been separated from her own mother very young in life. This meant that until Ember lost patience with his maternal role and sprang up the curtains, Molly tagged along behind him, nipping at his tail and trying to play. When he turned to box the importunate puppy's ears, she would fling herself onto her back, exhibiting the bare tummy of childhood. Ember would then flip her playfully around the ears instead of disembowelling her, and the dance would begin again. A bourrée de deux, with a little more physical contact than that dance of unresolved sexual tension which could set a whole bal musette alight and drive the couples closer together as the two danced, never touching after the first handclasp, shooting glances of dark Auvergnat passion through the smoky air . . .

Paris again. Phryne realised that she would not be able to suppress it now. Paris was returning, flooding back, and she had to go along with the waves or excise a part of her life forever.

And what was René, anyway? Just the man who broke her heart. As Lin Chung had said, that was what young love was *for*. And ever since then, no one had been in a position to do it again. She had seen to that, choosing her lovers carefully, paying attention to her own emotional well-being. She chuckled. She owed her astoundingly successful amatory career to René. And one day she might even be able to thank him fittingly.

With, as it might be, a handy piece of four-by-two across the ear.

Consoled by this thought, Phryne sat down by the window and picked up a book. The bookshop sent five new detective stories a week. She sipped at her last glass of wine and was halfway down the page before she realised that something was wrong.

'She half-fell, half-slid into his strong arms. She felt his heart beating wildly against her cheek. He stroked the silky hair back from her burning cheek. "There, there, little girl," he murmured.'

Unless someone got killed in the next paragraph, Phryne thought, she was going to strike this author from her list of writers. No one did. She closed the book and read the dust jacket. *Midnight of the Sheik*. Phryne refrained from throwing the book against the wall, because it was obviously Ruth's. The idea of the girl devoting herself to such drivel was uncomfortable, especially if she came to believe it. There was more to midnight with a sheik than someone murmuring 'There, there, little girl',

Phryne was sure. Raining kisses on one's burning cheek was one thing. No one in a romance novel discussed the difficulty of, for instance, getting gracefully out of a pair of knickers which you have just realised are torn across the crotch, or stockings which have potato sack holes in them. Or how to deal with the unexpected arrival of a menstrual period. Not to mention the surprise of all but the country-bred when the young woman discovers what is contained in the male underwear.

That led her to wonder about Lin Chung's fiancée, Camellia. What did well-brought-up Chinese girls know about men? Were they closeted away from anything with a penis?

Phryne put the book carefully back on the table, finished her wine in a gulp, and climbed the stairs to her own apartments. Tonight was dinner, and she would contrive to find out whether this alliance had the full consent of the girl who had braved such dangers to get here.

Detective Constable Hugh Collins left the train at Mildura and hefted his bag. He supposed that he should go, first of all, to the police station. He knew that he was supposed to stay there in a dormitory set up for firefighters, which he knew would be the height of discomfort. The more dedicated the officers, the worse the accommodation, hours, pay and food, he knew. Better to be on the spot.

He walked into the main street and headed for the Mildura Hotel. It was a large, imposing brick building, constructed when river boats brought hundreds of travelling salesmen, wanderers and workers along the Murray. It had elaborate iron lace on its balconies, a verandah deep in solid shade, and the sort of front door one expects in a castle. It was propped open.

He went in. A bosomy girl looked up from her contemplation of a yellow-covered novel. She was sitting in a highly polished wooden cubicle, and he was sure that he could smell a faint, attractive perfume. She had tightly curled blonde hair and heavily kohled eyes.

'Hello,' she said throatily. Must have been practising, Collins thought. That was just like Theda Bara would sound if she had sound.

'Room for the night?' asked Hugh.

'Staying long?' she drawled, fluttering her lashes.

'I don't know,' said Hugh, truthfully.

'Room 12,' she said, unhooking a ring with two brass keys. 'Dinner from six to eight. Breakfast . . .' the eyelashes swept down '. . . six to seven in the breakfast room. The door's closed at midnight. After that, ring the night bell and the porter will let you in.'

'Thanks,' he said. She shoved the large, blue-backed ledger across the polished counter.

'Sign the register, please,' she requested.

He signed and she read the information. 'Hugh Collins, commercial. You don't look like a commercial. My name's Ella,' she added, drawing out the syllables.

'Nice to meet you, Ella,' he said. He shook the pale hand heartily and mounted the stairs. It was his first solo investigation and he was determined not to make a single error. He wanted Dot to be proud of him.

And he could start investigating at dinner. Time for a wash and brush-up and then he could begin his very own investigation.

He tingled with pride as he bounced up the steps.

At seven p.m. Hugh Collins came down to dinner at the Mildura Hotel. The room was large and heavily decorated, but already the agricultural depression which the papers had been talking about for ages had set in. The dining room's red plush was shabby. Cigarette holes had been burned in the arms of red-velvet chairs. Spider webs hung from the portraits of past presidents of the shire and unpolished wood gleamed fitfully in the setting sunlight.

Dinner promised to be something of a trial. The only vacant space in the room was between a very large farmer and an equally large river-boat captain. Hugh sat down squarely on his bit of bench and wriggled, managing to push them aside enough to be sitting on both buttocks and with a reasonable chance at the edibles.

The Mildura Hotel was used to dealing with men who knew what they liked, and it happened to be just what Hugh Collins liked, too. A large plate laden with a very large steak, nicely burned on the outside and cooked to the consistency of wood, a heap of thoroughly boiled vegetables and four roasted potatoes, crowned with lashings of butter and gravy. He shook salt and pepper and Worcestershire sauce liberally over everything and began to eat, constrained only by the squared elbows of his co-diners in really getting down to absorbing the whole meal.

After ten minutes of hard going, the farmer wiped his mouth and said, 'Now that was a good meal to give a man.'

'Too right,' said the river-boat captain. 'My missus believes in all this Food Reform. Food Fad, I call it. Nothing but poached chicken and steamed vegetables. Won't even fry my Murray cod, and there's good eating on a Murray cod, just out of the river, fried in butter in a hot pan. Man needs food that'll stick to his ribs. But I got away from her tonight. She's at the Country Women's Association, probably learning about new ways to grate carrot.'

Hugh grunted an agreement. His own mother had flirted with Food Reform, until his father had threatened to walk out if he ever saw another pumpkin that wasn't roasted or seethed in butter. No jam, no pickles, no vinegar, no fried food, no alcohol, no sauces, no gravy, only a lot of oatmeal and chicken cooked in water. No wonder the old man had gone crook. Hugh said so. His companions laughed.

'Leaves! Bran! Rabbit food is for rabbits, and horse food is for horses, that's what I told her,' said the captain, introducing himself as Captain Max. 'If I wanted to eat grass I'd go out and graze! But she's a headstrong woman and there's nothing to be done on a river boat with a headstrong woman but to keep the peace.'

'That's true,' said the farmer, who had introduced himself as Alexander McLeod. 'But this Eat More Fruit campaign has done wonders for our sales. You know, the bloke in Melbourne, Mr Clapp, the Commissioner, he's got fruit stands on every station where you can buy a glass of fresh squeezed orange juice, or lemon or grapefruit or berry in season, melon, even banana, and the harvest looks good this year, God willing. Have a taste of this.' He poured a glass of orange juice from the iced jug on the table. 'Just have a sip. I watched the girl squeeze this jug only half an hour ago. Have a taste,' he urged, and Hugh found the juice very agreeable, fruity and fresh with a suitable bite which saved it from being oversweet.

'While you drink a few glasses of that every morning you'll never catch a cold,' said Mr McLeod. 'And you won't have to eat your way through a bale of leaves to get your vitamins, Captain Max. You tell your missus that and I'll throw in a sack of mixed veg when you buy a crate of oranges. Fruit of the Gods, golden as the sun. But you got to squeeze 'em fresh, mind.'

Mr McLeod was waxing lyrical about his produce. With the taste still in his mouth, Hugh remembered something Dot had read to the girls.

'The apples of the Hesperides,' he said. 'In this old legend. The Golden Apples of the Sun.'

'You're a young fellow with some learning,' said Mr McLeod, approvingly.

'What's your line?' asked Captain Max. 'What are you selling?'

'This and that,' said Hugh Collins. 'I mean, I'm looking for a bloke from round here, Thomas MacKenzie.'

'You're too late,' said Captain Max, easing his waistband. 'He a friend of yours?'

'No,' said Hugh.

'Well, whatever business you had with him, it's too late,' said the captain. 'He's dead. Fell into an irrigation ditch and drowned. Matter of a couple of weeks ago.'

'That's too bad,' replied Hugh. 'An accident?'

'That's what they said,' McLeod hinted darkly. 'I dunno about it, I got my doubts.'

'We all got our doubts,' agreed Captain Max. 'But that bone-headed cop kept going on about drunk and fell in the ditch and his brother-in-law agreed with him.'

'Why does that matter?' asked Hugh.

'His brother-in-law's the coroner.'

Hugh nodded. A lot of country towns tended to dynasties. Once you had the local policeman, the local schoolteacher and the local priest, it really didn't matter who was mayor.

'But why would the coroner want to cover up a strange death?' he asked innocently.

'Doesn't want any trouble,' McLeod told him. 'Because his brother's got his own irons in the fire, and a lot of townie cops poking around might upset him. Not all the fines that go through that police court go to the state,' he said, shaking his head.

Hugh was horrified. Things were, he knew, different in the country, but surely not that different.

'Does everyone know about this?'

'Of course,' said Captain Max.

'Why hasn't someone written to the police commissioner, then?'

'What, dob him in? You crazy?'

'Oh, of course, sorry,' muttered Hugh. He'd met this attitude before. It took a great deal of courage to inform on anyone in Australia, unless they had just murdered your brother, raped your wife, killed your dog and burned down your house, when it was allowed that you might become a trifle terse and tell someone in authority. Something was going to have to be done about the Mildura policeman and he was not going to be a lot of help in Hugh's enquiries about the untimely death of Thomas MacKenzie.

'Ah,' said Captain Max in quite another tone. 'Pudding!'

It was a huge, steaming, heavily glazed spotted dog, with custard in a jug.

'That's the stuff to give the troops,' admired McLeod.

After accounting for a lot of the pudding, a glass of port and a sugared orange for afters, Hugh dragged himself into the bar-parlour to digest. He felt like one of those huge snakes he'd heard about, which only eat one pig a year and then have to coil themselves around a tree and sleep it off for months. The girl behind the bar brought him a glass of fizzy salts.

'Thanks,' said Hugh, 'but I didn't order this.'

'You've just eaten one of Ma Humphrey's dinners,' she

replied, dimpling. 'Everyone who gets outside one of her spreads needs a glass of fruit salts.'

'Thanks,' he said, sipping. There really didn't seem to be any room inside him at all but the salts slipped down easily. The bar was otherwise empty. The girl, with a swift glance at the green baize door on her left, leaned on his chair.

'I heard you was asking for Tommy MacKenzie,' she whispered.

'That's right.'

'Why did you want him?'

'Just a friend of a friend,' said Hugh easily. He knew this situation. If nothing interrupted the girl, she would tell him something. What he had to do was to keep his temper, rein in his impatience, and keep smiling. It was a skill which he likened to what his grandfather had told him about salmon tickling. You wait for the fish to slide itself into your hand, caress it very gently, then one finger in a gill and flip!—it's out and on the bank. He had honed this skill on the Bad Girls of Brunswick Street and the even Badder Girls of St Kilda when he had been trying to catch a man who mistreated prostitutes. He knew that they had some clue to the attacker's identity, and that they would probably tell him if he allowed them to take their time, bought them drinks, and smiled. Old Jack Robinson had snorted and told Hugh that he had a way with women which would get him into deep trouble if he wasn't careful, son.

'Someone killed Tommy,' said the girl fiercely. She was small and bottle blonde, with dark brown eyes.

'Why do you think that?'

''Cos he wasn't drunk when he left this pub,' she observed. 'They said he fell into a ditch and drowned, dead drunk. He wasn't dead drunk when he left. I know he wasn't.'

'How do you know that?' asked Hugh, tickling his salmon.

He allowed just a suspicion of scepticism to seep into his voice, enough to flick the girl into further disclosure. She flushed with anger. Her voice rose a little.

''Cos I met him outside. We was courting. When his business was good enough, we was going to get married. I met him outside the back door at the gate. There's a seat there. And he wasn't dead drunk. He was only a little bit drunk and that's because he hardly ever drank anything. He said he'd just made a good deal and said he'd meet me the next day to buy my engagement ring. But he never came,' she said, her voice dropping back to a flat, grieved whisper.

'Why are you telling me?' asked Hugh, equally low voiced.

'You're a cop,' she breathed. 'Come to look into it. From the city. Well, ain't yer?'

'Yes,' he said softly. 'How did you know? And who else knows?'

'Just me. I got a message for you from Russell Street. Came through the phone exchange just before you arrived.'

'Then the whole town knows,' said Hugh, dismayed. Telephone exchanges were the central clearing house for all gossip in small towns.

'Nah.' The girl flicked her brassy hair from her face. 'My sister Elsie is the operator. She does the post office too. I asked her not to tell. She's a good sort. She won't tell.'

'What's your name?' Hugh sneezed at the effluvium of Paris Nights eau de parfum which surrounded the girl.

'Maisie,' she said. 'Gotta go. Here comes the Old Trout.'

A stout middle-aged woman came into the bar-parlour, shot a reproving glance at Maisie, who was polishing glasses behind the bar as if she had never left it, and asked for a small gin and tonic. She looked pointedly at Hugh, the sole occupant, and he stood up with some difficulty.

'Hugh Collins,' he said, 'Were you responsible for that magnificent dinner, madam?'

'Mrs Humphreys. I cooked tonight, yes,' she said, smiling. 'I reckon that travelling men need a good dinner. Puts meat on their bones,' she said, giving Hugh's massive shoulders and chest a quick, admiring once-over. He was not exactly flattered as he suspected that she might look at a bullock she had a mind to have slaughtered for the table with the same expression. 'You travelling in something, Mr Collins?'

'Just travelling, Mrs Humphreys. I was going to look up a friend of my brother's—Thomas MacKenzie—but they told me at dinner that he's dead.'

'That was so sad,' she said. 'And I told that stupid cop, he never got that load on at my house. Bar closes on time at six, sharp. Different for travellers and residents, but he wasn't neither. He was a nice quiet bloke, never drank much, never caused no trouble. I'm sorry he's gone. Still, bottoms up.' She drained her glass.

'Have another?' asked Hugh. 'Don't go leaving me all alone here,' he added, to entirely remove the notion that he might want to be alone with Maisie. Mrs Humphreys waved a hand at the barmaid and she brought another gin and tonic.

'You from the city?' asked Mrs Humphreys, sipping in a ladylike manner.

'Russ . . . I mean to say, Richmond,' stuttered Hugh. 'I've just finished a long stint at one job and wanted to wander about a bit, see the country. My brother used to live up here.'

'He was a Collins too?'

'Yes.' Hugh wondered what terrible coil he was about to wrap himself in. In the city you could claim to know someone in a suburb and not get caught out unless you named a street.

Here you couldn't assume that anyone remained unknown within a fifty mile radius.

'Must have been before my time,' said his landlady, after racking her brains. 'I've only been here five years. My husband bought a pub when he came out of the army. Then when he died I came over here. This was his cousin's pub. I took over the licence. Well, good luck, young man,' she said, draining the glass and getting up. 'The washing up doesn't do itself, you know. And I'm sorry about Tommy MacKenzie. If I were you, I'd ask the orange juice fellow. He was talking to him that night.'

'What orange juice fellow would that be, Mrs Humphreys?' asked Hugh, reverting to salmon tickling.

'Why, he stayed at this very hotel. I can tell you who he was if I can look at the register. Maisie!' she shrilled. 'Get the register!'

'All right,' said Maisie. 'If you mind the bar.'

'Sauce,' said Mrs Humphreys. She went behind the bar and absent-mindedly poured herself another tonic, to which she added gin in a way which conveyed that her left hand did not know what her right hand was pouring.

Maisie returned with the big leather-bound folio and Mrs Humphreys leafed through it.

'Here he is,' she said. 'Foreign gentleman he was, though he spoke quite good English. "Enchanté, madame," he said to me and kissed my hand. He spent a lot of time talking to young Tom MacKenzie.'

Maisie made a sound halfway between a sob and a snarl.

'I'm making allowances for you because it was your young man,' said Mrs Humphreys ponderously. 'You get yourself a double brandy now, my girl, drink it down quick, and pull yourself together.'

Maisie poured and gulped. Her gasp and choke informed Hugh Collins that she was not a hardened spirits drinker, despite the dyed hair and the make-up.

'Here he is. Nice curly writing, ain't it?' Mrs Humphreys shoved the book over to her visitor.

'Very nice,' said Hugh. He read the name. René Dupont. 'A French gentleman, was he? And an address in Melbourne, in Collins Street, I see. Well, perhaps I can talk to him when I get back to Melbourne. What did you say his business was, Mrs Humphreys? Another drink for Mrs Humphreys, Miss Maisie, if you please.'

'Oh no, I couldn't,' fluttered the licensee of the Mildura Hotel. Maisie sloshed impatiently and out of sight, and when the drink came it must have been close to neat gin. Mrs Humphreys did not gasp as she went on with the story.

'Orange juice, it was. He had an idea of freezing orange juice and sending it to Europe, like they freeze beef. Trouble with oranges is that they spoil, but frozen juice wouldn't spoil.'

'And when did Mr Dupont leave?' asked Hugh, gently.

'Day after Tom MacKenzie's death. Missed all the fuss. Nice gentleman . . .' Mrs Humphreys was definitely fading out. 'Well, I must go. Maisie! Take the register back.'

'Yes, Mrs Humphreys,' said Maisie with what Hugh guessed was unwonted docility.

The cook walked steadily out of the room—she had had practice, Hugh guessed. Maisie fled with the register and then came back and grabbed Hugh by the arm. He flinched a little. Years of hauling at brass taps had given Maisie a grip like an orang-utang.

'What did you see in that book?' she hissed. 'You saw something suspicious.'

'We shall have to get you into the Force,' responded Hugh,

freeing his arm before his fingers went numb. 'The name first of all: it's the French equivalent of Smith. And that address in Collins Street is the Melbourne Town Hall. I can see how I'm going to have to get a message to my boss about this Mr Dupont.'

'Wait until nine,' said Maisie, smiling for the first time since he had met her. 'And we'll go and see Elsie.'

The prisoner wept. No one heard her.

CHAPTER ELEVEN

Dot came in as Phryne flung the fifth and last dress onto her bed and swore.

'Hell's bells! Come and help me, Dot, do, before I throw all my clothes out the window and go down to dinner naked.'

'That would shock Mr Butler, and the poor little new bride as well,' said Dot calmly. 'What about mixing some of these up?' she suggested. Phryne watched as Dot picked up a pair of soft dark blue satin lounging pyjamas and laid next to them a decorous, high necked Chinese brocade tunic. 'That's what Chinese women wear, near enough.'

'Yes, but what if the girl has been dressed up in western clothes? I'd make her uncomfortable in her stockings and shoes,' objected Phryne.

'Then it's time for Madame Fleuri's latest,' said Dot. She unwrapped a dark purple, beautifully draped dance length dress. Phryne accepted it and Dot dropped it carefully over her head so not a hair stirred out of place. The dress fell into perfect lines, bias cut, flowing, high necked.

'There,' said Dot, smiling. 'Not Chinese and not western. Juste à la mode.'

'Good.' Phryne surveyed herself in the mirror and gave her face four precise licks with a compact. 'I'm late. Hand me the amethyst pin and the silver ring. And the amethyst fillet. Nice. What would I do without you? Are they here yet?'

The door bell sounded.

'There they are,' said Phryne. She dropped a scented kiss on Dot's cheek and flew for the stairs.

Dot stood with an armload of precious fabrics pressed to her bosom and said aloud, 'Good luck,' as Phryne vanished. 'Oh dear,' Dot added. 'Curse those Butlers! We haven't had a comfortable moment since he decided to quit.'

She smoothed the dresses lovingly as she hung and folded. Dot, an incurably virtuous person, would have presented prosecuting counsel in a putative divorce case with an insurmountable problem. To every loaded question, she had already decided, she would reply, 'I can't say,' and she would stick to it. It wasn't a lie. And nothing could make her testify against Miss Phryne. She saw no reason why Mr Butler, with the same recourse available to him, should have developed the megrims. She thought it unmanly and unworthy of him. And he was making the whole house uncomfortable.

Phryne came down the stairs at a more decorous pace as Mr Butler was greeting Mr Lin and his bride and escorting them into the drawing room. She followed them in and took the young woman by the hand.

Her first thought was, her hand is as hard as a washerwoman's. Her second thought was, she's so young. And so scared. Young was to be expected. But scared, so afraid that the hard little hand was wet and shaking, was strange.

'My name's Phryne Fisher,' she said gently. 'Come and sit down, Miss . . .'

'Li,' supplied Lin Chung. He urged the young woman along by the elbow. 'Sit down, Camellia, this isn't the den of the black dragon! She won't eat you, I promise!'

'Often have I entered the cave of the green dragon,' quoted Camellia, in a small voice and in very good English. Phryne relaxed a little. If her guest could speak a common language, this evening was going to be a lot easier. Camellia had the same breathy, slightly off-key accent as her soon-to-be grandmother, the effect of learning English later in life, after acquiring the multiple tones of Mandarin.

'Delusion,' said Phryne, who had not wasted her time in Shanghai either, despite the rival attractions of brilliantined young men and the famed dance bands of the Shanghai Hotel. 'To enter the cave of the green dragon is to be deluded by the glittering distractions of the world. I have always found them agreeably diverting, it is true. Would you like a cocktail, Lin dear? Miss Li?'

Mr Butler bent over her with a tray. 'Sherry or madeira,' he intoned, like a bishop offering a particularly fruity choice in eternal bliss. Camellia had been trained in western customs. She chose the sherry of the respectable lady, not the madeira of those loose in the hilts. Phryne looked at the girl as she sipped gingerly. She would have liked madeira better, Phryne thought, sweeter and not so foreign.

Camellia Li was small and slim with long hair in a chignon in which someone had set three small enamelled birds. She wore a cocktail dress of red silk, the colour of a bride, and dark stockings and high heeled shoes which must, Phryne reflected, be giving her hell. Her face was not the perfect oval required by the poets. Instead she had rather high cheekbones and a small, decided chin. She glanced up for a moment and caught Phryne looking at her. The thin, arched eyebrows rose a little. A strong face. Phryne smiled. Camellia smiled back, tentatively.

'I think we are going to be friends,' said Phryne, and Camellia, after a pause, nodded. Phryne liked the pause. It meant that the girl had considered the offer and decided to accept it. Mr Butler brought Lin his favourite cocktail, an orange juice, gin and bitters concoction.

'Are you a follower of the forbiddens?' asked Phryne, wondering if there was any dish on the menu suitable for a strict vegetarian. Camellia shook her head.

'No, but I like to read. My uncle thought that girls should be educated. He was a follower of the blessed Sun Yat Sen. I liked philosophy. My sister and brother also, so we had a tutor. My brother was more interested in commerce and my sister was more interested in the tutor, but I liked what he was teaching. Is Miss Fisher . . . surely Miss Fisher is not a Buddhist?'

'No, I like reading too. I spent a couple of weeks in Shanghai and visited a lot of temples. I listened when people explained things to me and then found translations of their scriptures.'

'It is good for a woman to have learning,' said Camellia stoutly, as though expecting opposition. Lin Chung laughed lightly.

'Certainly,' he agreed. 'You may learn as much as you wish, Camellia. I have already told you this. I am not the severe husband you might have had if you'd stayed in China. I would like you to enjoy your life here.'

'I should not have had a husband there,' said Camellia, softly. 'In China there is nothing but chaos and blood. And on the sea, too. Oh . . .' she remembered that Lin Chung knew all about the South China Sea pirates. She looked away, discomforted. Phryne said quickly, 'That is a superb gown. Was it made in Melbourne? If so, I would like the name of your dressmaker.'

'No, it was made in Hong Kong. I was seven months there, waiting for permission to come here. The Lin family were very kind and had my trousseau made for me,' replied Camellia, grateful for the distraction. 'Your own dress is very beautiful.'

'I will introduce you to Madame Fleuri,' said Phryne. 'Then, when he receives her account, your husband will know the true meaning of pain.'

'I already know what it means,' said Lin. 'I need no further education. Did you really read philosophy, Camellia?'

'Indeed,' said the young woman.

'Your uncle was a wise man,' said Phryne, running out of conversation and not feeling equal to philosophy before dinner. 'What else is taught to a young woman in China since the divine Sun began teaching?'

'Many things,' said Camellia. 'The usual, of course—how to supervise servants, how to keep household accounts, how to cook, embroidery and music.'

'I did the same subjects,' said Phryne, interested. 'Cooking, French, household management, fine needlework, and the piano.'

'And you excelled,' said Lin Chung, teasingly.

'I was good at accounts and household management, though you would never know it now,' said Phryne. 'I did nothing in needlework but stick needles into my fingers and bleed all over my poor sampler. And on the piano I was so abysmal that even the music master had to take it off the bill. He said it was "pure cruelty to the divine Muse" to make me continue.'

Camellia, whose eyes had widened at this confession of domestic incompetence, giggled. 'I was supposed to play the moon guitar,' she confessed, 'but I broke so many strings and made such noises—Uncle once sent to find out what was making the house-dogs bark so much!—that they let me stop "tormenting an ancient and delicate instrument in which were all the arts of love".'

'Sounds like the same music master,' said Phryne. 'But I liked cooking. My mother was always too tired to cook and, later, too indolent.'

'I, too, liked cooking,' said Camellia. 'It seemed magical that so many things which in their natural state are not at all nice—water chestnuts, for instance—become delicious when properly cooked.'

'I hope my menu is to your taste,' said Phryne. 'I was going to ask Lin to lend me one of his cooks, but I forgot.'

'Oh, I like western food,' said the girl. 'Except for some of the stranger things. In Hong Kong there are English restaurants. They make a strange food where mixed meats are forced into a skin made of—no, it is really too horrible.' The small reddened hands gestured helplessly.

'Sausages,' diagnosed Phryne. 'Each to his own. There's the gong,' she added. 'Come along and we'll see if any of this food is to your taste.'

'Oh, I'm sure it will be,' protested Camellia.

Dinner consisted of a clear soup, a sole bonne femme, a ragout of veal and a series of fruit sorbets. Mrs Butler had initially objected to sorbets as foreign but one mouthful of a well-made grapefruit sorbet had sent her experimenting with water ices. She had perfected her art. Lin took over the conversation as Camellia struggled bravely with the difficulties of using alien cutlery to eat alien food and a dinner which was the wrong way round, starting with soup (which everyone knows is the proper end to a meal) and ending with sweets, which start it.

Phryne saw that her guest would manage better if not observed, and dropped into a discussion about the missing girl, Elizabeth, daughter of well-known racing identity and grump, Hector Chambers.

'The car, I feel, is important,' said Lin Chung. 'Your Inspector Robinson will find it. He has eyes all over the city and hundreds of men at his command. Then we shall see what we shall see.'

'Yes, I suppose so. I'm worried about the girl. There's no clue apart from that ransom note and the rather confused and useless account of her blonde best friend. I took her to tea at the Windsor and stuffed her full of cakes but she kept wittering off into gossip and irrelevancies.'

'As good a way of escaping as any,' commented Camellia, so quietly that Phryne almost didn't hear her.

'Yes, I thought of that,' she responded. 'She might have been trying to lead me into the cave of the green dragon. But apart from a desire for pretty clothes and a settled future, I really didn't detect a lot of brain and absolutely no ambition. She is willing to marry this old curmudgeon just for his money . . .' Phryne wondered if this was a good time to stop talking and decided it wasn't. 'Even though she could earn a living beading dresses.'

'It must seem to you,' said Camellia, putting down her knife and fork, 'that I have made a similar bargain. My family was very poor. Now they are allied with the Lin family and are much more comfortable and secure.'

'No,' said Phryne. 'You're from a culture where this is normal. Here, it isn't normal. Here, we choose our own mates, all by ourselves.'

'Then how do you know who to marry?' asked Camellia. 'I am far too young to decide such an important matter on my own.'

'Good question,' said Phryne, taken aback. 'Perhaps I should just say that every culture agrees that it is the best in the world, and leave it at that?'

'As you say.' Camellia's head bowed in assent, but Phryne sensed that she was both curious and disappointed.

'Perhaps I can elaborate,' she said. 'Here, women go out alone, we work alone, we travel alone, unescorted, we mix with boys from early childhood and we are more used to . . . well, to men. When we find the one we want to marry, we take the advice of our elders and betters, but if the feeling is strong, we ignore them.'

'And these marriages, do they fail?'

'Some do,' said Phryne. 'Some don't.'

'In China, if the man is unhappy, he acquires another wife.'

'Yes, but if the woman is unhappy, she can't acquire another husband,' said Phryne.

'Oh!' Camellia was so surprised that she dropped her fork. Mr Butler materialised at her side with another one.

'Phryne, your ideas are too foreign for a well-brought-up young woman recently arrived in this den of vice,' protested Lin Chung.

'I am sorry,' murmured Camellia. 'But I never thought of such a thing.'

'And you need not,' said Phryne. 'Have some orange sorbet, it's really very good.'

The rest of the dinner was beguiled in general gossip and recipe swapping. Camellia, as her name suggested, was very interested in flowers and promised Phryne a root of a rare orchid which she had brought with her from China, when it was fully recovered from its journey.

Phryne swept Camellia away for a cup of coffee and a visit to the facilities. The young woman continued discussing rare orchids until Lin Chung was quite out of earshot. Then she caught Phryne's sleeve.

'May I come back and see you, by yourself, Miss Fisher?'

'Of course,' said Phryne, clasping a cold hand. 'Whenever you like. Is there something wrong?'

'Yes,' said Camellia, shaking her head so that the enamelled ornaments tinkled. 'Oh yes, there is. But I can't tell you now. I will be allowed to visit you. That is something which Grandmother will allow. She approves of you.'

'And I of her, if one can use the word "approve" for such an alarming old lady,' said Phryne. The clasp on her hand loosened.

'Yes, she is alarming, isn't she?' replied Camellia. 'I will try to send you a message before I come. Now, we had better go back.'

Phryne saw them out before eleven, mystified, and put herself to bed with a tot of brandy and a feeling that the world was reeling out of control.

It was rather exciting.

Detective Inspector Robinson was woken from a sound sleep at his desk—it had been an action packed couple of days—by an overexcited Cadet Quinn.

'Sir, sir,' he yelled.

'What?' Robinson had long mastered the art of coming instantly awake, a skill which had proved invaluable when his children were young. He could be out of bed, supplying nutriment, water or a story, before his wife turned over in her sleep. He attributed his long and happy marriage to the fact that, unlike most mothers, his wife got to sleep through the night when he was at home.

'We've found that car!' roared the cadet.

'Good,' said Robinson. 'Turn your voice down from a bellow to a gentle murmur or . . .'

Quinn didn't wait to find out what the 'or . . .' was. He immediately moderated his voice to that of a cushat dove calling to another cushat dove across a gentle pasture in spring. Quinn was very young, but an upbringing with three older sisters had honed both his survival skills and his sensitivity to raised voices.

'We've found that missing Bentley, sir,' he said mellifluously.

'Have you indeed?' asked Robinson. He rubbed both hot hands over his hot face. 'Slip down and get me a cuppa, will you, son? And some kind of food. What time is it?'

'Gone nine, sir,' said the cadet, halfway out the door. 'Two sugars, was it, sir? And you prefer ham to cheese sandwiches?'

'You're going to go far in the Force, boy,' said Robinson evenly.

Cadet Quinn reappeared with a cup of hot, strong tea, a plate of really fairly fresh ham sandwiches—the bread had barely begun to curl—and a constable with a notebook. Constable Burnett was a large, stolid, unimaginative looking constable. Traffic required a lack of imagination and the ability to stand in serious danger of being run down all day without shrieking. It attracted a particular type of person. This constable was typical.

'Report,' said Robinson, sipping. Constable Burnett opened his notebook, flicked to the right page, and began in his official voice.

'Well, sir, I come from Traffic and they said to look out for a black Bentley. I really like cars, sir, so I notice them. I was in hot pursuit of a handbag snatcher down an alley in St Kilda when I lost him in the lanes. He must have ducked over a fence, I thought, so I proceeded along the lane, looking over the garden walls. Didn't catch a glimpse of my man but I found a black Bentley, all covered up in an old bedspread, in the garden of this house. I was off my beat, sir, so I didn't know what house it belonged to. I could see the number plate and it was the right number that the Sarge had given us before we went out, so I went to the corner of the lane, counting back yards. Then I went along the actual street—Acland Street, it was—counting, and worked out where it was. Then I proceeded to the station and reported my finding—'

'Yes, yes, I'm sure you did it all by the book. Did you read the bit which said "Do not attract any attention and report to Jack Robinson as soon as possible"?'

'Yes, sir. We know the number of the house and we know that the car is there. My sergeant says just to report to you and not do anything else. Is that all, sir?'

'Yes, thanks. Good work,' added Robinson. 'Tell your sergeant that I said you did very well. Just give the details to the cadet here, will you? And keep quiet about this.'

'Yes, sir,' agreed the constable.

Acland Street. How had they got a car as big as a Bentley into one of those small back yards? And why would they want to? Robinson wished that Miss Fisher was not so economical with her facts. Well, now, perhaps she would tell him more, since he'd found the car for her.

The phone rang. He ignored it. Robinson did not like telephones. A necessary evil, he thought. Cadet Quinn answered it.

'Yes, he's here,' he said. Robinson glared. He took the phone and snarled, 'Yes?'

'It's Hugh Collins here,' said a cautious voice.

'Yes?'

'I'm in the Mildura telephone exchange, sir. I want you to find out about a man who was touting a plan to send frozen orange juice to Europe. He was here at the Mildura Hotel on the night of the death. He registered as René Dupont. His address was given as the Melbourne Town Hall.'

'Interesting. I'll call you at the police station when I find out.'

'Er . . . I'm not staying there, sir.'

'You're not at the station?' said Robinson coldly.

'No, sir.'

'Where are you?'

'At the Mildura Hotel, sir.'

'Ant is there a reason why you aren't staying at the police station?'

'Yes, sir, there is,' said Hugh with extreme care.

'Let me guess,' said Robinson. He might not like telephones but he was quick on the uptake. 'You suspect that he murdered the man?'

'No, sir,' said Hugh, shocked.

'Ah. In that case, you suspect that peculation is taking place.'

'That's the general view, sir. I don't think I'm going to be welcome there,' said Hugh.

'As welcome as the tax inspector,' said Robinson. 'I see. Well, gather up what you can tomorrow and then come home. We can't be paying out a fortune for you to stay in the Mildura Hotel, can we? And I'll be asking around about your Dupont. By the way, was that Dupont with a "t" or Dupond with a "d"?'

'With a "t", sir.'

'Good. Don't take risks and don't get into any trouble,' ordered Robinson. 'Those country towns can be chancy. Is everyone in the Riverina listening to this conversation?'

'No, sir, I've found the dead man's fiancée, and her sister runs the exchange.'

'Women will be the ruin of you, Collins,' warned Robinson.

'Yes, sir,' agreed Hugh, and rang off.

'Quinn!' exclaimed Robinson.

The head of close-shorn dark hair came up and the frank brown eyes stared into the Detective Inspector's, eager to be of service.

'Yes, sir?'

'Run down to records and have a look at that list of French arrivals. See if you can find a René Dupont. I wish I could believe that you will,' he added gloomily.

Quinn raced off down the stairs, aglow with delight at having some real detecting to do. Robinson sipped his tea and wondered if he had ever been that young. Probably, he considered, not.

He would wait until Quinn came back to telephone Miss Fisher and tell her that her car had been found. On second thought, he was lunching with her tomorrow at some French place. He could tell her then. If there had been any rush, she would have told him more about the case. One of her snobby friends could wait another night for his stolen car.

Hugh Collins watched the brassy girl—Elsie clearly shared a hairdresser with her sister—as she removed the plug and broke the connection.

'Are you sure that no one could have overheard me?' he asked, worried.

'Not unless they happened to be ringing in at exactly the same time, and then my board would have lit up,' said Elsie. She seemed sure of herself. Hugh relaxed a little.

'Did you know the decea . . . I mean Thomas, your sister's fiancée, Miss Elsie?'

'Yes. Nice bloke. I thought she was doing real well to have caught him. He liked her. She liked him, too. Used to natter away all the time about what sort of oranges they was going to plant. Soon as he made enough he was going to marry her. Pity he didn't.'

'Why do you say that?' Hugh leaned one hip on the edge of the desk. He was tired.

'Well, now she's heartbroken and she never got to find out what being married was like. If they'd gone ahead, then she'd be a widow. She'd have his little place and could plant her own orange trees.'

'True,' said Hugh. 'Did he leave a will?'

'I never asked,' said Elsie, a light of intelligence dawning in her eyes. She felt his disapproval and explained.

'It's just, she's my little sister, and I ought to look after her. It'd mean a lot to Maisie, not to have to work for someone else. She's too independent to really get along with the Old Trout, and she's not a bad Old Trout. But she rubs Maisie up the wrong way and then Maisie rubs the Old Trout up the wrong way and it's not nice.'

'I can see how that might happen,' said Hugh carefully. 'Did you ever meet this French gentleman?'

'Oh yes, he was in the pub the night that the party was on. He'd been there a few days before, talking about frozen orange juice. I never touch that muck. Raise blisters on your tongue, it would.'

'What was he like?'

'Not much taller than me. Now I like a big man,' said Elsie, eyeing Hugh with approval. 'But he wasn't much taller than a boy. Wasn't a boy, though. He had dark hair and dark eyes which kind of stared past you. Gave me the creeps, he did. I say,' Elsie was struck with an idea. 'You don't think he killed poor old Tommy, do you?'

'Enquiries are continuing,' said Hugh.

He thanked Elsie, handed her some money 'for her sister' and walked out into the fresh darkness. For a moment, he stood breathing deeply. He could smell river water and . . . was that orange peel?

Then someone hit him hard on the back of the head, and he pitched forward into the street.

The prisoner wept quietly, trying not to be heard. Her hands were bound securely to a bedpost and she dared not cry out. She knew that no one was looking for her. No one would rescue her. She knew that she was quite alone, at the mercy of a monster.

CHAPTER TWELVE

Phryne dreamed of a tea party in Thé Sybaris where she danced with Dolly Wilde. Dolly pressed close to Phryne, soft breast to flat chest, hoping to make Natalie Barney jealous. Natalie Barney was never jealous . . . and into the all female environment, steamy with sex and kettles, had come the beautiful twins, les enfants terribles, and the whole crowd became merely a background for their magnificence. Jean and Jeanne Bourgoint, doomed, inseparable, morphine-slender and golden. Dolly, in Phryne's arms, said in a waspish whisper, 'I've seen them far too often recently. Love never dies of starvation, but often of indigestion.'

Phryne woke laughing, wondering where Dolly Wilde was now. Probably in bed. There was nothing Dolly had liked more than a suitably luxurious bed, with free stationery and someone bringing chocolate, gossip, peaches and orchids.

What had she to do today? Answer some questions. First, what was wrong with the charming and educated young woman Camellia? Objected to Lin Chung as a husband? Disliked him on sight? Surely not, though she did seem frightened occasionally. In love with someone else? Certainly she'd had time in Hong Kong to meet people outside her family and the Lin family were probably replete with gorgeous men. One only had to look at the local specimens. Or—wait a moment. This girl had come across the South China Sea in a 'difficult' escape. What if she had been caught and raped? Therefore she was no longer a virgin as per specifications? That would be a difficulty. But surely not with the urbane and educated Lin Chung. If that was the problem, and Lin made any objections, Phryne was prepared to clip his ears.

She swung her legs out of bed and rubbed a thoughtful instep. Second question: where was Elizabeth Chambers? Time was running away. Fairly soon her father would be paying up, grudgingly, perhaps, but paying up. And, with any luck, might get his daughter back. No clue had leapt into Phryne's grasp. Mr Chambers hadn't found anyone in the underworld who might have arranged a kidnapping and he could be relied upon to rummage rather thoroughly. Especially with a payment of five hundred pounds in prospect. Unanswered subsidiary question: what had been missing from Miss Chambers' room? Her passport and her pocket money she might have had on her. Possibly a few of her clothes. Possibly a book. The ones on the bookshelves had been tumbled down. Who would break into a lady's boudoir and only pinch a book?

Phryne shook her head. Who would know which book? Surely not the incurably blonde Julia. She might be able to read, but Phryne got the impression that fashion magazines were challenging enough for her.

And where was René? That reminded her. She scrabbled through the pictures she had found in her kitbag when talking to the ex-soldiers. Sarcelle's studio, light flooding through the multifold panes. Morning. And there they were: Edouard the Englishman, Sarcelle himself, Madame Sarcelle, Anton, LeBain from downstairs, both picture dealers Sardou and Dupont, and René. What was René doing there?

René never came to Atelier Sarcelle. He had always refused to have anything to do with Phryne's career as an artist's model. He had been jealous that other men would stare at her naked-ness and had always been cross when she came to see him after posing, until she produced her fee and took him out to dinner in the Rue de Gaîté or down in the Rue de Vaugirard for pancakes and cider at the Breiz. Phryne examined the picture more closely, taking up the magnifying glass which Dot used to mend stockings.

Yes, that really was René, next to Madame Sarcelle, with Sardou and Dupont behind them. Phryne knew Sardou, of course. When René had persuaded her to re-establish contact with her family, she bought pictures for her father from Sardou. Her telegram 'Hello family having fun in Paris how are you?' had not been answered by the outburst of parental fury that she had almost hoped for. Her mother had sent a long telegram (which must have cost a fortune) full of concern and affection, after which Phryne could hardly refuse further contact. Her father had even told her that he was proud of her ambulance work and glad that she was amusing herself among the artists but she should come home. When Phryne refused, he asked her to buy him some pictures, since she was so undutiful. He had purchased a Picasso dancer in London and believed that he was a fine artist. Though the Hon. Fisher didn't know a lot about art, he knew what he liked. Each bank draft was accompanied by a stern order to buy so many francs worth of late Impressionists and that fellow Picasso, and then come home.

Sardou liked Phryne and although he had not sold her any paintings cheaply, because that was contrary to his code, he had always given her a ten per cent discount for, he said, her beauty. He offered to pay her for standing in his shop, nude, to attract buyers, but that was too close to pneumonia for Phryne to consider. Sardou kept a vast collection of paintings, only a few of which were on display. When pressed, he would grumble and drag out canvases from cupboards—all the light and joy of Renoir, sprinkled with flowers—and mutter, 'Don't want to sell this one, pretty, very pretty, but if you insist . . .'

Phryne had insisted to the limit of her father's purse. She had visited Picasso herself, bidding for his exquisite line drawings.

'Bah,' the artist had scowled. 'Facile. See, here is a line . . .' and he had plopped a brush full of Indian ink down on a big sheet of butcher's paper and flicked it without even looking, producing a cat. It arose magically out of the paper. One line, the brush never lifting from the surface.

'Facile, but only you could do it,' Phryne told him. He smiled at her, a supremely seductive smile, compounded of Spanish Dominant Male and a curious detachment, a seeing eye. At that point his wife always moved gently between Phryne and the artist and concluded the deal for a sheaf of line drawings. Phryne had been fascinated by the portrait of Gertrude Stein which he would not finish. There she sat, Doyenne of Patrons, as heavy and blocky and impressive as the Venus of Willendorf, her hands dangling on her knees. Miss Stein was in Belgium with her constant companion Alice B. Toklas, distributing food to the starving, and Phryne had yet to meet her.

She looked at the photograph again. There was René in the Atelier Sarcelle, where he had no business to be. What had he been doing there?

What did she really know about René, anyway? That he was clever, skilled, attractive, ruthless and cruel? That was probably enough. In any case, he was not relevant to the third question: who was killing the ex-soldiers? Or was he? And if he was in the same picture as the Sarcelles, could René have had anything to do with the death of Sarcelle? Surely not . . .

'Things to do today: find René,' Phryne said aloud, hoisting herself to her feet and walking to her bathroom where Dot had drawn her bath, scented with chestnut blossoms. Interesting choice, Phryne thought. She used this exquisite scent to make herself feel better if she was unhappy. Dot must think that she needed it. She probably did.

Phryne sank gently into the bath and closed her eyes, breathing deeply.

Hugh Collins groaned. His head hurt. He tried to move and found that his hands were bound and so were his feet. The world appeared to be wobbling, or rather, surging. Nausea roiled over him in a blood-warm wave.

All he could do for his immediate ease was roll on one side to be sick. He retched helplessly, even after his stomach was empty, and wished he had a drink of water and the key to the handcuffs. This never happened to Sexton Blake.

Handcuffs? The ache in his head was lessening a little. He moved his wrists experimentally. Yes, definitely handcuffs, though it was so dark in his little world that he could not really see them. A momentary fear that he might have gone blind was dismissed as he sighted little stripes of light coming through the boards that constituted his roof. Not blind, then, and not dead. But captive. In a boat.

Who had a reason for hitting Hugh Collins over the head and kidnapping him? The local cop, what was his name? Smith? Yes, Smith. He might have overheard Hugh's conversation with Robinson, not by any telephonic means but by standing outside the door. And he might have decided that Hugh was surplus to requirements and biffed him with a handy brick. But handcuffing a fellow officer . . . it seemed extreme.

By a complicated manoeuvre during which he wished that he was a stone lighter and had studied acrobatics with some serviceable circus, Hugh managed to get his hands in front of him and reached up to examine his mistreated head. Yes, patch of blood matting the hair, tender to the touch, and a goose-egg swelling. Nothing worse than he had got in many a difference of opinion on Fitzroy Street or Little Lon. Now to get the handcuffs off.

He began to grope around on the floor. Sexton Blake would have found a bent nail or even a complete set of skeleton keys on his prison floor. This floor, however, apart from certain unpleasant detritus, was bare, slimy, and entirely devoid of the means to pick a handcuff lock. But wait a moment. Had he been searched?

Trying to reach his own pockets with handcuffed hands was the sort of physical challenge which only Houdini could have truly relished, he decided, after bending his body into a number of painful contortions. He finally got his fingers into his pockets and found that all of his possessions were there, which included his penknife. This was the sort of careless oversight which one could only approve of in a kidnapper. Hugh prised the awl free with his teeth and bent to his task.

Phryne ate her excellent breakfast and sat down in her parlour with all the information she had gleaned from the police department. Dot had taken the girls out to the pictures. Mr Butler was consulting with the wine merchant in the kitchen and Mrs Butler was remonstrating with the cleaning woman about dust left in corners. Ember was curled on Phryne's desk and Molly had collapsed asleep on her feet. Molly favoured this place of repose because it made the sittee stay peaceably in one place and not force Molly to follow them all over the house until they settled again.

Phryne was staring over Ember's head at a small oil, one of the pictures which had come from Paris in 1918 and which she had claimed as commission. It was a Sarcelle nude: Phryne herself, not recumbent and iconic but a swift, rough sketch of her. She was leaning on a windowsill, talking to someone in the yard outside. Her body was pearly, her buttocks as square as a boy's, her hair swinging forward to hide her face. Her small breasts rested on her crossed arms. Light gushed through the window and flooded the figure. It was considered un-acceptably non-cubist and Sarcelle had asked only twenty francs for it. Phryne remembered the day it was painted. November the twenty-third, 1918, one of those sunny clear days which Paris turns on to deceive the populace about the freezing winds and lowering skies to come. The lightly sketched trees outside the window were bare. Yes, nearly Christmas. Papa was paying for paintings, she no longer needed to model, and she wasn't hungry. And she had been talking to . . . René. So, he had come to the Atelier Sarcelle. Her memory had been at fault.

She gently slid the first paper out from under Ember, who moved his paws obligingly. A list of French people who had come into Australia in the last six months. The last time she had looked at this, she had baulked at René's name. Now she could scan it carefully.

One thing stood out immediately. René Dubois had been accompanied by Madame Dubois. Not that this should have come as a surprise. René had always been on the qui vive for a rich wife. For a while, until that terrible night, he had thought that Phryne would suit him admirably. Rich Papa, title, beauty. Everything he wanted in a spouse, including a doting, unconditional passion. René had always required a life in which he could play his music until three a.m., sleep until one p.m., and drink, smoke, gossip and flirt for the rest of the time. René, to the horror of his respectable peasant parents, was a ne'er-do-well.

And it wasn't that everyone hadn't told her. 'Oh, my dear,' La Petite Madeleine had said, fanning herself, 'if you had to find a lover, chérie, and I acknowledge that one does need a lover once in a while, did you have to embrace René? Everyone knows he is a bad hat.'

'Phryne, my darling,' Dolly had whispered in her exciting, breathy voice, 'my princess, my damsel in a tower, did you have to come down into such unworthy arms? René is no knight in shining armour. René would have been following the Crusade, tooting on a crumhorn and plucking plackets. He would have been thrown out of Sherwood for cheating Robin Hood. They would not have allowed him within a clothyard shaft of any real money or he would have been off to the High Sheriff of Nottingham with the gold and claimed the reward for turning them in . . . really, René is not a good idea.'

Phryne had protested, and Dolly had turned her exquisite wrist to make a Wildean gesture.

'When will you learn, my dear girl,' she said coolly, 'that inadvisable is not the same as undesirable?'

Toupie had called him 'that bastard'. Toupie did not habitually mince words and was not susceptible to roguish charm (male). Natalie Barney, the only person willing to tolerate René, had viewed him with such penetration that he had avoided her. The artists considered musicians nothing more than background noise which interrupted important discussions on Modernism. Only in the Rue des Trois Colonnes had René been welcome. In the dark and smoky atmosphere the shrill and gleam of the accordion had dominated the night, seeming to contain not only music but the sibilant mutter of Auvergne voices, the scent of cheap tobacco and the eau de mille fleurs which the prostitutes wore to cover the odours of their trade.

And when Sarcelle had paid her fee into her hand, he had told her not to spend it all on René, as he objected to paying souteneurs. And he was a pimp, that was true. He was living on Phryne's earnings and had every intention of going on doing so until she ran out of money, when—the Sapphics said—he would find another fool to pay for his pleasures.

Phryne's mind shied away from René again and she forced it sternly back. She had had enough of this. She had suppressed the memory of that night for ten years and now she was going to remember it: remember it, and get over it.

It had been a sullen, icy day, and Phryne was cross. She had a cold coming on. Sarcelle was working on a big nude for which he had a commission from Sardou, and he wanted to finish it. Because the stove had smoked unendurably, he had opened a window, and his model had lain in the draught for hours. When she stood up, instead of offering her the usual cup of chocolate, Madame Véronique had given her a lecture on

166

why handing her money to René was not good. Phryne had flounced out into the street without her fee. She was in the mood for a good dinner and some sympathy.

Instead, she had found René half drunk and half asleep, lounging in her bed and drinking the last of her private bottle of cognac. La Petite Madeleine was not there. René had reached for her but she was not in the mood and had pushed him away.

Then he had erupted into astonishing violence. Phryne found herself on her knees, her hair twisted in his fist, while he snarled, 'You will do as I say, woman!'

'Let me go!' Shocked, Phryne began to cry.

'You will do as I say,' he insisted. 'Where is the money?'

'I haven't got any,' she said through a bitten lip.

He hauled her up and slapped her hard across the face. The bitten lip split.

'Go out and walk the street,' he snarled. 'I want another bottle and then some dinner. What use are you if you haven't any money?'

Phryne, recovering her wits, wrenched herself free. She was still astounded.

'René, what's come over you?'

'Time you learned your place.' He spat at her feet.

'I know my place,' said Phryne. Sidling, she crossed the room, reached into a drawer and produced her service pistol. Panting, bleeding, weeping, she levelled it in hands which hardly shook at all.

'Get out,' she said. René laughed. He had never been closer to death than he was at that moment. Phryne fired into the wall beside him. Plaster fell like rain. Voices protested. Windows slammed open. René scrambled away towards the door.

'What about your papa?' he yelled, as the pistol came around again. 'You will pay well so that I do not tell Milord Papa what you have been doing!'

'You're giving me more reasons to kill you,' said Phryne. 'You may tell my father anything you like. Not one sou more do you get out of me! Goodbye, René!'

'I'll be back!' he shouted.

'I wouldn't,' said Phryne. She closed the door behind him, locked and barred it, then sank down on the floor and wept as though her heart was broken, because it was.

When Madeleine returned and coaxed her into opening the door, she did not say a word about the bloodstained face which was turned up to her. Instead, she applied a cold wet washcloth and made hot chocolate with cognac. When Phryne had recovered enough to walk, La Petite smuggled her downstairs and through a maze of lanes into the Quartier Latin, where she could go to ground amongst the women.

Phryne stayed indoors at Toupie's, playing solitaire (and occasionally poker with the mannish Standard Oil heiress Joe Carstairs) until her face healed. She won eleven hundred francs and got warm at last. Toupie had a large house, an American view of central heating, and no objection to guests, as long as they had no objection to her habits. No man ever entered the portals and that was all right with Phryne. She never wanted to see a man again.

Fortunately, she had contracted a cold, so she could stay in bed, sneezing voluptuously, drinking Mariette's chicken soup and feeling thoroughly sorry for herself in comfort. No one said 'I told you so'. Dolly Wilde called (when Phryne was presentable again) and brought hideously expensive grapes, which Dolly ate, tucked up cosily beside the invalid, comforting her with her silly, clever, enchanting fantasies.

La Petite Madeleine called, bringing all Phryne's possessions, as René had been seen lurking. Madeleine told Phryne that René had also called on Sarcelle and collected her fee for the nude, and that last piece of gratuitous meanness had cured Phryne of loving René.

It hadn't stopped her wanting to kill him, though. This must have leaked through the gossip network which connected the bohemians, because she never saw him again. He fell out of her life and she had only a small scar on the inside of her lip to remind herself of him. That was, of course, enough.

Soothed in the company of women, Phryne returned to modelling. Sarcelle made no comment but 'My Muse has returned to me!', and Madame Véronique had resumed supplying her with chocolate. The weather turned snowy but the stove had been fixed. Soon it would be Christmas. The 'flu was dying down and more food was getting through from the provinces. Cheese appeared in the shops again, and unsalted meat, and even marzipan. She had dined that day, she recalled, with Toupie and the girls, on the first post-war tournedos made of real beef and Normandy pommes de terre, and drunk red wine of the Languedoc with farmer's cheeses wrapped in vine leaves and bread made of wheat, not pease flour.

Phryne lit a cigarette and smiled. She had done it. René was reduced from a towering monster to an ordinary bastard of about five foot six. René was no longer a dreadful image to haunt her sleep, and Paris was her own again. Ember allowed her to remove the next sheet of paper. Mr Butler entered with her morning coffee, made to her own specifications. Sunlight flooded in through the parlour window, lighting up the small, swift, terribly charming sketch, and the Indian ink Picasso cat beside it. Phryne had stood and watched Pablo draw that cat in one effortless sweep of the brush. She had been very fortunate to be in Paris, very fortunate indeed. A thought struck her.

What were Sarcelle's paintings worth these days? She must call on a picture dealer on the way to take Jack Robinson to lunch.

The price she had been quoted from the crowded but fascinating picture dealer's shop in Bourke Street had staggered Phryne. The acting proprietor, Jacob Stein, offered her a chair and asked if he could fetch her a glass of water. He was attentive, as young salesmen who scent a woman with a stash of French Modernist paintings usually are. He was just starting in his father's business and wanted to make an impression on his parent. Old Papa Isaac Stein thought his son far too interested in girls to learn his hallmarks correctly, much less value paintings. Jacob only had sole control of the shop because Papa had had that heart attack. He reported on the day's trading every night, over dinner.

'If you would allow it, madam, we could call at your house and make a catalogue for you,' he offered, as a scurrying black-clad woman brought iced water in an eighteenth-century crystal tumbler. Phryne took a deep gulp. 'At a most reasonable fee. No obligation to sell, of course,' he added. 'But Sarcelle is all the rage at the moment and sometimes these fashions do not last. Our commission is very moderate, and I'm sure you will be pleased with our estimates.'

'I don't want to sell,' said Phryne. 'But a catalogue is a good idea. I had Father send all my favourites over when I bought my house and they're insured, of course.'

'But not for nearly enough, if you have a Sarcelle,'

suggested Jacob Stein, going so far as to pat Phryne's hand. She sat up straight.

'Very well. When can I expect you?'

'On Monday, madam? At ten?'

'Good.' Phryne gave him her card. She wasn't going to mention that she actually owned seven Sarcelles in case someone was listening and decided to burgle the house before the insurance could be raised. 'Your fee for the catalogue?'

'Five pounds,' said Jacob promptly. He saw Phryne out of the shop and heard the bell tinkle. It rang for success. Papa would have to admit that this was a coup, and he was sure that he could persuade the lady to sell a Sarcelle, even if it was only one. He wrote her details in his appointment diary, humming to himself. Miss Ellis, the business's most aged and trusted retainer, had brought the water in the eighteenth-century crystal. That meant that she agreed with his estimate of the customer's taste, discernment and wealth. It was going to be a good day, he felt sure.

Phryne Fisher collected Jack Robinson from outside his police station and executed a thoroughly illegal turn to take the car onto St Kilda Road. Robinson, who (on the grounds of not seeing anything of which he might have to take official notice) always kept his eyes shut when driving with Phryne, opened them cautiously.

'You ever heard of road rules, Miss Fisher?'

'No, you must tell me all about them,' yelled Phryne over the slipstream. She slowed down enough to allow pedestrians to get on and off the tram before roaring past it. They were in Fitzroy Street before he opened his eyes again.

'You'll enjoy this, Jack,' said Phryne as she allowed the big car to slide into a space occupied by a van moments before. 'This is the best French cooking in Australia.'

'If you say so, Miss Fisher,' said Robinson. He was resolved. If someone offered him snails, he was—by gum!—going to try them. The same did not apply to frog's legs, however. In a parental prospecting foray into the outback, young Jack had gotten lost and been rescued by some Aborigines. They had offered him something flaky which tasted vaguely of fish. When his father had found him he had been informed that he was eating snake. He had retained the snake because manners are manners and a rescue in the desert is a rescue in the desert, but he had decided to omit reptiles, and that included amphibians, from his diet thereafter. It was no use offering Jack Robinson a crocodile sandwich, even if it was delivered very swiftly.

Café Anatole was almost full. Jean-Paul greeted them at the door, smiling a professional smile. It broadened when he recognised Phryne.

'Milady, m'sieur, this way.' He led them to a small table in an obscure corner.

'Feed us,' said Phryne, waving away the menu.

'Snails,' said Robinson bravely.

'Escargots au beurre,' said Jean-Paul. 'A little fish, perhaps? Today we have sole. And the chef's special, mousse de saumon. Then perhaps chateaubriand?'

'Yes,' said Robinson. 'Snails and then a steak.'

'I'll have the salmon mousse,' said Phryne. 'And chateaubriand, rare, with Béarnaise sauce.'

'With pommes de terre paille. And we have the new broad beans, tiny, tiny ones . . .' hinted Jean-Paul.

'Some of them as well,' said Robinson recklessly.

Ten minutes later, Phryne watched, fascinated, as he

chewed his first escargot. 'Not bad at all,' he said judiciously. 'Doesn't really taste of anything but this butter sauce. I reckon you could put that butter sauce on India rubber and get the same effect.'

They chatted amiably through the snails.

'Oh, by the way, we've found your car, Miss Fisher. It's just around the corner, hidden in a back yard. Don't you think you ought to whisper in my shell-like what this is all about?'

'I think I'd better,' said Phryne. She outlined the kidnapping of Elizabeth Chambers, the enquiries she had made, and the total lack of progress she had met with. Robinson chewed his steak. It was very good. He averted his eyes from the blood-seeping spectacle on Phryne's plate and said, 'Kidnapping's always bl . . . extremely difficult. I can't say that we would have fared any better. The old man's done his best to comb through the underworld and there ain't many gangs who'd risk kidnapping, especially not a young girl. It's got to be amateurs, and they're always chancy.

'We'll need to raid the house,' he went on. 'But we can do it real quiet. If I take a few more blokes than usual we can get through the door and into the whole house before they have a chance to get rid of their prisoner. We'll do it tonight,' he said. 'And no, I ain't going to talk to Hector Chambers. You've got all you can out of him, probably more than I would have got. And that blonde girlfriend sounds useless. We'll just get a warrant, not a hard job because there's a stolen car in the yard.

'And for our other news,' said Robinson, 'young Hugh Collins has found a bloke who was seen talking to the deceased just before he got to be deceased. And his name was in the register. René Dupont. And you'll not be surprised to know that no René Dupont is registered with Customs and Immigration.'

'Oh dear. So, is Hugh back?'

'I told him to poke around a bit more but not get himself into any trouble. He should be on his way home.'

'Well, that's a bundle of news,' said Phryne. 'Come along, let's congratulate the cook.'

She entered the kitchen, bowed in by Jean-Paul. M'sieur Anatole was teaching the washing-up boy to make sauce blonde. The boy's hands were very quick and the sauce was compounding as he watched it, egg yolks performing their alchemy, thickening under the whisk.

'Hello,' Phryne signed under the boy's nose.

Startled eyes lifted, the boy saw Robinson behind her, dropped the whisk with a soundless yelp and fled out of the back door, which was open. Phryne heard his flapping shoes resound on the cobbles.

M'sieur Anatole caught the whisk and returned to the sauce, which must not be allowed to boil. 'Quelle affaire!' he said.

'What just happened?' asked Robinson.

'You scared him,' said Phryne.

'Can't imagine why,' Robinson replied. 'I've never seen him before in my whole life.'

CHAPTER THIRTEEN

Phryne took a bemused Robinson back to the station. So much for that theory. Billy the Match, if he was still extant, wasn't working at Café Anatole. But the Chambers' Bentley had been found, and tonight, with any luck, Jack Robinson might free a prisoner.

Phryne had not been able to finagle herself into the raiding party. She would have to wait outside to find out what had happened in the Acland Street house.

That sorted, she went home with an unshakeable conviction that what she had to do was find René Dubois, without the faintest idea of where to go searching for him. French consulate? René detested officialdom. Hotels? If René had money, he would choose the Ritz. But if he was staying for a while, he would rent a house. His peasant ancestors had made René very shrewd with money.

Phryne went home, hauled out the telephone directory, and made a list.

Hugh Collins had just got his hands loose and was working on his ankles when he heard someone coming. Heavy footsteps pounded what he was now convinced was a deck. He twisted the awl frantically and the shackle clicked open. His ankles were free.

Hugh crouched. He had no weapon except a penknife but he was now so very thirsty, hungry and angry that he was not concerned about minor details like weapons. He wanted to grab the man who had hit him and stuffed him in what were (probably) bilges. When he did grab, he planned to hang on and twist, until his captor gave up or his head came off. Hugh did not care which happened first.

The cover slid off the bilges, or possibly it was a hatch, and Hugh erupted into the fresh air like a Jack-in-the-box. He heard a startled shout and something clipped at his shoulder, then he was on his feet. Not with one bound, like Sexton, but pretty close. He turned on the man, intending to crunch and rend, and found himself confronting a shotgun.

'Captain Max!' exclaimed Hugh.

Captain Max was looking sorrowful. 'What did you have to come interfering for?' he asked. 'Now I have to kill you, son, and you're a nice young chap.'

'Why do you have to kill me?' Hugh was surprised at how steady his voice was. This was the first time anyone had tried to shoot him. He was attempting not to look down the double barrels of the shotgun and going cross-eyed. He dragged his gaze away.

'You know,' said Captain Max scornfully.

'No, really, I don't know,' shouted Hugh.

He was on the other side of the boat. He could always dive into the river. Then he'd be half dead, because he couldn't swim very well, but staying up on deck with that shotgun meant that he would be all dead, and half dead was better.

'I picked you first go,' said Max. 'No, don't move! Knew you were a cop! Knew you hadn't come about that other business. No city cop would come 358 miles to look into a soldier settler getting drunk and falling in a ditch, even if someone pushed him into it. No, you didn't fool me for a moment.'

'I can see you're a wise man,' said Hugh carefully.

'Only took me a moment to suss you,' said Captain Max. 'Then I had to decide what to do with you. I waited until you'd finished wooing them yeller-haired girls in the telephone exchange, then I swings me bit of four by two and you were out like a light. Then I just carried you here.'

'I follow you,' said Hugh. 'But I still don't know why.'

'Stands to reason,' said Captain Max complacently. 'You must have been investigating the stolen jewellery. Was it the Toorak house, or the shop in Flinders Lane?'

'Neither,' said Hugh, thinking about it. 'But it's a good way to dispose of stolen jewellery, a fine way. The thieves just pack it into a case with a lot of other stuff, consign it to the railways, they bring it here, you pick it up at the station and off it goes across the river, out of the Victoria Police jurisdiction. You've got the local policeman well bribed, so he's not going to enquire. Yes, a really good scheme.'

Captain Max beamed. 'Bonzer, isn't it? And then you had to come poking your nose in.'

'And you know the really funny bit, Captain?' asked Hugh. His foot had struck against something heavy and round. It rolled a little.

'No, what?'

'I didn't know anything about it until now,' said Hugh as he simultaneously stooped, grabbed, and hurled an unopened tin of Best Seville Orange Marmalade straight into Captain Max's face.

Hugh threw himself flat as the gun roared. Then he dived across the deck and, after a fierce struggle, managed to get Captain Max to go down and stay down. He scrabbled in the hold for his manacles and applied them, securing the dazed assailant to the taffrail. He dropped the gun overboard with profound pleasure.

He went forward to what he thought of as the driver's cabin and found a thin middle-aged woman with one hand on the tiller, pensively eating an apple.

'Hello,' he said, keeping both hands free in case Mrs Captain Max was in on this enterprise. She looked up, startled.

'What are you doing here? Max didn't tell me there were any passengers.'

'I'm a police officer,' said Hugh, producing his badge.

'Max has been doing something he shouldn't, hasn't he?' she asked resignedly.

'Yes, I'm afraid so.'

'I knew it. Whenever he gets that grin, he's been doing something he oughtn't.'

'I must ask you to turn the boat around and get us back to Mildura.'

'All right, but it'll take a while. If you're in a hurry to get back to Melbourne, you'd be better getting off at Echuca and catching the train.'

Hugh thought about the well-bribed Constable Smith in Mildura. 'Maybe you're right. Let's do that, then. Er . . . full steam ahead?'

Mrs Captain Max did not smile. She took a final vengeful bite out of her apple and tossed the core from the window.

'What's he done?'

'Receiving stolen goods, I think.'

'It's his diet, you know,' she said sternly. 'All that refined sugar will be the death of him.'

Hugh pondered the irony of a Food Reform resister being felled by an illicit tin of jam and smothered a smile.

'I'll read him his rights when he wakes up,' said Hugh. 'Meanwhile, can I get a drink of water? Something to eat?'

Mrs Captain Max tucked back a strand of iron grey hair and replied calmly, 'There's banana bread, just out of the oven, inside. It's a bit scorched. I just got the recipe from the Country Women's Association at our last stop. And you can squeeze yourself some oranges. I don't carry no coffee nor tea. Poisons, they are. Rank poisons.'

The galley was very neat. He sipped water as he cut and squeezed oranges and when he drank the juice it removed the taste of sickness and fear from his mouth as if by magic. After that the banana bread was chewy and nutty, precisely what his stomach would have ordered. The boat surged through the water. He cut himself another slice.

Hugh felt that, after all, there was something to be said for Food Reform.

'Miss?' asked Dot, coming in to the drawing room at about three o'clock. 'Can I help?' she added, seeing the bits of paper strewn all over the desk. Phryne was not being assisted by Ember, who had an uncanny ability to ascertain which book, reference or note she was going to need next and then sitting on it. This meant that Phryne had to politely request that he move and stroke him before retrieving her information.

'You can remove Ember,' she said.

Ember, who had picked up quite a lot of English, drew himself onto his paws and stalked out of a room where the barbarians did not appreciate his company. Besides, he had heard the clang of the ice-box door and knew that Mrs Butler was preparing dinner.

'Never mind, he's removed himself.'

'I think he understands every word we say,' said Dot dotingly.

'Probably. At least, as far as it concerns him. Dot, I am trying to find a passenger who came in on the *Stranraer*, and I don't know where to start. He's here for a while and he has his wife with him, so he's probably rented a house.'

'Or maybe a room,' said Dot, looking at the scatter of papers. 'There must be hundreds of people renting rooms in Melbourne.'

'Yes. Where do we begin?'

'At the beginning,' said Dot briskly. 'Where did he go when he got off the boat? Station Pier is the place to start. Would he have friends in Australia?'

'I shouldn't think so,' said Phryne. 'Never had any while I knew him.'

'Don't aliens have to register with the police?' asked Dot.

'Quite right, Dot, they do. Here are his registration details.'

'René Dubois,' read Dot. 'Place of birth, Riom, Auvergne, France. Date of birth, 21st February, 1890. Occupation, gentleman.'

Phryne snorted. 'I wonder what they do to you for lying to Customs,' she mused.

'Probably something nasty. Why, isn't he a gentleman?'

'René Dubois is many things,' said Phryne grimly, 'but he isn't, and never has been, a gentleman.'

'Oh.' Dot didn't feel that she needed any more information. The trouble with Phryne was that if you asked her for further details, she would probably give them, and Dot knew that she didn't want to know. 'Well, the new arrivals usually go to one of the hotels on the foreshore. Just until the ground stops rocking under their feet and they've got their bearings. The Port Melbourne, that's the biggest. Then there's the Maritime and the Sailor's Rest.'

'If it's René, it'll be the cheapest, and the nearest to any source of sly grog. I don't know those hotels.'

'I should think not,' said Dot tolerantly. 'But Mr Bert would.'

'So he would. But can you imagine any hotel clerk giving Bert any confidential information?'

Dot giggled. 'I bet he knows all of them,' she said. 'Very close together, those Port people. All in the family, like.'

'You have a point. I don't want to ask him, Dot. I'd be putting him in danger. I think René is the murderer. It's an absolutely groundless suspicion, and I can't really tell Jack Robinson, because when he asks me for my proof, I haven't got any. And when he asks me how I know this Dubois, and I tell him that he broke my heart in Paris in 1918, then he'll laugh.'

'He wouldn't,' said Dot indignantly.

'Your clever Hugh has found out that a small, dark Frenchman was talking to poor Thomas MacKenzie just before he was murdered. And the man signed the hotel register as René Dupont. Dupont is the French form of 'Smith'. And don't people who take on false names usually keep their initials and sometimes their first names? Something to do with losing their identity.'

'Mr Robinson would accept that,' said Dot.

'Maybe. I want some more proof before I go to him with such a mad idea, though.'

'Were there any other Renés in the list of people coming into Australia?' asked Dot.

Phryne ran her finger down the list. 'No. Lots of Jean-Pauls, Jean-Baptistes, Jean-Lucs, Michels, Edouards, Raouls and a sprinkling of Henris and Guillaumes, but no other Renés,' replied Phryne, scanning the list again.

'I think Mr Bert could find out,' said Dot. 'And he won't be in danger if he knows about it.'

'Hmm,' said Phryne. 'You're right, I suppose. Let's get Bert on the phone and ask him.'

After the usual difficulties of persuading a willfully deaf landlady to locate Bert and usher him to the phone, Phryne put the matter to him.

'So you think this Dubois character is our murderer?' demanded Bert gruffly.

'I think so, but I've got no proof and only a lot of guesses. We need to find him, and Dot suggested that you might be the person who could get information out of the clerks at the Station Pier hotels.'

'Yair, well, as it happens, Cec's cousin's nephew is clerk at the Port, Cec's brother's daughter is a housemaid at the Maritime, and me auntie works at the Sailor's Rest. But there's a lot of boarding houses round here. P'raps we try the hotels first. And you don't have to tell me to be careful, Miss Phryne, in case you was thinking of it.'

'Well, actually, Bert dear, I was thinking of asking you not to kill him until we find out if he's the murderer. Not because I don't think the world would be a cleaner, sweeter place without René, because I do, but because if you should, quite without meaning to, sort of bludgeon him to death and he *isn't* the murderer, then we'd be back to the beginning with a false sense of security. If you follow me.'

There was a pause while Bert sorted this out.

'I follow yer,' said Bert at last. 'Good point. I'll make sure we don't do him, carelessly, until we know it's him. I'll take Cec with me to mind my back. It's not as if we haven't done that trick before, and it'll give us something to do. These other blokes are drinking us out of house and home. It's like the good old days round here. I'll call yer when I know something. Bye,' said Bert, and hung up.

'But there's another thing we could try,' said Phryne.

'Yes, Miss?' Dot was pleased to see the light of curiosity back in Miss Phryne's eyes. She'd been miserable the last few days, crying out in her sleep. Dot had learned that she was worried about Mr Lin, and the Butlers' defection, and something to do with Paris. Dot had tried to express her sympathy by service; mended stockings, nice baths, choice of dresses. But she felt helpless against this avalanche of memories. However, now it appeared that Miss Phryne had gotten over whatever it was that had been giving her nightmares. Her green eyes were sparkling, her cheeks were pink, her hair was a shiny, patent-leather black and she looked like an animated Dutch doll, which was how she should look. Her frank conversation with Bert did not shock Dot as it might have done in her early days with Miss Phryne. If Phryne said that the world would be better without a certain person, then she had a reason. Anyway, she had been asking Mr Bert *not* to kill someone. Dot's conscience, never particularly elastic, could accept that.

'Music,' said Phryne. 'I cannot imagine René abandoning music. It was the only thing he loved. He and that button accordion were joined at the hip. He even used to go to bed with it—no need to look shocked, Dot dear, just in the middle of winter to keep the reeds from freezing. Assuming that he has moved with the times, where would we find him in these jazz conscious days?'

'You know all the best places,' said Dot. 'But you shouldn't go alone!' she added quickly.

'Quite,' Phryne replied. 'I propose taking you and Hugh with me. Hugh for decoration and you to back me up in case there's trouble. Real French accordion players are worth their weight in plantinum. Isn't Hugh supposed to be back by now?'

'On the train today,' Dot replied. 'Mr Robinson said.'

'And Jack is going to raid the house in Acland Street tonight, so it may be a fatiguing evening,' said Phryne. 'I might retire for a nap. The bookshop should have sent some more detective stories. Is Ruth still reading those ghastly romances, Dot?'

'Yes,' said Dot. 'But I don't think they're doing her any harm, miss.'

'And it's better that we know what she's reading rather than have her boggling at *The Awful Adventures of Maria Monk* under the covers, I suppose,' said Phryne. 'But she's always seemed such a sensible girl.'

'She'll grow out of it,' said Dot firmly. 'We all do.'

'I never started,' said Phryne. 'But if a sensible person like you read them, Dot dear, then I shall stop worrying.'

'Oh yes, I went through all of the romances in Miss Mudie's Lending Library,' said Dot. 'And all them three-volume novels too—*The Rosary* and *The Daisy Chain*. They didn't do me any harm. You'll see. After a while she'll find out they're like eating too much Turkey lolly. All sweet pink fluff and no food. And she's keeping up her studies, she got an A for her chemistry exam yesterday.'

'Excellent.' Phryne picked up *The Clue of the Skeleton Key* and went out of the room, collecting a glass of water on the way. This evening would require a clear head.

She debated as to whether she should call Mr Chambers and tell him not to pay the ransom, but continued her climb towards her own apartments. It was never wise, she had found, to count her chickens before they had tapped their way out of the egg.

Bert and Cec did not bother with the front door of the Port Melbourne Hotel, which was their first destination. They did not like front doors. They went straight to the kitchen door and asked for Jimmy Clarke. The kitchen was such a scurry of white aprons and seething, steaming, boiling and roasting that they were driven back into the anteroom where the vegetables awaited their transformation into food. Bert leaned on a sack of potatoes.

'My old man told me, never get into a trade where you have to feed people,' said Bert.

'Like being a taxi driver,' commented Cec. 'Changed minds, contrary cusses and lots of going crook.'

'S'pose,' agreed Bert. 'But a hotel can't just tell their customers to shut up and pay up or walk home.'

'Yair, but a taxi driver can't drop fag ash into the soup,' said Cec, watching a cook do precisely that.

'True,' agreed Bert. 'Bloody heavy, the murphies,' he added. 'I remember being black and blue necking them hundred and forty pound bags.'

'Worse'n wheat,' agreed Cec. 'Even though wheat's heavier. It sorta moulds to your back, where the murphs are all knobs.'

'You reckon the wharf strike'll be over soon?' asked Bert, taking a butt from behind his ear and lighting it.

'Nah,' Cec replied. 'I reckon it'll go on for a year. Ah, here's the young feller. Jimmy Clarke, is it?'

'Who's asking?' The boy had long outgrown his suit. He was an anatomy lesson in wrists and ankles. He had a belligerent cock to his fair head and the remote Scandinavian ancestor who had bequeathed his pale blue eyes and flaxen hair had also handed down a reasonable modicum of Viking aggression.

'Me, I'm your sort-of-cousin Cec.'

'Oh yair. I saw you at Betty's wedding. What can I do for you, gents?' The clerkly manner was quite convincing.

'I want you to go and look at the register and find out if you had a René Dupont or Dubois staying here on the night of the fifth.'

'I can't take the register away from the desk,' he protested.

'You don't need to,' urged Cec. 'Just go and flip through it and see who came in off the *Stranraer*. You can do that,' said Cec encouragingly.

'Yair, all right.' The boy was evidently convinced. 'Back in a tick.'

Bert sat down on the potatoes. He pinched out his cigarette. The kitchen resounded with shouted orders.

'I wouldn't do this for quids,' he said.

'What, finding out things?' asked Cec, helping himself to a piece of bread from a tray.

'Nah, working in a kitchen.'

'Too right.'

They waited patiently until Cec's relation came back with a scribbled list.

'Sorry,' he said. 'No French people at all. I've made you a list of everyone off the *Stranraer*.'

'Thanks, son,' said Bert.

'Give my best to your dad,' said Cec.

They left the kitchen, avoiding a flying pot by inches.

The Maritime proved more difficult. Cec's brother Aub's daughter was called Terebinthia, a fact which Cec explained by telling Bert that her mother 'had fancies' and had been reading a romance in which the main character was called by this name at the time young Terebinthia made her appearance. She was known generally as Bintha. The staff in the kitchen of the Maritime did not appear to wish to cooperate in calling her, and as Bert was trying not to attract attention, he restrained himself from more forceful methods and went around to the front.

'Bloody unfriendly place, this,' he commented to Cec. 'Good afternoon, miss,' he said to the woman at the desk. 'We want to see Miss Terebinthia Yates, please. She's a housemaid here.'

'Who's asking?' The glasses slid down a ski-run nose. The lady had grey hair ironed into waves and glacial grey eyes. She looked Bert and then Cec up and down and it was clear that their advent in her nice clean hotel gave her no pleasure.

'Cecil Yates,' said Cec quietly. 'I'm her uncle.'

'Even so,' said the Manageress, Mrs Jones, 'I can't call the girl away from her work just because someone off the street comes asking for her. Is it an emergency?'

'Yes,' said Cec. His limpid eyes and air of sincerity apparently won his point. The Manageress rang a bell and ordered a boy to find Bintha and bring her here right now. Bert examined the foyer.

The Maritime was the second hotel in Port Melbourne, but it did not try harder. It had been built in the spacious days when half an acre of foyer was just about adequate, and decorated by someone with a lot of plush, gold foil, cupids, naked marble statues and a forest of aspidistras to spare. The chairs were spindly and gold-legged, and Bert was unwilling to trust his frame to any of them. There was an air of about-to-be-shabby genteel about the Maritime which Bert did not like and he was glad when another tall, long-legged and blonde member of the extended Yates clan came hurrying out, wiping her hands on her apron.

'Yes, Mrs . . . oh, hullo, Uncle Cec!' she said, her face lighting up. Cec had always been her favourite uncle, one who could be relied upon to advise on the feeding of baby birds fallen out of the nest and to be properly sympathetic when they died, which they always did.

'You have five minutes, Bintha,' said the Manageress, ostentatiously consulting the large brass clock.

Cec hustled the girl into a corner under a very sad aspidistra.

'Bintha, I gotta ask you to do something for me.'

'Course,' said Bintha, pressing her hands to her starched bosom.

'It might cost you your job,' warned Bert.

'I'm sick of it anyway,' declared Bintha stoutly. 'What do you want me to do?'

'Can you get at the register?' asked Bert.

'If we can distract her. What do you need?'

'We're looking for a René Dupont or Dubois who came off the *Stranraer* on the fifth. Can you look it up for us?'

'Of course.'

'Good girl.'

'Mrs Jones, my Uncle Cec knows all about aspidistras,' said Bintha, moving to the counter. 'I'll mind the desk if you want to talk to him.'

Mrs Jones did not like the look of Bert or Cec, but she had

been very worried about the droopiness of her aspidistras. She slapped open the flap and allowed Bintha inside.

'Just for a moment, then,' she snapped. Cec took her arm very courteously, turning her so that her back was to the counter. Bintha leafed frantically through the register and pencilled details on a small piece of card, which she flicked across to Bert, who trousered it quickly.

'You oughta clean aspidistras with salad oil, not milk. You're gonna kill 'em all if you keep on cleaning 'em with milk. And water 'em only once a week, and only when they're dry,' instructed Cec. 'Bit of a wash and dry and a lick of oil and they'll be fine. They'll come up right as ninepence in a month, you'll see,' he assured her.

Mrs Jones unbent sufficiently to thank him.

'Will you come on, Gardening Tips,' snarled Bert.

They left as Bintha informed the Manageress that one of her relatives had died, but there was no immediate need for Bintha to cut short her work and go home. This pleased the Manageress so much—she still had fifteen rooms to clean—that she resolved to accept Cec's advice about the aspidistras. Salad oil might cheer them up, at that.

'In on the fifth, out on the seventh,' Cec read the note. 'No forwarding address.'

'She's a beaut girl, your niece Bintha,' said Bert.

'Too right,' said Cec.

The Sailor's Rest was not about-to-be-shabby genteel, it was downright shabby. Even when it had been first port of call for men off the deep-sea ships with money to spend and six months sobriety and celibacy to undo, it had never bothered much with appearances. Or legalities. Bert walked in and the first person he saw was his Auntie Joan.

'Bertie!' she exclaimed. 'Come in and have a drink!'

'That's a nice welcome, Auntie, don't mind if we do,' said Bert thirstily, sitting down beside her at the desk. 'You remember Cec?'

Auntie Joan hitched up her bosom and yelled, 'Three beers, Wally, and don't you go supping them on the way! So, Bertie, tell me all the family news.'

'There ain't much that you don't know already, Auntie Joan,' said Bert, embarrassed. Not even his mother called him 'Bertie'. The beer came, cold and fresh, and he sipped for a while.

'You don't just drop in to say hello,' said Auntie Joan. 'What can I do for you, Bertie?'

'I need to know if a bloke came in here from the Maritime on the seventh,' said Bert.

'Take a look,' said Joan. Her hair was a startling shade of henna red and she was wearing far too much make-up, but Cec decided that she was a kind old body, except possibly to defaulting sailors. Bert examined the register, which was considerably blotted.

'You look,' he said, passing it over to Cec. Not to anyone was Bert going to admit that he needed glasses. Cec turned over a couple of pages.

'Bingo,' he said. 'Came here on the seventh, out on the ninth. René Dupont. And Mrs Dupont.'

'Good-o. You remember this bloke, Auntie?'

'Him?' Joan's mouth pursed. 'Yair. You after him, Bertie? Then you keep your wits around yer. He was a charmer, that one. You remember your Uncle Jim?'

'Yair,' said Bert. 'He was a charmer, too.'

'He was a snake,' said Joan vehemently enough to blow the froth off her beer. 'And since he passed away I've got a nose for

'Where you fucking come from, bitch? Fucking get out of it! This is my fucking beat!'

'I'm not working,' said Phryne calmly. 'I'm waiting. Why didn't you grab either of those sailors? I sent them your way.'

'Too fucking drunk,' said the woman. 'To get that drunk, they'd have already fucking spent their pay. One of them social workers, are yer?' She scanned Phryne's clothes and her air of sophistication. 'Nah, not in that hat. Got a fucking smoke on yer for a working girl?'

Phryne produced a cigarette case, and lit both their cigarettes. It was dark now, with a hot, uncomfortable wind that carried dust into their eyes and caked on the prostitute's make-up, which looked to be an inferior form of whitewash.

'There has to be a better way to make a living,' muttered the woman. 'What you waiting for?'

'How much do you make in a night?' asked Phryne.

'Fucking what's it to yer?' the woman snarled. Then she seemed to shrink. 'About a pound. I can't go home without a pound or me old man'll go fucking crook. And I only made seven bob and a deener tonight. And I found the fucking deener.'

'Here's a pound,' said Phryne, producing it from the recesses of her costume. 'Take a night off.'

The whore's face cracked in a disbelieving grin. She suddenly seemed much younger, a ghost of the vigorous, lusty young woman she had once been.

'I ain't had a night off since . . .' The woman grabbed the note and tucked it into her bosom. 'I'll—I'll go home early— nah, that won't do. Me old man'd just send me out again, he's a fucking mean bastard. I'll go over the caff and swank about me generous Jack. Ta ra, miss,' she said, and walked off quickly, her high heels tapping the pavement.

Having cleared the decks, Phryne peeped into as much of the cake shop window as she could see through the shutters and listened to the St Kilda night: wailing ships' sirens summoning missing crews from the fleshpots with a weary 'Oh, come *on*, you blokes' persistence, a police whistle, the smash of a bottle, the shout of a drunken man and, somewhere quite close, the chanting of children playing skippy. What were they doing out at this time of night? Shouldn't they be home in bed?

Possibly they had no beds. The economic forecasts were bad, especially from America. Phryne reviewed her investments: beer, food, land, jewellery, gold, art works. Should yield some income as long as Australians continued to drink, which she thought a reasonably safe bet. She had three houses now, apart from the one she lived in, all in good suburbs. They ought to retain at least some of their value if the whole world fell apart. But what would happen to the poor?

What usually happened to them. They would pinch and scrimp and starve if they had to, in the hope that they would eventually see better times. Which was unlikely. The future, she thought pessimistically, was bleak.

She was distracted from her gloomy meditation by the unmistakable noise of a police officer applying the nine pound key to a door. Nothing else in the world sounded like a sledge-hammer.

The smash–thud seemed to echo. Someone yelled, a noise abruptly cut off. Phryne heard feet pounding, and a man came around the corner at speeds of Mach number. He had the lead and he was going to keep it and once he got into another maze of lanes he would escape like a rat up a drainpipe. If he had information which Phryne needed, she would have to stop him. He was a big, solid man with muscles on his muscles, and he must have weighed sixteen stone. A bit much to tackle unassisted.

Well, there was always good old reliable gravity.

Phryne extended a delicate ankle and he performed a neat half somersault, slamming face-down on the ground with force enough to jar out all his remaining wits, as well as teeth. She placed a thoughtful foot on his neck as the other set of pounding feet were revealed to be a pursuing policeman.

'Er,' he said, skidding to a stop. This was the Mystery Woman who visited Jack Robinson. The entire station was dying to know who she was and what she wanted with him. Especially since it was well known that he loved his nice, calm, plump wife Rosie even more than he loved a good pinch or his cattaleya orchids. Now did not seem to be a good time to ask the Mystery Woman for any personal details. His malefactor was reposing under her dainty foot and didn't look like he was going anywhere until his head stopped spinning. How had such a small thin woman done that to a big solid bruiser like Jimmy the Hook? She mightn't like answering personal questions. It would be the act of a nitwit to irritate a woman with such remarkable martial arts skills.

'Thanks, miss,' he said politely, hauling the recumbent man to his feet and applying handcuffs. 'I'm Constable Davis. I'll take him off your hands.'

'Who is he?' asked Phryne, inspecting the groaning man as though he was an anatomical specimen. Of a particularly nasty disease.

'Jimmy the Hook,' said Constable Davis, eager to please.

'He seems to have both hands.'

'They call him that because of this,' explained Davis, pulling a wharfie's hand tool, a long sharp metal hook set in a wooden handle, from his prisoner's belt. 'He always fights with a hook. Lucky he didn't gut himself when you . . . did whatever you did to him.'

'You're from Detective Inspector Robinson's raid, aren't you? And so is this . . . person. Anyone else in the house?' asked Phryne.

'Dunno, miss. Jimmy came haring out of the back door as though devils was after him and I thought I'd better collect him, or the boss'd go crook. So come along with me, Jimmy,' said the constable. 'You're in big trouble this time,' he added affably as they turned the corner. 'Car theft. How much d'ye reckon that Bentley was worth? Ten years in jail, I reckon, when the magistrate reads through your priors.'

Jimmy replied briefly but pungently on the subject of cops and sheilas in league with cops. 'I would'a got away if she hadn't tripped me,' he snarled.

'Where is the girl?' asked Phryne in a sub-zero voice.

'What girl?' asked Jimmy. 'I never saw no girl. What're you on about?' He looked at Phryne and added, 'Lady?'

'Who was in the house?' asked Phryne.

'You asking me to dob in me own mates?' demanded Jimmy angrily.

'Yes,' agreed Phryne. 'If you want any mercy from me.'

Jimmy the Hook had never been wise, but he had elements of self-preservation. This thin little female had not only brought him down but kept him down, and that much strength required respect. Not many people could say that they'd brought Jimmy the Hook down. He thought he might be in love.

'I dunno!' he wailed. 'There was just Dusty and old Almonds and Blue. Never was no girl. I don't know anything about any girl.'

'Dusty is Miller, the car thief,' said the policeman. 'Almonds is Terence Bailey. They call him Almonds because he eats almonds all the time. And Blue is John Pollack, who had red hair, when he had hair. Plus Jimmy the Hook. That was everyone, Jimmy?'

'Yair.' Jimmy subsided when they came round the corner into the lane. A police van was there, into which three other men were being loaded.

'Bugger,' Jimmy spat. 'They got all of us.'

'In you go.' The police officer shoved him up the steps and into the dank interior.

'Hello, Miss Fisher,' said Jack Robinson. He was almost dancing with joy. 'You've done me a bit of a good turn by making me look for that car.'

'Oh? How?'

'We got all of the makings for a fine little prosecution,' enthused Jack, rubbing his hands together. 'We got the names and addresses. We got the car numbers. We got a fine collection of naughty persons and we've got three cars. They gutted the bottom storey of the house and just drove 'em inside. One of which is, as you see, your missing Bentley.'

He waved an expansive hand. There, indeed, was the Bentley. Gratifying, but Phryne had other fish to fry. That prominent racing identity Hector Chambers would be pleased to get this expensive collection of metal back, but he also wanted his daughter. Where was Elizabeth Chambers?

'Have you searched the house?' she asked.

'I was about to invite you inside,' said Robinson, offering her his arm with a courtly gesture which made the rest of his men stare.

Phryne laid a hand on his elbow. 'Let's go then, shall we?' she asked.

The path through the back yard was strewn with things which crunched and rolled underfoot. On examination, they proved to be nuts, bolts, spark plugs and unidentifiable bits of ex-motor vehicle. Phryne reflected that she was walking on a geological stratum of car parts, and wondered what a competent geologist would think of this—and what he would call it. The vehicular belt?

'We reckon there's the remains of at least ten cars here, maybe more,' said Robinson, as excited as Phryne had ever heard him. 'We've been looking for these blokes for a couple of years. Steal the cars, repaint them, change the engine numbers and drive 'em to Sydney. Never a clue as to who was doing it. Well,' said Robinson, pushing aside the broken remains of a back door, 'here's the house.'

'What a hovel,' commented Phryne. It stank of poverty, oil, paint and dirt. The only furniture appeared to be four broken armchairs and a case of beer. 'Is there an upstairs?'

'This way.' Robinson indicated a staircase littered with cigarette ends and other debris into which Phryne was not minded to enquire. The upper floor windows, festooned with cobwebs, looked over Acland Street. There were three rooms. They were all empty.

Empty, that is, of a kidnapped heiress. Actually they were rather full. They were filthy and crammed with bits of engines and pots of paint and tools. No one was hidden there. There was nowhere to hide anyone. Phryne tapped walls, looked for a way into the roof, moved various larger bits of pressed metal, but not only was there no sign of the young woman, there was no sign that she had ever been there.

'A cellar?'

'Not in this house,' said Jack. 'And when I was having a little chat with Blue—Pollack, that is—he told me that they found the Bentley with the keys in the ignition and the doors unlocked in Barkers Road, Kew.'

'How very curious,' Phryne commented. 'Let's get out of here,' she added. 'You will search this place in daylight, won't you? Thoroughly?'

'I'll take it to pieces myself,' said Robinson, chuckling.

'Then if you will excuse me . . . and congratulations on your coup.'

Phryne walked home, thinking hard. This had been an operation whose stated objective was to steal cars, not girls. Someone had taken the Bentley to Barkers Road, Kew and left it there, practically with a 'Please Steal This Car At Your Earliest Convenience' label on the windscreen. Who had taken it there? And where, oh where, was Elizabeth Chambers?

'Miss Fisher!' Jack Robinson leaned out of the window of a police car which had crept up beside her. 'You walk fast! Coupla bits of news. We found Billy the Match. Working as a furnace tender at Hume's Pipes. Never leaves the fire and never been happier, he reckons.'

'That's nice,' said Phryne. 'I was rather sorry for Billy the Match.'

'And I forgot to say, your Miss Williams' young man will be late back. He broke a stolen goods case in Mildura but he'll be home tomorrow. And he found your René Dubois had been there, staying at the same hotel, talking to the dead man just before he got to be dead. And Collins found out that this Dubois bought a whole bottle of some heathen spirit from the pub keeper. Called vodka.'

'Oh,' said Phryne. 'That would explain how Thomas MacKenzie got so drunk. Vodka has almost no taste.'

'Yair, so my Russian sergeant told me. This Dubois was s'posed to be there on a frozen orange juice lark. He fills the glass with this vodka and the orange juice, tells the poor bloke to bottoms-up and he's half-pi full of ink already.

Wouldn't be hard to lay him down in a ditch with all that inside him.'

'How very . . . ruthless. What about the other murder?'

'I'll come and tell you about it tomorrow, but it's much the same. They should'a found the knock-out drops in the body but it's too late for that now. Luckily they found the bottle they was in, once the lazy hounds searched that yard properly. He was laid out under the car and then it was dropped on him.'

'Efficient,' murmured Phryne.

'Yair. I reckon it's someone who isn't real strong. Both the victims've been knocked out before they was killed.'

'Not so much not real strong,' observed Phryne, 'as not real brave.'

Jack Robinson gave her a shrewd look.

'I reckon this ain't such a surprise to you,' he said. 'I reckon you're going to tell me all about it tomorrow.'

'Do you?' said Phryne. 'Goodnight, Jack dear.'

She walked on and the police car, after a pause, roared away. Jack had his car thieves, and Phryne had—what?

Not a lot, and that was plain.

Phryne had always enjoyed walking at night and after she was free of René she had reclaimed the streets of the Quartier Latin for her own. Phryne was not going to allow the fear that she might set eyes on her faithless, brutal lover again debar her from the streets of Paris, which are the most interesting streets in the world . . .

To begin with, it had been fear. People had beaten Phryne before. It was not the pain. It was the humiliation. The messy, dirty, squalid fact that she had been slapped around like a whore disciplined by her pimp. That someone—that her lover—could think of Phryne like that made her shudder with disgust.

But the fear faded. Sarcelle and his atelier were delighted to see her and had given Madame la Concierge strict orders to never, never, allow René in, regardless of any bribe which he might offer. The Quartier Latin women were quite capable of carrying out their collective threat, which was to deprive René of his masculine attributes and make him eat them. If ever they laid their hands on him he might suffer the fate of Pentheus, and even Natalie Barney had said that she would join in the Bacchic rout if René was the object. She added that her Temple of Friendship could be dedicated anew if necessary.

Toupie declared that if she saw the louse René she would run him over, and Joe Carstairs said the same. Both had fast cars and a cavalier attitude to driving which would have made it easy to explain to the French police that they just looked away for a moment and he dived under the wheels, and would the gallant officer of the law accept a little present for his kindness? Sapphic Paris was of the view that they would get away with it and it was just what the repulsive Auvergne peasant deserved for betraying and humiliating one of Toupie's girls. Who, moreover, was a succès fou as an artists' model.

Phryne found, to her amazement, that these generous, eccentric, surprisingly interesting people liked her and were willing to go to considerable lengths to comfort, amuse and defend her. She had never been liked in her life. She had been tolerated at home, much oppressed (and frequently expelled) at school, and patronised by her own family when they became wealthy and disliked by all. Until she had come to France. There, in the middle of a war, she had found kindness and appreciation and love and, in her new-found freedom, Paris unfolded before and around her like a blossoming flower.

She walked down the boulevards when the chestnuts were in bloom. Sweet petals dropped all around her, decorating her hair, paving the ground so that she trod on flowers. It was like walking in a scented dream. She sorted through prints and books on the promenade by the Seine, bargaining for posters by Steinlein or Toulouse-Lautrec. She sat on an iron seat in the Jardin Luxembourg while three artists sketched her with the elegant flower-arrangement beds shouting with cannas and lilies as a background and climbing geranium crawling down from the marble urns.

She paced—a little unsteadily—down the edges of cobbled lanes, the sound of dancing in the little square receding behind her, alight with movement and cognac, arm in arm with Dolly or Joe or Kitty or that clever American girl—what was her name?—ah, yes. Sylvia, who wanted to open a bookshop.

And when she was tired, she would sit down at any one of a legion of cafés and order coffee and always find someone interesting to talk to, while the poets argued about Modernism and the patron roared for more Pernod and a white-aproned waiter made grenadine syrup for the children.

Paris was a moveable feast, like Easter. It was full of marvels.

Phryne came to her own front door in an elevated frame of mind.

The house was quiet. In the parlour, two good girls were doing their homework. Phryne sat down in her own chair, eased off her shoes, and Mr Butler brought her a cocktail. Jane and Ruth looked up eagerly.

'Did you find her?'

'No, and there's no sign that she was actually there. Girls, do you remember being poor?'

Both abandoned their geography abruptly. Ruth pushed aside a map of Africa, printed with colonies in red and blue and yellow. It slid to the floor, rainbow-coloured.

'We remember,' she said quietly. Phryne observed that they were both tense. Damn. Ruth had been rescued from domestic slavery and Jane from a much darker fate and they were not entirely secure in their safety. Not yet, at any rate. Possibly they never would be. Phryne cursed her tactlessness.

'It's all right, you don't have to be poor ever again. You already know how to be poor. I have a job in mind, and I'm wondering if you might be just the people to do it.'

'Part of your investigation?' asked Jane eagerly. 'Oh, do let us help.'

'It might be . . . well, I don't think it will be dangerous, but it might be embarrassing and it might come to nothing.'

'We don't embarrass easily,' said Ruth. 'We'd love to help. What are you thinking, Miss Phryne?'

'Of the curious reaction of Sam, the deaf-mute dishwasher in the Café Anatole,' said Phryne, and explained. They listened carefully.

'So he isn't this Billy the Match,' said Ruth, who had a logical mind.

'No, Jack Robinson was sure that he had never seen him before in his life,' Phryne told her. 'And he's found the real Billy, working as a furnace tender. A natural for the job if ever there was one.'

'Yet Sam ran away when he saw Detective Inspector Robinson,' confirmed Jane.

'Yes. Or me, of course, but I'd seen him before and he didn't run away then.'

'And you'd like to know more about him,' said Jane.

'Yes. If anyone else tried to follow him home, he would twig at once. He's small and fast on his feet and he always goes out through the lane, so he'd notice anyone following him.'

'Except a couple of shabby girls playing, as it might be, skippy,' said Jane, who had leapt to the conclusion. 'Or hopscotch,' she added, not wanting to be seen to be exclusive of any useful theory. Phryne reflected that Jane would make a very valuable medical practitioner when her time came. She agreed.

'Or, as you say, hopscotch. He always goes out through this lane. We don't know where he goes after that. I'm curious. He's the only new person in Café Anatole since the kidnapping and since the attacks on the café by arsonists. I thought I had him all worked out but I haven't. I'm curious about him. You might have to take trains or trams and you might lose him, and if you do, I won't be angry, I won't be disappointed at all, girls, do I make myself clear? Following people is very difficult and even full-grown and experienced detectives lose people sometimes.'

'We won't lose him,' promised Ruth. 'We'll follow him like hounds.'

'No one notices anyone under five feet high,' agreed Jane. 'Not if we look poor. But what if we have to follow him to somewhere—well, somewhere rich?'

'Good point. Old clothes will do for the lanes of Fitzroy Street but not for Toorak—if he should go that way. What about this; Jane shall have a basket.'

'Me,' said Ruth. 'I'm stronger. I used to haul home all the things from the corner shop which that old bi . . . which my previous employer used to forget to order. Always used to be lots of tins, and how she'd thump me if I wasn't fast enough! I used to get two rounds of the kitchen and a belting with a broom.'

Jane's hand stole out and took Ruth's.

'That will never happen again,' she said solemnly.

'I'll say it won't,' said Phryne very firmly. 'If this is going to awaken too many bad memories, girls, then we'll find another way.'

'No,' said Ruth. 'I don't have nightmares about it any more. I'm safe now. It'd be fun to do something for you, Miss Phryne.'

'Do you still have nightmares, Jane?' asked Phryne.

'No,' said Jane. 'I've forgotten about it, mostly. It seems like I've lived here with you for such a long time. That other time is like a dream. We can do this, Miss Phryne. What would be in the basket?'

'Good clothes,' said Phryne. 'Just a coat and hat each. You can wear your old-fashioned boots and stockings, they'll pass in the dark. If you have to, you can split up. That might be best. If, for instance, he takes a tram, you can get on it, one girl near and the other at the other end, and then he might not notice. But you need to be careful. If he meets up with anyone who looks at all chancy, abandon the chase, come home right away or ask a policeman for help. I don't want you running any risks, Jane, Ruth, do you hear? As I said, if there is any trouble, you're to come straight home.'

'Yes, Miss Phryne,' they said, lowering their eyes like good girls.

Phryne did not believe them for a moment.

'And if you find, as you probably will, that this sourd-muet is the sole support of a poor old widowed mother, you are to come away without attracting attention and we'll look for some other way of solving the puzzle,' instructed Phryne, holding out her glass for a refill. Mr Butler materialised in his usual spectral way and obliged.

'Yes, Miss Phryne,' chorused her adopted daughters,

projecting 'good girl' so effectively that she could practically see their haloes.

'We'll try it tomorrow night. You must go to bed after dinner and get some rest. Then we'll go down to the lane behind Fitzroy Street at eleven, when the café closes, and see what we shall see. Now, any messages while I was gone?'

'Mr Collins called Dot,' said Ruth. 'She was blushing when she was talking to him.'

'What did he have to say?'

'He'll be home tomorrow and he's solved some case about stolen jewellery,' said Jane, disapprovingly. 'Miss Dot says he said something about river boats and Food Reform but I was thinking about something else. He was really pleased, Miss Dot said.'

'Good. I heard a summary of that from Jack Robinson. Anything else?' asked Phryne, wiggling her toes. She wanted a bath.

'Mr Bert and Mr Cec rang and left a message. Mr Butler has it,' Ruth told Phryne.

Mr Butler entered with a silver salver on which reposed a message written in his clear, round script. The writing, Phryne had always thought, of someone who was not interested in calligraphy but who wanted the reader to have no doubt about the content of the message. It was as easy to read as print.

'Tell Miss Fisher we found her Frog under name of Dupont come in on the *Stranraer* like she said and stayed at the Maritime. After he left there, he went to the Sailor's Rest with his missus. My auntie didn't like him and said she was sorry for his poor wife. She's a good hearted old chook, Auntie is. She sent him to talk to a letting agent called Slyme just down the road about a house or flat or maybe rooms. We're leaving him to you, you might have to grease his palm, all these landlords is thieving bastards and all property is theft. Watch your back like I'm watching ours, Albert.'

'Well, that's my task for tomorrow,' sighed Phryne. 'Greasing palms in Port Melbourne.'

'I'm sure you'll be very good at it, Miss Phryne,' said Jane, stoutly.

Phryne laughed and sipped her cocktail appreciatively. She was really going to miss Mr Butler.

CHAPTER FIFTEEN

Phryne could tell, from the moment she entered his office, that she would decline all invitations to go on any long walking tours with Mr Slyme.

It wasn't that he was fat. She had liked a lot of fat men. She doted on every chin on the absurdist playwright Georgiev's face and she always liked hugging her Uncle Vivien, who was as warm as toast and a lovely chubby armful for his numerous mistresses. They must have loved him for his beauty, in view of his perpetual conviction that sooner or later a rank outsider must come in at 100–1 and repair his fortunes, which in turn meant that he was always skint. She had waited breathlessly for Father Christmas as a child.

It wasn't the avoirdupois, it was the curdled cream complexion, the scraped-over threads of dark hair on the bald scalp, the unbecoming tie of some private school which almost looked like Geelong Grammar but wasn't, and the reaction to her advent.

He had snarled, 'No use whining, Mrs Johnson! Out by noon!' without looking up. Phryne had coughed politely. When Mr Slyme had taken in the vision of style, fashion and, above all, wealth which decorated his office, he had writhed like Uriah Heep and begged the lady to take a chair while he put all the resources of his office at her complete disposal.

No, Phryne considered. The only reason to go on a long walking trip with Mr Slyme would be if one had brought along a convenient flat iron, or if the route was designed to pass a suitable crevasse. Preferably bottomless.

When Mr Slyme had offered tea (politely declined) and a cigarette (accepted and instantly regretted—cheap and nasty) he inquired as to what had brought Miss Fisher to his humble agency.

'I am looking for a friend of mine,' she said, blowing a smoke-ring. 'He came in on the *Stranraer* a few weeks ago and was going to rent a house, or possibly a flat. He told me his new address, but I have misplaced it.'

'How unfortunate. But you must know, Miss Fisher, I can't disclose any business dealings I might have had. I wouldn't stay in business long if I did, ha ha.'

'Ha ha,' echoed Phryne politely. 'I really am anxious to locate my friend. Perhaps if you could consult your books and just copy out some information for me? I could pay any reasonable fee, naturally.'

There was a pause while poached-egg eyes looked into green jade ones. Phryne went on the offensive. She knew all about letting agents and their little lurks. She entirely agreed with Bert's estimation of them. This one was undoubtedly an oppressor of the poor, because they were easier to oppress. She asked, 'Why did you think I was Mrs Johnson?'

'It's nothing,' said Mr Slyme hastily.

'Is she about to be evicted?' asked Phryne carefully. 'Because, as it happened, she couldn't pay your little extra fees? Perfectly proper, a man must live, of course, and naturally the landlord will understand should he hear that you are adding a little to the rent, to cover your very reasonable expenses?'

'What a suggestion,' huffed Mr Slyme, without conviction. He wasn't used to this. Landlords were only too anxious to rent their hovels, the property market being what it was, and tenants regularly grovelled to him to obtain a little more time on the rent. He was not used to cold-eyed fashion plates making insinuations in bored voices in his very office. Blowing insolent smoke-rings with his very cigarettes.

'Some people would call that peculation, Mr Slyme,' purred Phryne. 'Or even nastier words. Blackm—'

'Who are you trying to find?' asked the agent abruptly.

'René Dubois,' said Phryne promptly. 'He came in on the *Stranraer*. With Madame Dubois. Or—my friend likes his little jokes—he might be using the name René Dupont. Did he come to see you?'

'Yes.' Mr Slyme opened a ledger, scribbled rapidly, and laid his large puffy hand flat on the note.

Phryne took out another note, a banknote, and transferred his palm from one to the other. He allowed her to do this. She cast a swift glance over the paper.

'I see,' she said. 'And just for luck, you can give me Mrs Johnson's address, too.'

He gaped again, then scribbled. His most fervent wish was to get this insouciant woman out of his office and forget that she had ever existed.

Phryne folded the papers and put them in her purse. She stood up and stubbed out the cigarette.

'Well, nice doing business with you, Mr Slyme.'

She was gone before he could make his mouth form an adequate reply.

Phryne puzzled out the fast, uneven writing, a sign, she had always heard, of an unbalanced mind.

Fitzroy Street, St Kilda, she thought to herself. Well, well. Mr Slyme does spread his net widely. A house, how extravagant of René—it must be someone else's money. Now, it would be wise to go home and tell everyone where I am going, so I will do that. I am not going to put myself into a situation where I might be able to kill that louse without being observed. If the murderer is René, and I still can't imagine why it should be, then he's doing what he always did, the craven. He's making sure that he runs no physical risk. He's stupefying his victims before he kills them. Drinkies with René are not indicated. And before that, I'll just drop in on Mrs Johnson.

The house was just around the corner. Phryne stopped abruptly. Two exquisitely embarrassed policemen were supervising the removal, onto the dirty pavement, of a whole household. There wasn't much. A dresser in which china rolled and smashed, a big bed and three small ones, bundles of bedclothes and a table. A chair cracked as it was shoved roughly out the door and a sad, patched stocking flicked along the street and wrapped itself around Phryne's ankle.

Mrs Johnson stood with a baby in her arms and two children clinging to her apron. The worst thing, Phryne thought, the very worst thing about this scene was the woman's face. It was blank with catastrophe. The children were crying, but Mrs Johnson just stood, looking like a statue of Grieving Motherhood. This could not be borne.

Phryne detached the stocking. She strode forward and said decisively, 'Stop,' and even though she had not raised her voice, everyone stopped.

'This is a legal eviction, miss,' said one of the bailiff's men. 'For non-payment of rent. You can't stop it.'

A crowd had gathered. They muttered. The two policemen looked nervous. This was not what they had signed on to the police force to do. Throwing women and children into the street. But there was a threatened breach of the peace. Last week two bailiff's men had been beaten up by the angry mob. By the looks of it, this mob was about to get angry. Perhaps this immaculate lady might have a solution.

'By a surprising coincidence, which I am sure you will agree is timely, I have some money for Mrs Johnson,' said Phryne. 'How much does she owe?'

'Matter of eighteen shillings and threepence. And a half-penny,' said the leading bailiff, consulting a clipboard. Men in these positions always had clipboards, there must be an agency which supplied them, Phryne thought. Another small bully.

'Well, well, these five one-pound notes,' Phryne waved them in the air and the crowd gasped, 'are hers by a small inheritance. Whether she will want to stay in your grubby little slum dwelling house is another matter. What do you think, Mrs Johnson?'

'My man's away at the road building,' said Mrs Johnson, her voice forced through lips set so firm that they had trouble bending enough to speak. 'He needs to know where we are. I'll stay here, miss.'

'Good, well, I am sure that your men will be delighted to take all that furniture back inside. Carefully. I am, of course, intending to instruct my lawyer to visit your Mr Slyme to demand repayment for all that broken china and the damage to her effects, of course,' added Phryne, beginning to enjoy herself. 'And the shock and humiliation she has endured at your hands.'

'No, lady, hang on, no need to act the goat. No need to bother the boss. We'll knock, say, ten shillings off the rent, shall we, call it quits?' pleaded the larger of the bailiff's men, really worried now.

'Ten shillings? asked Phryne, and Mrs Johnson nodded. Phryne counted out the balance, eight shillings and threepence halfpenny, into his hand.

'Receipt,' said Phryne firmly, and watched the man write it out and sign and date it.

The crowd shifted as the furniture was carried back into the house, with a wincing delicacy otherwise only awarded to Meissen or Ming. It did not take long. There wasn't much.

'Now, we'll be on our way,' said the large one hastily. 'Sorry you were troubled, missus,' he added to Mrs Johnson, who had recovered enough to accept the receipt and shove it into her corsets.

'Come along,' said Phryne, giving the rigid woman a little push to set her moving. 'I think that concludes the entertainment for today,' she added to the disbelieving, relieved policemen, who awoke to their duty.

'Move along,' they said to the crowd. 'Nothing more to see here. Haven't you got homes to go to?'

'No, but Mrs Johnson has!' shouted a wit, and the bemused Mrs Johnson entered her home to cheers and almost good-natured hisses for the retreated, foiled bailiff's men. The woman sagged down into one of her own kitchen chairs.

Phryne grabbed the oldest child, whispered some instructions, and handed over some coins. His thin face lit up with delight. Phryne watched the fleet bare feet skip across the scrubbed floor on the way to fetch some refreshments.

'Is this your cat?' asked Phryne, when Mrs Johnson did not speak. The cat floated up into the woman's lap, poked an enquiring nose into her ear, and purred loudly.

'Oh, Tabby!' said Mrs Johnson, and started to cry. 'I thought I'd lost you!'

This set the baby off. Phryne found the kettle and set it on the fire, which was almost out. Phryne tipped the scuttle and loaded the remaining fuel into the grate.

'We ain't got no more coal than that,' observed the smaller child. 'Mum said we had to be careful.'

'Tomorrow,' said Phryne, 'she can buy some more coal.'

'What's your name?' asked the child, uncorking a grimy thumb in order to speak.

'Miss Fisher,' said Phryne.

'No,' said Mrs Johnson, mopping her face on her apron and rocking the baby. 'She's an angel sent straight from heaven.'

'Where's her wings then?' asked the small child, quite reasonably.

This gave rise to a complicated theological argument which allowed everyone to feel more settled.

The kettle was boiling by the time the boy came back with a heavy basket. He found the teapot, put in newly purchased tea and filled a wooden bowl with sugar. To crown his achievements, he produced a paper bag full of unbroken biscuits.

'I've been thinking,' Mrs Johnson said as she put down her cup. 'I can't recall any relatives who might have died and left me some money.'

'Distant cousin, I believe,' said Phryne with such conviction that she was instantly believed. 'Humphrey was the name. Were you dealing with that snake Slyme?'

'Yair. Wanted a shilling every week over the rent, and I had enough trouble paying the rent as it was. My husband was a soldier and work's hard to find. He's off on the roads, they're building an Ocean Road, and he sends me what he can, but it ain't much. And we miss him something cruel. That Slyme would never have dared to ask for extra if my Dan had been at home. But Dan'll be back end of the month,' she said, actually smiling, 'and he'll find us where he left us.'

'But much better fed,' said Phryne.

Phryne distributed sixpences to the children and left on a wave of goodwill.

In the street outside she met a worried man in a shabby black suit.

'Is Mrs Johnson gone? I came to see how she was getting along.'

'You're a bit late. If I hadn't come along with her legacy she would have been out on the street,' said Phryne, a little acerbically.

'They told me you paid it,' said the shabby man. 'That was kind.'

'And your interest in the matter is . . . ?'

'Oh, I beg your pardon, should have introduced myself. I'm Edward Dunne. I like to keep an eye on the poor people in this street. Hand out a bit of money, a bit of advice, pair of boots sometimes, that sort of thing.'

'Do you? Why?' demanded Phryne with extreme scepticism.

'For the love of God,' he said simply. 'I have a concern.'

Phryne had met people who used that term before. She smiled. 'You're a Quaker, aren't you? I recognise the phrase. I met Friends ambulance drivers in the war.'

'Yes. Will you still talk to me?' He smiled, a pleasant, serene smile.

'Just the man I was looking for,' said Phryne. 'I want to do something to Mr Slyme, and you're the person who will know all about him and his horrid ways.'

'Yes,' said Mr Dunne.

Phryne took his arm.

She had time to take Mr Dunne into the station to talk to a policeman about fraud, peculation and theft and to sign a few cheques for his good works. She returned home and concluded a phone call to Bert just before Detective Inspector Robinson arrived. With him was Hugh Collins, who seemed to have grown. He had always been large. New confidence made him massive. Robinson was still in an excellent humour.

'Two prize pinches in two days,' he said. 'I got the car thieves and the boy here broke as nice a little ring of jewellery fencing as I've ever seen. All because he allowed himself to be hit on the head and shanghaied, of course, but it's a hard head and a few cracks might let in some caution.'

He smiled as he delivered himself of this opinion. Hugh Collins did not seem cast down by this criticism. He had a piece of sticking plaster over a shaved spot on the back of his head but seemed otherwise uninjured. Dot gave a small concerned cry when she saw him.

'No, really, Dot, I am all right,' he said hurriedly. 'Just a bit of a bump. And I've got all the information the boss sent me to find and a river-boat captain who was a fence into the bargain. And a corrupt police officer,' he added in a low voice, as though such things were not to be spoken of in mixed company. 'That's worth a bit of a bump on the coconut.'

Dot, evidently, did not agree. Phryne ordered tea and they all sat down.

'I've already dealt with ex-Constable Smith of Mildura,' said Robinson vengefully. 'He won't trouble us no more. And I had a look at Mrs Chambers' death certificate. It all looks in order. She had a heart problem. Her doctor confirms it.

'Well, here's the gen on Mr Eeles. Neighbours saw a small dark man hanging about for a few days before the death. He even knocked at the old lady next door's house and asked her if it was Mr Eeles, who used to be a soldier, who lived there. The old lady said he was very foreign and charming and kissed her hand like foreigners do. And she told him that Mr Eeles had been a soldier and was such a nice man. She told him that Mr Eeles was often seen working on his truck.'

'So she gave him the idea,' said Phryne.

'Perhaps. She's a harmless old chook, bit lonely, glad to have someone to talk to, so I didn't tell her that, poor woman.' Robinson sipped his tea.

Dot had managed to find a seat next to Hugh Collins and had already passed an anxious hand over his skull to check that it was not, as his superior had said, cracked. She had managed to do this without the boss noticing. Phryne gave her marks for tact. To make sure that Robinson did not look around, Phryne asked, 'Anyone else see him?'

'Two other people. Woman hanging out washing and a child coming back from doing the messages. The descriptions agree. Small, dark, dark brown hair and eyes, well dressed. Not carrying anything. Mrs Eeles didn't see him. She also didn't notice what sort of voice it was at the door, just that it was male, because the baby started crying. The autopsy was faulty. They didn't test the stomach contents for drugs. But we found a bottle of chloral hydrate mixed with alcohol in the garden. The murderer must have offered the victim a little nip to keep out the cold and, once he was unconscious, jacked up the van, dragged him under, then knocked or kicked away the jack. No dogs in the surrounding yards. Then he legged it out the back gate and was gone. As you said, Miss Phryne, ruthless. And efficient.'

'And cruel. He left the body to be discovered by the wife. She'll never get over that,' said Collins.

'And what did you find out, Hugh dear?' asked Phryne, pouring more tea for the proud young man.

'Same kind of feel to the case, if you take my meaning, Miss Fisher. He enticed MacKenzie out of the pub with a scheme about providing frozen orange juice to Europe, then must have offered him a big glass of the supposed product—perhaps he said it was juice which had been frozen and thawed—and when MacKenzie drank it down he would have been legless. I tried quarter of a glass of that vodka in orange juice and you really couldn't taste it and it was deadly strong.'

'Ethanol,' said Phryne. 'A Fitzroy cocktail, without the meths. It seems to work on the local derelicts, poor souls.'

'Yes. Then he just pushed MacKenzie into a ditch and stood on him until he drowned. And MacKenzie had a fiancée. Her name is Maisie, she works at the hotel. She was real fond of him. She's in a bad way now that he's dead. They were going to buy the ring the day he was found in the ditch.'

'Yes, cruel,' said Phryne.

'So, Miss Fisher, are you going to tell me all?' asked Robinson, putting down his cup.

'I'll give you a photograph,' said Phryne, handing it over. 'Ask your witnesses if they recognise anyone in that picture. The third from the left is a man called René Dubois. I knew him in Paris in 1918. He's in Australia now. I have an address for him. I'm thinking of seeing him tomorrow, if you will lend me a big strong man to go with me.'

She grinned in a predatory manner. Robinson returned the smile.

'All right, you can have Collins. He's been given three days off to recover from his head injury. Just don't get him into trouble, mind. And if this is our man, I'll come back and you can tell me all about him.'

'Yes,' murmured Phryne. There were people she was intending to tell first, but Robinson did not need to know that. He believed in her deference just as much as Phryne had believed in the girls'.

'Oh, Miss Fisher, there's a little problem I thought you might like to help with,' said Hugh unexpectedly.

'What's that?'

'Like I said the deceased had a girl he was about to marry, like I told you. She was dead gone on him, poor girl. She hates working at the hotel and she was going to be an orange farmer. Her sister said Thomas MacKenzie might have made a will. Can we get someone to find out if he did, and maybe something good might come out of all this?'

'I'll talk to my lawyer tomorrow. There must be ways of finding out if people have made wills. There's probably a stock agent or solicitor in Mildura. If there's a will, we'll find it. That was a nice thought, Hugh.'

'Definitely needs a few days off,' said Robinson. 'Told you: women'll be the ruin of you, boy. Present company excepted, of course. Right, we're off.'

'See you tomorrow,' said Hugh to Dot, and kissed her on the cheek in front, as Dot later said, of everyone.

After that it was hard to settle down to anything. Dot put on her hat and took herself out for a brisk walk. Phryne idled away the afternoon playing jazz records. It would be pleasant to revisit some of the jazz clubs again. And this time she wasn't looking for a missing girl, but a missing musician, and he should prove easier to find.

The girls came home, agog with excitement. They packed their basket with good clothes and, on Dot's insistence, a bottle of cold tea, a couple of sandwiches and two headscarves.

Then they dutifully ate a light meal, one of Mrs Butler's excellent omelettes with tomato and bacon, and lay down for their rest.

Ruth fell asleep at once, a legacy of her life as a domestic drudge who slept when she could and was always tired. Jane tried several times to talk to her but nothing was as adamantly asleep as Ruth. Jane reflected on hibernating animals and dropped off in the middle of her meditation on the strangeness of going to sleep in autumn and waking up to find that it was already a quarter past spring.

When she woke them two hours later, Phryne gave both girls a cup of half-strength coffee and Dot looked over the initial disguises. 'Good,' she said.

The stout boots were carefully scuffed and the stockings thick. Jane's dress was a skimpy black skirt and a winceyette shirt which had bagged in the wash. Ruth wore her own dress from when she was rescued, which she had kept as a trophy of her liberation. It was now much too short and too tight and had irreparable stains all down the front. Treacle, as Ruth remembered it.

'You look perfect,' said Dot, tweaking at Jane's shabby skirt. 'Got the skipping ropes? This is a very brave thing to do, girls. Now remember that you've got pennies in your kicker legs and some money in the basket and if you get into trouble ask the nearest policeman, or get into a taxi and come home. Good luck, now,' said Dot, kissing each of them.

'Don't be careless,' said Phryne on the way to the car. Then, out of earshot of the anxious Dot, she added, 'And have fun.'

Jane smiled and Ruth grinned. This was, indeed, going to be fun.

CHAPTER SIXTEEN

The prisoner had been untied. Now she sat in a chair. It was a hard chair and she was very thirsty. There was water in the tap and it was only five paces away, but he had told her not to move and he would know if she did. He always did, somehow. So she sat, dully noticing that the night was continuing. It seemed to last forever.

Eleven o'clock was not an hour for good children to be on the street, but these were not good children. They skipped nonchalantly down the side street and into the lane behind Café Anatole, where once the night men had plied their odorous trade. The cobbles were uneven but almost any surface allowed for skipping. They heard a back door open, and then the creak of a back gate.

'My mother said I never should,' began Jane, swinging her rope.

'Play with the gypsies in the wood,' responded Ruth.

Someone came out of the back gate. A boy with straw-coloured hair and oversized shoes plodded past them without even glancing their way. Jane and Ruth kept skipping behind him, not getting too close, continuing the chant. As they passed lit yards and dark ones their prey silvered or darkened and their footing became difficult.

They reached the end of the lane, where it came out onto the street, and saw the straw-head walking quickly north. Ruth hefted the basket, Jane fell in ten paces behind her, and they trailed the spiky hair down past the row of shops to the station.

He was walking differently, Jane noticed. In the lane the boy's back had been bent, the shoulders hunched as though expecting a blow. Now he was walking freely, like a dancer. Jane put the basket down behind a pillar before groping in her knicker leg for the first of her hidden pennies. St Kilda was a very plush station—the only one with a chandelier—and she and Ruth were out of place.

Ruth joined her. They pulled on their good coats and hats and Jane took the basket as Ruth fell in line behind the boy. Up close, he exuded a pleasant scent of cooking, as though he had been steeped in kitchens all his life. On his shoulders was a light dusting of flour. He asked for a half price one-way ticket to the city.

Ruth bought two of the same and managed to drop her ticket into Jane's basket as she passed her without catching her eye.

The train might be difficult. Ruth decided to get into the same carriage as the boy. A city train came in, one of the new electric ones, and the boy suddenly ran like a rabbit from where he had been standing to the other end of the train and dived inside as though seeking his home warren. Ruth hoped that Jane was in place and stepped into the carriage.

Now—would he get out at South Melbourne, Albert Park or Middle Park instead of Flinders Street? The train clunked and chunked over the track, clickety clack. Ruth was suddenly sleepy. This was very late for her to be out. She must not fall asleep! She wished she had the basket with the food in it. Food always kept Ruth awake. Middle Park. No one got off the train.

There were few other passengers at this late hour: some young men out on the town with brown-paper wrapped bottles in their pockets, a couple of women in headscarves who were probably cleaning ladies, a fireman in full uniform. Ruth occupied herself in counting his buttons until they came in at Albert Park. There the young men left, laughing and shoving each other at the door. Ruth did not approve of young men. So noisy.

South Melbourne and she was at the door, scanning down the length of the platform. No boy and no Jane. Good. The cleaning ladies were watching her and one called out to 'Mind the doors!' Ruth sat down again. The night was a black glass plate, studded with rhinestones. Flinders Street. The platform slid past. Ruth got out. So did the cleaning ladies. So, far away, did Jane.

But no boy. She couldn't see him anywhere. Where could he have gone? Jane stood with the basket at her feet, staring. Then she snatched it up and ran to Ruth.

'Come on,' she said breathlessly. 'He's got out the other side of the train, Ruthie, and he's only got two ways to get out of this station and we have to watch both of them. Take a scarf,' she said, shoving one into Ruth's hands. 'Watch down the street for me. If I've got him, I'll wave. If it's you, you wave.'

'All right! I'll run down to the Degraves Street exit, you're puffed.'

They gave up their tickets and Jane sat down with her basket on the steps, under the clocks, with an assortment of indigents and young men waiting for young women. Under the clocks was where everybody met their friends, Jane knew. She was now convinced that there was, indeed, something wrong with this boy, as Miss Phryne thought. Why should he take the risk of jumping down onto the track? He had a ticket. Ruth had seen him buy it. Therefore he was evading pursuit. Jane didn't know if he had seen either or both of the girls and marked them as his pursuers. Perhaps he did this every night. She edged around a little on her step, making sure that she could scan the pedestrians as they left the domed station concourse. Many people came, but not a straw-headed boy with a scarred face.

Ruth belted down to the Degraves Street exit as though she was playing hockey, then leaned into a doorway to straighten her hat and still her fast breathing. There were many people on the streets. This was a help in that it provided cover but a hindrance in that Ruth had to peer around them and that looked suspicious. She had to watch two exits at once. There was the back gate of the station, on Flinders Street, and there was the tunnel under the street which came up on the other side of Flinders Street. Tricky. She took out the little mirror Phryne had given her and stood so that she could see the reflected people coming up out of the ground. The crowd had died away. Surely he hadn't evaded them? Where else could he go?

Ruth's heart sank. She knew where he'd gone. Back into the station, of course, and onto another train. They had failed. She looked so stricken that a kindly passing lady gave her a penny and told her to go home to her mother.

Ruth accepted the penny. It was never a good idea to discourage a charitable impulse, Miss Phryne said. Suddenly she caught sight of a flash of scarf mounting a tram.

Thanking the nice lady, Ruth gripped the penny and boarded the Wattle Park tram, sitting boldly in the open carriage with the night air rushing in. She had seen Jane and the basket tucked away at the back and, almost hidden by the conductor, the boy with the straw-coloured hair. Except now he didn't have straw-coloured hair, but darkish red short curls, sweat dampened from being confined under the blond wig, and he was carrying a canvas bag. Aha! A disguise!

He still had the terrible scar which made people's eyes slide off his face, though. Poor boy.

The tram clacked along St Kilda Road—back the way they had come. The boy's destination would have to be somewhere fairly close. This must be almost the last tram. Ruth knew that they stopped at midnight.

She surrendered her penny to a jovial conductor whose ticket bag rested at an angle on a fine solid belly. He patted her and asked her where she was going and did her mother know she was out this late?

'Certainly,' said Ruth in her best imitation of her schoolmates. 'But it is very civil of you to enquire,' she added. The conductor chuckled and moved on. Where on earth was this boy going? This was like one of those paper-chases which they had at school. A game of hare and hounds. Ruth and Jane always came in first at hare and hounds because they worked so well together. Now they were doing it in real life and it was unbearably exciting. If only she wasn't so *sleepy*.

Swan Street, Richmond. The boy was engrossed in a big heavy book. Ruth was too far away to read the title. Past the railway bridge's inky shadow, Colliseum-Treadways loomed, still brightly lit though the shop, of course, was closed.

Jane was trying terribly hard not to look at Ruth. Where was this chase going? This tram was taking them completely off Jane's mental map. She was journeying into an unknown region. It was very exciting.

She had stowed the scarf, a bright, metallic blue, in case the boy had noticed it. He was paying very close attention to his book. Jane puzzled out the title. *Ma Cuisine*. By Escoffier. A cookery book. Not surprising in a cook's boy. Perhaps the deaf-mute wanted to be a chef. At least he wouldn't yell at the staff, as Miss Phryne said was common in cooks. Though he could still throw pots.

The tram was almost empty. The boy shut the book and pulled the cord. Neither girl moved. The scarred face scanned both of them. Jane wished she had brought a book, too. It's easier to avoid attention when you are reading. Ruth looked back at him, allowing her mouth to drop open in a way deplored by her teachers, then abruptly looked away. That should simulate a good 'horrified' response so that he wouldn't suspect that she had been looking for his scarred face for what seemed like hours.

It seemed to work. When the tram stopped, he got off. So did Ruth. Jane was to stay on the tram one more stop and then walk back, as arranged. Where were they?

Glenferrie Road, the sign said. It was empty and dark. Ruth watched the boy walk to another tram stop and collected Jane as she hurried past. They broke into a run in order to reach the next stop before the tram came.

Jane surrendered the basket to Ruth, who ran better. She took off her hat and put on Ruth's unused headscarf.

'Different enough?'

Ruth surveyed her critically. The plaits were tied at the back of Jane's neat head. She had no basket. Her coat was an ordinary shade of navy blue. Her scarf was a prissy shade of pink. Nothing notable about her.

'I think so. Your hair's hidden. And you can take off your glasses.'

'Then I can't see,' said Jane, taking them off and folding them.

'Don't need to see fine detail,' said Ruth, giving her a friendly push. 'Go on! Here's the tram! I'll be right behind you,' she added, hefting the basket and stepping back into shadow.

Jane managed to get up the steep tram steps without disaster, surrendered yet another penny—this trip had cost a terrible lot of pennies—and sat down with her back to the body of the tram. The boy was there. On they clacked into the night. Jane was wondering where this would end. Were they going to wander forever, like gypsies? My mother said, I never should, play with the . . . her head nodded.

Three stops later, end of the line. Cotham Road, Kew. Jane had never been to Kew. Ruth would be on the next tram, which would probably be the last one for tonight. The boy paced slowly up the road under the streetlights, as though he was tired now, and confident that he had eluded all pursuit. Jane trailed after him, keeping to the shadows of high fences and dark trees. These were the biggest houses she had ever seen. Biggest fences, too. Great iron constructions which might have fended off invasion from a Norman keep. Who did the people in these houses think was going to attack them?

The boy paused at a corner. Jane froze in the shadow of a huge plane tree. She was close enough to see the boy actually shrug, then turn away and proceed down the street.

Jane was tiring, as the boy was. When he came to one big, dark gate and swung it open, she was glad to sit down on a convenient fire hydrant cover two doors down. She heard the boy stumble as he went down the side way, and a door opened and closed. He was home at last.

Jane went to the corner of Cotham Road to intercept Ruth and lead her to the place. Ruth walked wearily along and then plumped herself down beside Jane on her fire hydrant cover.

'We got him,' breathed Ruth. 'This basket is flamin' heavy. How did you carry it so far on your own?'

'I wasn't thinking about it,' said Jane vaguely. 'Have you got my glasses?'

Ruth handed them over and Jane blinked as the world came into focus again.

'I'm starving,' said Ruth. 'We'd better wait here a while to make sure he doesn't come out again. Have you looked at the number?'

'No,' said Jane. 'I can't see without my glasses. You look at it.'

Ruth did so. There was no light in the huge house. She came back. Jane offered a rather squashed brown paper packet.

'Have a sandwich. They're egg. Or there's ham. Which would you like?'

'Both,' said Ruth, grabbing. 'Hard work, this private detective lark.'

They ate companionably for a while in the warm darkness under the huge trees. When they finished the sandwiches they rolled the paper bag and put it tidily into the basket. Ruth took a long swig of cold tea.

'Well, we've done as she asked,' she observed. 'How do we get home? I think I can remember the way, but I definitely caught the last Cotham Road tram, the conductor told me so. What did Miss Phryne want us to do next?'

'She will have thought of it,' said Jane comfortably. 'Isn't it nice to sit down? My feet hurt.'

'Mine too,' said Ruth. 'So we just sit here, then?'

'We just sit here,' said Jane, with perfect faith.

Ruth drank some more tea. She wasn't good at perfect faith. The plane leaves rustled overhead. A breeze was picking up.

'I can hear a car coming,' said Jane.

'Probably one of the people who live in these houses. You know, we probably go to school with some of them. I never realised. This is really rich country, Jane.'

'It's a taxi,' said Jane, and walked into the middle of the road, holding up her hand.

'He's not going to stop for us,' said Ruth scornfully. 'Two little girls out on their own in the middle of the night?'

'He'll stop,' said Jane. 'Because he's Mr Bert. And Miss Phryne.'

'Oh,' said Ruth. 'Well, that's different.' Jane's perfect faith appeared to have been justified. Ruth filed the fact for future reference. The taxi drew to a halt. Phryne got out and hugged both girls with admiration.

'Oh, well done, my dears!' she exclaimed. 'You shall think of a really nice present as a reward. Bert's been trailing that boy for days and always lost him—how did you manage to follow him off the train?'

'Because there were two of us,' explained Jane. 'I think he might have seen Ruth, because she was closest to him on the tram, but when I took off my glasses he didn't know me.'

'And on the train,' said Ruth, 'he didn't notice Jane.'

'You're very, very clever,' said Phryne. 'Now, are you so

tired that you want to go straight home, or would you mind waiting for about—oh, I don't know, half an hour? You can have a picnic with our co-conspirator while I interview the people in that house.'

'Miss Phryne,' asked Ruth tentatively, noticing that her benefactor was wearing black trousers and soft shoes, a black pullover and headscarf and was holding a soft canvas bag, 'are you really going to burgle the house?'

'Yes,' said Phryne. Were these sterling young women going to disappoint her by developing scruples? Had all that public school education actually changed their attitude to a little light crime in a good cause? Surely they weren't going to tell her that burgling houses was unladylike? Ruth's next words relieved her adoptive parent's worried mind.

'Can we come too?' asked Ruth.

Phryne laughed and hugged her again. She might be dressed in men's clothes and about to commit a felony, Ruth thought, but Miss Phryne always smelled of Jicky or Floris Honeysuckle. Her voice was brisk and amused.

'Not for the moment. One person is quieter than three. But don't be cast down. You're my rescue party. If something goes wrong, I'll shine my torch through a front window, and you can come and rescue me. All right, Bert dear?'

'All right,' grunted Bert.

Phryne left them, sliding through the gap in the unclosed iron gate without stirring a leaf. They watched until she was swallowed up in the darkness.

'She's got a lot of cat in her, I reckon,' said Bert, roused to the need to entertain the girls. 'Can see in the dark and move like a shadow. No need to worry about Miss Phryne, girls. Never needed to be rescued in all the time I've known her. But that doesn't mean we don't follow her instructions. One of us has to keep watching the front of the house in case she shows her light. You can take first watch, Ruthie. Jane and me'll get us some food. And you can tell me how you followed that young hound to his kennel. I always used to lose him in Flinders Street.'

'We might have been lucky,' said Jane, sorting out a box of the little pies which Mrs Butler always made for parties. 'Ruth thought that he might have gotten out onto the track, climbed onto another platform and taken another train.'

'P'raps,' said Bert. 'I like these eggy pies, they're grouse. You want one, Ruthie? But another train wouldn't get him anywhere near Kew. Capitalists don't want trams belting down their expensive streets. Only sensible way is the bus down Studley Park Road or the tram. And if he wasn't trying to lose followers, why would he come into the city anyway? Easier to catch a tram in St Kilda.'

'Not to mention crossing the tracks, which is very dangerous,' said Jane with her mouth full. 'Ooh, good, ribbon sandwiches. This is a very nice picnic. Ruthie? Salmon mayonnaise or ham and lettuce?'

'One of each,' said Ruth, who had not taken her eyes off the huge house. Not a spark lit the darkness. 'And is there anything to drink?'

'Raspberry vinegar,' said Jane, handing it over. Mrs Butler had provided cups but it was more fun to drink out of the bottle.

'How did you follow us?' asked Jane. 'Were you in Flinders Street?'

'Yair. Been up and down dunno how many times, trying to nail the boy, but I never could see him. So when I saw Janey here wave that scarf, I just trailed the tram. Then it was easy to follow either one of you, even when you changed your hat and took off your glasses. But I never twigged that straw hair was a wig. That's why I never caught him. I was looking for that hair. Got any more of them pies for a starving man?'

'We were looking for it too,' said Ruthie, extending a hand without looking. Jane gave her another ribbon sandwich. 'We only got him because we were on foot and close. It was a good disguise.'

'My turn to watch the windows,' said Jane.

Ruth leaned back against the smooth leather seat. 'But why was he disguised and working in the Café Anatole?' she asked.

'Miss Phryne knows,' said Jane, taking off her glasses, polishing them and staring at the darkened windows.

'And maybe she'll tell us all about it,' agreed Bert. 'Pass over the raspberry vinegar, will yer?'

Phryne walked very carefully, toe first and then heel, as she had been taught. Stalking was an exercise in patience, the handsome young ghillie Hamish had told her one long, sunlit summer in the Highlands. The beast has no appointments to keep. It is not concerned with time. So we have to forget time, too.

Phryne was not in a hurry. The undergrowth yielded, as Hamish had taught her, to a slow gentle advance, when it would have tripped the feet and torn the face and arms of haste. Leaves and tendrils flowed around her. The trick was a sort of benign self-confidence which allowed the stalker to move through the landscape like a slow, unthreatening shadow. The path was both under- and overgrown, but she negotiated it with no noise that a moderately alert guard dog would have heard. It brought her to the side door.

She explored the surface with gentle fingertips. Usual sort of door, usual sort of lock, scent of . . . she sniffed a finger. Sewing machine oil. The door was in use. No cobwebs over the latch. The hinges had been recently oiled.

How very charitable to adventitious burglars. She took out a lockpick and worked slowly, her ear against the door listening to each tumbler fall, trying to feel her way into the mechanism. Deprived of sight, her hearing had become acute. Somewhere a small beast was moving, probably a cat, possibly a rat. Phryne hated rats. She tried not to think about it.

Then a pounce and squeak told her that another silent hunter was abroad in the night. The rat threat had been removed by a feline associate. The door yielded at that moment and Phryne allowed it to open then glided inside like a shadow.

She stood perfectly still, regulating her breathing, and listened.

There was no light, but the faint vibration of speech trembled on the air. The house smelt of mould, dust, disuse, with an overscent of—was that cooking?

Yes, somewhere someone was consuming onions. And they probably weren't doing that in the dark.

Phryne risked a brief light from her electric torch. She was in a hall. It was filthy, hung with years of cobwebs, but the floor was swept clean. Fallen plaster was piled neatly in one corner. Beside her a staircase went up into blackness, and—she moved and sniffed—down that staircase the smell of onions was wafting. Phryne's stomach growled. She had been too excited to eat much supper.

She shut off the torch as soon as she had her foot on the first step. She laid a hand on the rail and walked up very slowly, keeping to the balustrade side of the treads. It was well known that stairs creaked, if they creaked, in the middle.

Up twenty stairs, the scent of onions was strong, and there was a bar of light bright enough to hurt her sensitive eyes under one door.

Phryne opened the door and said, 'Good evening.'

CHAPTER SEVENTEEN

Three faces looked up in the most absolute horror that Phryne had seen in a life rather replete with people looking horrified when they saw her.

'May I come in?' she asked. 'I've brought a bottle.'

'Miss Fisher?' asked Julia Chivers through numb lips.

'Miss Fisher?' quavered the white rabbit, Mr Jenkins, still holding a slice of onion tart in one trembling hand.

'Miss Fisher?' asked a girl with short curly auburn hair and a red mark across her face, dressed in a silk robe covered with dragons.

'The very same and a long dance you've led me, I must say.' Phryne, keeping away from any grabbing hand, though the company appeared to be too appalled to think of attacking her, unslung her canvas bag and extracted a bottle of champagne.

'It shouldn't be too shaken up,' she commented. 'Miss Chambers, will you do the honours? And I'd love a slice of that tarte à l'oignon, s'il vous plaît,' she added.

'Avec plaisir,' replied Julia Chivers with automatic courtesy, handing over a plate. Phryne took a bite. It was very good. Miss Chambers dealt with the cork and suppressed the ebullience of the escaping Veuve Clicquot with an adroit thumb. Phryne accepted a tea cup and sat down to look at her company.

So this was the missing girl. Elizabeth had cut her hair as short as a boy's. It curled rather attractively. Without her trademark scowl, she was a charming figure in her gorgeous dressing gown. Radiantly blonde Julia in her sky blue silk looked like she was made of spun sugar and ice. Mr Jenkins looked terrified. They sipped for a moment in silence.

'You know, I have been looking all over for you,' said Phryne without heat. The champagne was too good to quarrel over. 'I worried about you. One always worries about young women who vanish unexpectedly. Now, since the intelligence of my adoptive daughters has saved me from having to trawl for you through all the brothels in St Kilda, don't you think you ought to tell me what this conspiracy is about? I'm not your father's employee, by the way,' she added.

'N-n-no,' stammered Mr Jenkins. 'She isn't. The boss was going crook all day about her refusing to take his money. He likes people to take his money. Then he can control them.'

'Precisely why I didn't take it,' said Phryne. 'Well?'

'I noticed two little girls playing skippy in the alley behind the café tonight,' said Miss Chambers slowly. Her voice was perhaps rusty from disuse. 'Then there was a girl in a grey hat on the train. I thought I'd shaken her by crossing the line. Then there was a girl—Lord! Were they both your daughters?—

one on the tram, in a pink headscarf. One with a basket and glasses. And they followed me all the way here?'

'All the way,' confirmed Phryne. 'If it makes you feel any better, I've had a man in a car following you for days, and he always lost you when you took off the wig. Where did you learn to elude pursuit like that? You're very good.'

'John Buchan, the *Thirty-Nine Steps*,' said Elizabeth Chambers, with spirit. 'Who taught you to burgle houses?'

'A burglar,' said Phryne, as though surprised at the question, 'of course. Now, you were saying . . . ?'

'Jig's up?' said Elizabeth, appealing to her co-conspirators. They nodded.

'All right. I want you to understand this first, Miss Fisher. I only ever wanted to be a cook. That's all I want. All I did at that finishing school was learn everything I could about cooking. The teacher thought I showed promise. I need to get an apprenticeship with a good chef. M'sieur Anatole is probably the best chef in Melbourne, so when Father told me I ought to marry him I didn't mind, though he is old, but I wanted to find out what he was like. I'm not going to trust my career to a cruel man.'

'Or your body,' said Phryne. Elizabeth nodded.

'That, too. So I asked Father if I could go and work in the kitchen at Café Anatole for a few weeks to find out what the chef was like. A kitchen is a very high pressure job. The character of the chef always comes out with twenty dinners to cook and the boy late with the salad vegetables and the fish going off and the ice-chest melting . . . you can imagine.'

'Seems like a reasonable request,' murmured Phryne encouragingly.

'Not to Father. He puffed and roared and yelled that no daughter of his was going to work for a living and I was bringing disgrace on him and that's what came of sending girls overseas to get foreign ideas. He went on and on,' said Elizabeth, wincing at the memory.

'Yes,' said Phryne. 'I can imagine.'

'Then he forbade me to go to the café again, shut me in my room and told me to play with my new clothes. He told me that I was marrying M'sieur Anatole at the end of the month and then he was marrying my school friend, Julia. He told me it had been agreed with her parents and it was all settled and he was only waiting to get rid of me before he married her. I was a bit upset.'

'If you hadn't been upset I'd be worried about your mental health,' said Phryne. 'What happened then?'

'I'd just picked up an armload of those rotten French clothes and thrown them on the floor when Bunny came tapping.'

'That's me,' said Mr Jenkins, smiling a very sweet smile which completely changed the tension in his face. 'She's called me that since she was a child. She said I looked like the White Rabbit in *Alice in Wonderland*.'

'More than anyone I've ever met,' agreed Phryne. 'What had you to suggest?'

'Well, you see, I've worked for Mr Chambers since I was a boy and I know about him. He's not the husband for a young woman. Or any woman, perhaps. And I knew that with a bit of capital, both young ladies might set up on their own and escape from him completely. I'll never escape,' said Mr Jenkins in a resigned tone. 'But they could. I'd heard Miss Julia talking to Miss Lizzie about that marriage. I knew she was being forced into it.'

'I was in despair,' confessed Julia. 'I'm not strong minded like Lizzie. My mother and father think this marriage settlement is their due for raising me and their last chance to get back to where they were before the war. They would nag and nag and nag and eventually I would do what they wanted just to get some peace. I couldn't see any way out of it until Bunny came up with his scheme. It was a corker.'

Lizzie went on. 'So I told Father that I wanted to go to a party at Julia's cousin Raoul's, and he was pleased because he thought me properly cowed and obedient—he really doesn't know me at all well. Julia called and took away with her some of my clothes and my money and passport and things.'

'You forgot something, though,' said Phryne. 'Was it a book?'

'*Ma Cuisine*, by Escoffier,' said Elizabeth. 'Can't try and be a chef without *Ma Cuisine*, it's like trying to be a priest without a bible. Bunny pinched it back for me. It was so brave of him.' She leaned over and hugged an embarrassed Mr Jenkins. 'And he faked a burglary in case anyone noticed. As you did, Miss Fisher.'

'So you went to the dance,' prompted Phryne.

'I went to the dance, waited until Albie went off for a drink, which he always does if he has to wait, then I pinned the ransom demand on the lamppost, pinched the car and drove it to Kew. Father doesn't know I can drive. We all learned at the school on a cranky old Deux Chevaux. The Bentley's a beautiful car. I nearly ran a red light until I worked out how fast it went. I changed my clothes in the back and bundled up my things in a suitcase. I left the car unlocked in Barkers Road with the keys in, hoping someone would steal it. And they did. I walked here, got in by the side door into this disused bit of the house and went to ground. Then it was up to Julia.'

'And you know what I did.' Julia blushed a little, looking like a fairy princess who has been caught out fibbing to her fairy godmother. 'It went off like clockwork.'

'And you came here, adopted the guise of the deaf-mute, and worked in the kitchen. What were you going to do if Mr Chambers called in the police?'

'Reappear, say that I couldn't remember a thing, and start plotting again,' said Elizabeth quickly. 'But we were rather banking on him being too fly to bring in the police. He wouldn't want any of his dealings being examined too closely by the law. And we would have had warning of it from Bunny here.' She smiled on the white rabbit Mr Jenkins.

'How did you hit upon your disguise?' asked Phryne. 'It was very good. People never look too closely at a scarred face.'

'Sir Arthur Conan Doyle. *The Man with the Twisted Lip*,' said Elizabeth. 'The scar is cobbler's glue. Only problem with it is that you have to take it off with turps and it's burned my skin a bit.'

'Yes, and that's what put me onto you,' said Phryne. 'I knew of another person who made his scar with glue. In another case, a long time ago. And it wasn't Jack Robinson you were scared of, was it? It was me. Why?'

Elizabeth chuckled.

'I don't know deaf-and-dumb language. I couldn't return the signs. I was afraid that you'd come over all charitable and send a real deaf-mute person around to teach me. I thought the man with you was him.'

'Shrewd,' commented Phryne. 'I *was* thinking of doing something about the deaf and dumb boy.'

Julia sighed, and Elizabeth sighed with her.

'All we had to do was keep our nerve and we'd be five hundred pounds richer. Except that you worked it out, Miss Fisher. Now we'll have to think of another plan.'

'Not so fast,' said Phryne. 'As I said, I am not your father's employee and I can't see that any crime has been committed. How do you feel about M'sieur Anatole now?'

'He's a darling,' said Elizabeth enthusiastically. 'He almost never throws things, he's patient and he's kind. Look at how nice they all were to the deformed sourd-muet. He was even teaching me how to make sauces, and I was the most un-attractive creature alive. His family is very close but I reckon I'll fit in like Mary and Janey, the other girls that have married in. He wants his wife to work in the kitchen and that's what I want too, more than anything. And I will be a very good cook,' said Elizabeth, elevating the firm chin.

'Mr Jenkins, how did you dare to carry this out? Weren't you afraid of being caught?' asked Phryne.

Mr Jenkins raised his white face. His nose twitched.

'Oh yes, Miss Fisher, but I'm always afraid, it's my natural state. He wasn't going to notice anything different in my manner. I'm always stammering and terrified. Some of us have courage,' he said sadly, 'and some of us haven't.'

'I don't agree,' said Julia. 'I think you're very brave, Bunny dear.'

Phryne needed more information before she made her decision.

'And what were you going to do, Julia? Surely you weren't going to try to buy off your parents?'

'But that's just what I was going to do,' said Julia. 'I'd give them the money and they'd leave me alone. I'd get a flat or a little house, and have enough to live on until I decide if I want to marry anyone. I'm not sure that I do. And I'd never have to go to one of those terrible saddling-paddock gatherings again, where all the mothers bridle about all the other mothers' daugh-ters and no one says anything but vicious gossip and silliness.'

'It won't work,' Phryne told her brutally. Julia gasped and

put her hand to her mouth, a fairy princess who has just sat on her favourite gnome. 'How are you going to account for where you got the money?'

'An inheritance,' said Julia. 'Do you really think that they won't leave me alone even if I give it to them?'

'What do you think?' asked Phryne gently. 'This is about power and rights, not just about money.'

'What should we do, then?' asked Elizabeth. 'Are you going to turn us in?'

'No,' said Phryne. 'I am not. And my advice, if you would care to have it, Miss Chivers, is to develop religion. Go to church every day. Refuse to wear bright clothes. Decline all frivolous gatherings, go to no parties, don't wear jewellery, give something your parents value to the poor. You have a real talent for acting, so use it. Pray a lot. Punctuate your evenings with long readings from the more tedious parts of the bible. Try the Epistles, that's my advice, or all those begats in the Old Testament. Go and work in a soup kitchen. Be seen in the street in your worst dress, praying with passers-by. Get some church leaflets and hand them out to the neighbours. Suggest that you are thinking of entering an Anglican Sisterhood if they make you marry anyone at all. If they are still resistant, fast on bread and water. That's an old female blackmail method.'

'How long for?' asked Julia uncertainly. 'I can do it. But I don't want to actually starve to death.'

'Until Miss Chambers marries M'sieur Anatole at the end of the month. But they'll crack before that,' said Phryne confidently. 'You can't beat them if you are obeying their rules. Embarrass them and they'll fall to pieces. Then I suggest that you stay with your friend Elizabeth for a few weeks while you find yourself a nice little house. Collect the ransom, of course.

Well invested in the sort of trusts which Mr Bunny will tell you about and you'll have an income for life. Then you can look about and consider what you want to do.'

'That's good,' said Julia. 'I'm sort of . . . I mean, I like . . . my friend is Tim Purcell. He's nice. But . . . I don't know how he feels about me. Oh, this will work.' A gleam of malicious mischief sparked in her bright blue eyes. She looked like a fairy princess who has just got the goods on the wicked queen. 'Oh yes, that will work. Thank you.'

Phryne got up to leave but Julia caught at her black pullover. 'Miss Fisher?'

'Yes?'

'When did you know I had Lizzie hidden here?'

'I suspected as soon as I saw two used cups on a tray when breakfast had been cleared away, you had had no other visitors and there was no more metho in the primus,' said Phryne. 'I suspected more when I was listening to your excellent imitation of a giddy Miss. But I only knew when I opened this door,' she added, opening it again. 'Goodnight, my dears.'

Phryne left the house with care—after all, somewhere in this ruin the Chivers parents were asleep. She tiptoed down into the street and found that Bert was watching and her two daughters were curled up in the back of the taxi, fast asleep.

'All right?' asked Bert, starting the car. 'We watched for your light.'

'All right indeed, Bert dear.' Phryne got in beside him so as not to disturb the sleepers in the back. 'Home now, if you please. That's one mystery cleared up. One lost girl off my mind. Now, Bert, we need to find out who killed your mates. And to do that, I have the strongest feeling that we need to find René.'

'Got a few whispers out,' said Bert. 'Might have something

for you tomorrow. Got a few mates who play jazz. Not my kind of music, but. And them musos drink like wharfies, a man can't hardly keep up with them. I'll come round about lunchtime tomorrow, all right? Today, I mean,' said Bert, noting that the church clock said half past twelve.

There was no reply from beside him. Bert's taxi was full of sleeping women. He drove to St Kilda in a calm and circumspect manner, so as not to disturb their slumbers.

Phryne's morning started with a cup of inky coffee and someone at the front door. She accepted the cup from Dot. It was ten a.m. and she had been woken by the doorbell, and had heard Mr Butler go to the door.

'I suppose Mr Butler hasn't changed his mind, has he?' Phryne asked, without much hope.

'No,' said Dot sadly. 'Mrs Butler is real cut up. They've been fighting about it every night.'

'I think that must be the dismissed butler from Mr Chambers' house,' Phryne remembered. 'What was his name? Something to do with fish. Sole, that's it, Mr Tobias Sole. Such a butlerine name, isn't it? I asked him to come for an interview. Fling me some clothes, Dot dear. Something bright. I don't want this butler to have any illusions about what sort of household he is joining.'

'Go down in your dressing gown, then,' said Dot. 'It's perfectly decent.'

'So it is.' Phryne eyed Dot suspiciously. 'Are you up to something, Dot?'

'Me, Miss Phryne?'

'You have been practising your innocent expression,' said Phryne severely. 'Very convincing. Slippers. Hairbrush. Mirror, please.' She watched the ruffled black hair fall into its accustomed smoothness, wrapped and tied the gorgeous dressing gown around herself, and descended the stairs into the smaller parlour, where a tall young man leapt to his feet.

'Miss Fisher?' he asked, as though someone else might be walking into Phryne's parlour at ten of the morning in a dressing gown. 'I'm Tobias Sole. Delighted to meet you,' he said. His widening eyes indicated that this was the truth. Phryne, just woken and newly supplied with coffee, in her royal purple double damask gown figured with golden phoenixes, was a sight to gladden any male eye.

'Good morning, Mr Sole, do sit down. Mr Butler, coffee for me, if you please. And you, Mr Sole?'

'Oh yes, coffee by all means,' said Mr Sole.

Mr Butler, who had come in as usual, took the order without blinking. But Phryne thought that she surprised, just for a second, a look of deep offence on his bland face.

'Now, I know who your previous employer was, so I am not asking him for a reference,' said Phryne. 'Why did you leave him, Mr Sole?'

'He was intending to marry, Miss Fisher.'

'And you object to marriage, Mr Sole?'

'Not as such, Miss Fisher,' said Mr Sole. He had a pleasant baritone voice and a handsome, slightly tanned face. 'But I like a little life, Miss Fisher. I like a well-staffed house where we have parties, where we dress for dinner, where there is an exciting air of culture and good paintings and music and . . . well, fun. A house with a wife is soon a house with a child, or even,' he shuddered slightly, 'children. Then there are the nurses, governesses, teachers and little play mates. The standards of cleanliness plummet. The food invariably goes downhill right away, because few good cooks like houses where children may wander into their kitchen at any time, and they do not like making bread and butter pudding instead of sole à la meunière. Within a few months, Miss Fisher, the cuisine has become abominable, the noise is appalling and the whole tenor of the household has become—you understand—domestic.'

'Dear me,' murmured Phryne. She sipped her coffee. 'What about the all male or all female household, Mr Sole?'

'An all female household, madam, can become a little touchy and precious, prone to tantrums and slammed doors on bad days, but it is generally a pleasure to inhabit. An all male household is rougher, of course, and more boots are flung at attendants' heads, but as long as the cook is good, there is no reasonable objection to them.'

'And a household where the lady of the house consorts with a married man? Are you not afraid of appearing in a starring role in the Divorce Court, Mr Sole?'

'No, Miss Fisher,' said Mr Sole, also sipping. 'For several reasons. The character of both the lady and the gentleman must be taken into account, of course, and the character of their household. But should any upstart of a barrister ask one questions about the working of one's employer's household, one can only be compelled to answer from one's own knowledge. I have, Miss Fisher,' continued Mr Sole, bowing slightly, 'a terribly bad memory for such goings-on, should I have noticed them, which I haven't, and should they have happened at all, which, to my knowledge, they haven't.'

'You are a valuable man, Mr Sole,' Phryne told him. 'Did you have to spend a lot of time not noticing things that never happened in the household of Mr Hector Chambers?'

'I was thinking of purchasing myself a serviceable blindfold, Miss Fisher. With matching ear-plugs.'

'Your opinion of the Chambers daughter, Miss Elizabeth?'

'An unhappy young woman with an unfortunate manner.'

'Her kidnapping?'

'Most mysterious. Mr Chambers was ropeable.'

'Mr Jenkins?'

'An unfortunate man with an unfortunate manner. In both cases I believe that the hearts, Miss Fisher, are in the right place.'

'And your employer?'

Mr Sole gave her a wry smile. 'I really cannot comment, Miss Fisher.'

'Quite right. All other things being equal, you're provisionally engaged. Hand me your references and I shall check them. Just ring the bell for me, will you—oh, Mr Butler, there you are. Standing behind me all the time. This is Mr Sole, whom I have provisionally engaged for your job. Take him into the kitchen, please, introduce him to Mrs Butler, and give him all the gen about the way the house is organised. As always, Mr Butler, I greatly value your opinion.'

Mr Butler bowed fully a quarter of an inch to his replacement and led the way out of the smaller parlour.

Phryne went into the breakfast room rather puzzled. She took an egg and some toast and wondered what Dot was up to. Another cup of coffee brought her no nearer to an answer.

She breakfasted well, lit a gasper, and wondered whether Julia Chivers would dare to follow Phryne's suggestions as to her future religious conversion. To keep up the pretence of having no one in the house she must have a fine natural talent for intrigue, doubtless fostered by a good finishing school. Could she carry it off? People like her parents would never give up on getting their fairy princess Julia suitably married, however she tried to bribe them. But people who cared so much about social position were terribly vulnerable to embarrassment, and by this method Julia would embarrass them finely. The future looked like it could be very amusing.

There was still René, though. Hugh Collins was due in an hour and she had to get dressed, so she stubbed out the cigarette and went to the stairs.

From the kitchen she could hear a hum of conversation.

CHAPTER EIGHTEEN

Hugh Collins, in plain clothes, looked like an out-of-place wrestler. His honest face shone with soaping and his hair was combed so flat that his head looked like a billiard ball. His suit, however, was bought off the peg and, as Madame Fleuri would have said, 'fitted where it touched'. It strained over his mighty chest and squeezed his impressive biceps. A new suit for Hugh would have to be one of Dot's wedding presents. Made by Mr Rosenstein in Flinders' Lane, a charming and excellent tailor of Phryne's acquaintance.

Phryne had adopted a dark blue suit of restrained cut and a hat with only one feather on it. Dot wore a terracotta cardigan over her oatmeal dress, though the day was promising to be hot, and a hat with geraniums, making her look like an ambulant window box. She carried a large loose-weave basket.

They both stood obediently, listening to Phryne's instructions.

'Now, we are going to stroll along with a nonchalant air until we get to the corner. Then Dot is going to the door with that handful of charity appeals—you have the parish leaflets, Dot? Good. We need to know who is in the house. I am going to go to the side window and Hugh is doing the back door. Now, we haven't got any official standing, so if we strike any real opposition, we may have to retreat.'

'If we see anything which could be considered a crime or which constitutes a breach of the peace, I can intervene,' said Hugh. 'I'm a police officer.'

'Not on private property when we haven't been invited in,' said Phryne.

Hugh nodded. It was not a long walk. The street looked down to the sea. It had been a Good Address once. Now it was fading and falling with the fortunes of St Kilda. Once immaculate facades were cracked and patched, windows were replaced with neat pieces of cardboard and there was a proliferation of bells at each door. Many people lived in Fitzroy Street now. Most of them poor.

The morning was bright and the air fresh. Phryne walked along ahead of Dot and Hugh, ignoring them, looking like a woman with bills on her mind. She walked straight past the house. It was a small watchman's cottage which must once have belonged to a large house before the city had crept up like a tide and engulfed the mansion.

Phryne stopped, pantomimed that she had forgotten something, and went back to the house as Dot managed to open the gate. Hugh passed Phryne on his way to the back door, huge feet clumping like a dray horse. Phryne reminded herself not to take him on any sneaky expeditions unless she needed a battering ram.

She tried not to touch the peeling paint of the window. It was uncurtained. The room inside was empty. Damn! Did that mean that the snake René had somehow heard that she was looking for him and had already basely fled? René was good at fleeing basely. She had not heard whisper of him in Paris again after Toupie had threatened to run him over. Dear Toupie . . .

Next window. The scullery. Dishes piled in the sink. Didn't mean anything. René wouldn't do the washing up if he was basely fleeing. In fact, he wouldn't do the washing up ever, under any circumstances. Two of everything, plates, cups, glasses. He was here with someone else. Probably Madame Dubois.

Third window. Another empty room. Not even any furniture. Damn again, round the house, past Hugh standing like something from Easter Island by the back door. The side fence had almost fallen and it was a squeeze to get past it. I am spending altogether too much time in the jungle lately, she thought crossly, freeing a strand of hair. If I want jungle, I'll go to Africa. Next window. I believe this house is empty. I can hear Dot knocking from here. And another window. Dear God in Heaven.

Hugh was shaken out of his policeman's resting trance by the smash of glass. Miss Fisher had done something impulsive, he thought, as he shoved past the lolling fence and completed its fall. Just in time to see her legs vanishing through the window.

'I'll open the front door,' he heard his fiancée's excitable employer shout. He tramped to the front, brushing off leaves and plucking twigs out of his hair. He heard the door tried, then another noise; someone was picking the deadlock. The toll of unlawful activities was mounting. What would the boss say?

Still, the boss knew Miss Fisher and he might be angry but he wouldn't be surprised.

The door yielded and Phryne flung it back, gesturing to them both to come in. They followed her to the parlour.

'Ditch the parish magazine, Dot, and get me some water. Hugh, have you got a knife? These ropes have bitten into her wrists and ankles.'

A woman was tied to an armchair. She was moaning faintly. Hugh, galvanised by a fierce glare from Dot, dropped to his knees, producing his handy folding knife with the attachment to extract stones out of horses' hooves. It had a useful sharp blade and he sliced through the bonds, pulling them away. Dot came back with water and managed to make the woman drink.

She opened her eyes, coughed, saw Phryne and blinked. Then she said, 'Alors,' and Phryne knew her.

'Véronique? Véronique Sarcelle? What are you doing here? That is a stupid question. The first thing to do is to make sure that you are no longer here. My house is close. Come with me.'

Véronique raised a clawed hand to her face. 'He will follow,' she warned.

'Then he will be really, really sorry,' said Phryne grimly.

'He is afraid of you,' said Madame Dubois, shakily.

'He has reason,' said Phryne.

Hugh had never learned French and Dot's was not adequate to follow these fast exchanges. He looked at Dot. Dot looked at Hugh and shrugged. Phryne looked up and gave some orders.

'Dot, find the rest of her clothes and possessions. Stuff them in a suitcase. Look also for her passport. Too much to expect that there is any money in the place—René always keeps money next to what would be his heart if he had one. Find me paper and a pencil, too, if you can. Véronique, drink some more water. How long have you been sitting there?' she asked, switching to French.

'Since he went out before dark,' said the woman.

'Will you come with me?'

'Yes,' said Madame Dubois. 'But I don't know if I can walk.'

Dot returned with a suitcase, a passport, and a piece of butcher's paper. She had a pencil between her teeth. Phryne extracted it, wrote 'Adieu cochon noir. Phryne et Véronique' on it in block capitals, and turned to Hugh.

'Pick her up,' ordered Phryne. 'If René comes in, just step on him.'

'Yes, Miss Fisher,' Hugh thought it best to reply. No one disobeyed Miss Fisher when she used that tone. The woman was light enough, all bones and rags.

A taxi drew up as they reached the street. Hugh loaded Madame Dubois, Dot, Phryne and the suitcase inside then squeezed himself into as small a space as possible. Dot would have eased the tight fit if she had agreed to his perfectly rational suggestion that she sit on his knee, but she gave him Madame Dubois instead, which was not what he had had in mind.

'This is where he lives, Bert,' said Phryne. 'But he isn't here.'

'Yair,' said Bert. 'Noticed that. This his missus?'

'Yes,' said Phryne.

'Poor cow,' observed Bert. 'I'm leaving a couple of us to mind the house. And I know where he'll be tonight.'

'Oh?' asked Phryne. 'Where?'

Bert told her and she started to laugh.

Madame Dubois did not object when she was stripped, bathed, bathed again, dabbed with iodine, examined by a gruff Scottish female doctor, anointed with expensive scented unguents and clothed in a silk petticoat and dressing gown. Dot washed and combed the coarse dark hair, shot through with grey streaks.

She only revived when Phryne sat her down in her own boudoir and offered her a glass of strong red southern wine, a sausage out of which the garlic beaded in oil on the red surface, a baguette and some imported brie. Véronique, once Madame Sarcelle, took two mouthfuls and burst into tears.

Phryne let her cry for a long time. Finally she managed to stop, sniffed, dried her face and blew her nose, and then took a gulp of wine.

'It is you, isn't it?' she asked in wonder. 'La Petite Phryne? Or has René finally killed me and I am in heaven? I am sorry to see that you are dead too, mademoiselle. You have died far too young.'

'No, we are alive, you are in my house and eating my bread and drinking my wine. And you need never see René Dubois again,' added Phryne.

'But no,' said Madame Sarcelle-as-was. 'He will find me. He always does.'

'Do you know what he has been doing in Australia?' asked Phryne gently.

Véronique began to tremble. 'I cannot say.'

'But you know,' insisted Phryne.

'Yes,' said Madame Dubois.

'Then you know that when we catch him, he will hang. René cannot find you after he is dead, and he will not go to heaven. Not unless the requirements for admission have changed dramatically.'

'You do not know what he can do.' The clawed hands came together again in a tight clasp. The bruised eye sockets seemed too deep to house eyes which could see.

'He doesn't know what I can do,' said Phryne. 'And he has murdered some men with very strong-minded friends. And also annoyed a lot of policemen in what would be rather an uneasy alliance, which is why I'm not telling them about each other—it would only lead to trouble. This is my own house, Véronique. No one gets in unless I let them in, and René is not invited. This,' she said, 'is my companion, Dot. She speaks much more French than she thinks she does, but talk to her slowly. Dot will stay with you every minute. If René comes to get you and manages to get through the locked doors and the barred windows and the guards, she will shoot him.'

Dot caught the last line of that sentence and looked at Phryne, who handed over her own small pearl-handled revolver.

'You know how to use it,' she said. 'And you will have Hugh downstairs. Can you do it, Dot? I can't leave her with a man for the moment, not until she recovers a bit. I doubt she ever wants to see a man again.'

'I can do it,' said Dot stoutly. 'But I hope I don't have to. Where are you going to be tonight?'

'At the Lord Mayor's Ball,' said Phryne. 'I had quite forgotten. With, as it happens, Jack Robinson and his wife.'

'Oh,' said Dot. 'Of course. I came up to tell you, Miss Phryne. That nice Chinese lady, Mr Lin's intended, she's come to see you. Will you talk to her?'

'Of course. You stay with Madame. Make sure she eats some food and give her as much wine as she likes. I'm personally dying to find out how she ended up married to that absolute bastard René, but I don't think she can tell me that yet. When she gets sleepy, give her my bed. Don't leave her alone. She's under René's thumb and might go back to him, just to reduce the stress of knowing that he's going to come for her. She used to like handcrafts. Show her your knitting.'

Dot went downstairs to get her knitting bag and when she returned found Madame Dubois looking a little better and eating brie. Dot couldn't stand the stuff—cheese should not be runny—but it, or the wine, was putting some roses back into Madame's cheeks. Dot tried a sentence in French, suggesting more wine, and Madame agreed. And Dot understood the answer. She was overwhelmed by the idea that all that grammar, all that laborious learning of joujoux, hiboux, cailloux, genoux and so on was actually meant to facilitate communication with a foreign person. Flushed with success, Dot tried a comment on the weather, and Madame asked how long Phryne had been in this house.

She was speaking French to a Frenchwoman. Dot was delighted.

Camellia was sitting in a corner of the smaller parlour, tense as a wire. Phryne felt that she was surrounded by tense women. She offered Chinese tea and rang, only to find the bell answered by Mrs Butler.

'Where's Mr Butler? Left already?'

'He's still talking to Mr Sole, Miss Fisher,' said Mrs Butler with a concealed air of—what? Smugness? Pleasure? 'I'll fetch the tea and some of my ginger snaps directly. They're just out of the oven.'

'Right you are, Mrs B,' said Phryne. 'Camellia, let's cut this short, I'm having a strange day. I solemnly swear that I won't relate anything you tell me to Lin Chung unless you say that I can. Now, what is it?'

Camellia looked down at her clasped hands. 'I . . . am finding this very hard to say.'

'Then all you need to say is yes or no. You object to Lin Chung?'

This directness seemed to steel the young woman. She leaned forward, answering the questions eagerly and quickly.

'No, he seems a fine person, a nice man, gentle. I like him. And my family are now allied with the Lin family. Everyone is made more secure by this. In fact, that is my first problem. What if . . . if I like him too well?'

'Sorry?' asked Phryne.

Camellia explained. 'You have the prior place, and might become angry if Lin Chung and I . . . become too close.'

'I am perfectly aware that one man can love two women without them being jealous of each other,' Phryne told her. 'I lived in such a ménage à trois myself in complete amity. Do not let it concern you, Camellia. Love Lin as much as you like. But that isn't all, is it?'

'No,' said Camellia.

'Then is it that the pirates got you on the way and you're not a virgin?'

'Not . . . not the pirates. And I'm not . . .' she faltered.

'Not a virgin?'

'No, but also not . . .'

Mrs Butler handed over the tea and biscuits. Phryne did not want to be interrupted as she felt that she was at the nexus. She pushed the tray aside.

'Not what, Camellia?'

The answer came out in an almost comic squeak. 'I'm not Camellia!'

'Oh,' said Phryne. 'That is a bit of a surprise, I admit. Who are you, then?'

Confession had unchained Camellia's tongue. 'I am called Camellia, but I am not the Camellia the Lin family thinks I am. They contracted a marriage between my cousin Camellia and Lin Chung. At a distance, of course, and communications in China are very bad. They did not hear that my cousin Camellia was killed by bandits. So the family thought . . .'

'Ah, I see. They had a spare Camellia, and you were substituted. So far I don't see a problem. Cousin Camellia is dead, poor girl, and you are here, and a very intelligent, well-spoken, personable young woman you are. And Lin Chung likes you, too.'

'But I'm a widow.' Camellia began to weep. 'I'm no virgin. My husband died of typhoid two years ago. I'm nineteen, not seventeen.'

'Had you children?' asked Phryne, lighting a meditative cigarette.

'No. Well, yes, one, but she died at birth. It was a bad year for typhoid.'

'You should tell Lin,' said Phryne.

'I don't think I can.' Camellia buried her face in her hands. Phryne took them in her own.

'Look at it this way. You wouldn't have had much of a life in China. Widows are married off again as soon as possible, aren't they? And half of China is ruined and the other half is killing each other. Correct?'

'Correct.'

'And what sort of a wife would a scared seventeen year old virgin have been for an urban sophisticate like Lin Chung? You are doing him a favour, Camellia. And we are going to get him to come over right now and we are going to tell him. And if he repudiates you, my dear, I'll eat my newest Spring Racing Carnival hat. And the artificial hydrangeas on it. Without salt.'

The look of settled despair was leaving Camellia's face. 'You really think so?'

'I do,' said Phryne, and marched to the telephone. Some

things were going to be cleared up right away so that she could concentrate on the evening's entertainment, which promised to be engrossing.

Camellia expressed interest in Phryne's garden while they awaited Lin's arrival. This was a relief. One geranium was much like another, in Phryne's view, and she could not take the guest upstairs to inspect her Lord Mayor's Ball dress because a distraught Frenchwoman was occupying her bed.

Phryne's garden consisted of mown weeds, a couple of dustbins, Mrs Butler's hen-run (in which the inhabitants clucked and pecked) and a few dispirited shrubs. It was patently the garden of someone who didn't like gardening.

Camellia considered the space underneath the back verandah and recommended ferns. Phryne replied that ferns might be nice but she had never got over seeing her grandmother feed those horrible buck's horn things with banana skins, the small Phryne being under the impression that perhaps those sinister projections of vegetable menace might also eat little girls.

To this Camellia assented. 'One of my uncles collected carnivorous plants,' she confided. 'He used to feed them flies. The leaves would just slap shut over the insect. Horrible. I hated them. What about orchids, then?'

'Too much trouble. I have black thumbs.'

Camellia looked startled until Phryne explained the idiom.

'Maidenhair, then, and some of the tougher ferns. You could make a fernery and sit here on hot days. And an arbour, with roses and vines. The house and the high fences shelter it from the salty winds and you could plant a bamboo hedge to hide the chickens and the dustbins. This could be a nice little garden. It seems a pity to do nothing with it.'

'You design it,' offered Phryne, 'and I'll have it made.'

'Deal,' said Camellia, so reassured by the exercise of her art that when Lin was shown through by Mrs Butler, she did not flinch.

'Mr Lin, I am not the person you thought I was,' she said bravely.

'I was beginning to think that you were not,' he said carefully. 'But you are such an improvement I was not minded to enquire. They told me I was to have a village girl with no education and no English, and I have on offer an intelligent, well-bred, clever young woman who speaks better English than me. I think I'm doing remarkably well out of the swap,' said Lin, smiling.

'My cousin Camellia is dead, so they sent me. I'm called Camellia as well.'

'Good,' encouraged Lin. 'That means you will always remember your name.'

Camellia stood up straight, took Phryne's hand for support, and said with deliberation, 'And cousin Camellia was seventeen and a virgin. I'm nineteen and a widow.'

'Then I must ask Grandmother for the phial of chicken's blood which is customary on these occasions. Some customs are really barbaric but the family will expect it,' he said equably.

'Phial of chicken's blood?' asked Phryne, amused.

'Well, yes, Phryne, not all maidens are virgins and not all virgins bleed, so to stop any gossip, we use chicken's blood. All blood is equal on bed sheets. My dear Camellia, I am delighted that it's you,' he said, offering Camellia his hand. She took it. 'Are you also pleased that it is me?'

'Yes,' said Camellia. 'I am.'

'Good. Now, Miss Fisher is busy. I know that look of barely restrained ferocity. I propose that we thank her very nicely for being so kind and helpful, because she is both, and take ourselves off. Do you have Grandmother's car? I'll escort you.'

'How do you know that Miss Fisher is busy?' asked Camellia, allowing herself to be guided into the house.

'Because she is working on a case, and tonight I am taking her to the Lord Mayor's Ball.'

'What a nice man you are, Lin dear,' said Phryne affectionately, and saw her visitors out.

Véronique woke in a dream of comfort. She was lying on a soft bed with the taste of real southern wine in her mouth. She was clean and combed and without male company. A sleek black cat had joined her and was asleep, warm against her cold ankles. A young woman was sitting by the window, knitting placidly. It was clear from looking at Dot that she was not anyone's jailor. She was a nice girl who was thinking of her lover, and that alone made her beautiful.

Madame Dubois sat up against a wealth of pillows and found her handkerchief. She didn't want to weep any more. The young woman had informed her that this was the house of the only person René was really afraid of. When he treated that one harshly, as he treated all women after the first, blissful three months, she had not stayed and clung and cried so that he beat her again. She had escaped, taking all her money with her and had gone to hide among the Sapphics, whose threats of revenge had frightened René into going home to the Auvergne and staying there until 1923.

But unfortunately—how very unfortunately—he had taken Véronique with him, and however she tried to run away, whatever desperate plans she made, he always found her, beat her, and dragged her back.

But not this time. When Phryne returned, Véronique smiled at her. 'I am beginning to believe in you, Madame

Phryne,' she said. Phryne noted that she had been awarded Madame instead of La Petite Phryne, which was an indication of growing respect. What had Dot been saying about her?

'Good. How do you feel?'

'I creak a little,' said Madame Dubois. 'It is to be expected. Perhaps—there might be coffee?'

'There shall be,' said Phryne. Dot folded her knitting and went downstairs. Madame Dubois laid a hand on Phryne's knee.

'I will tell you all,' she said.

'I think I know most of it,' said Phryne. 'But I would be honoured to have your confidence.'

'It was when we went to the bal musette that I fell in love with him,' confessed Madame Dubois. 'He was so charming, no? So funny, so insolent, so . . . whatever it was, I fell in love with him like falling down a well. I was angry when he took up with you. I kept warning you about him but you would not listen. I knew he was a scoundrel by then, but I still loved him. I adored him, I doted on him. Sarcelle never knew, not until the day he died he never knew.'

There was a silence. Phryne remembered how fervently Madame had urged her not to give her earnings to René. She had known what she was talking about. He must have been wooing Madame while he was courting Phryne. No wonder he hadn't wanted her to come and live with him. Véronique was wringing her hands and her voice rose to a wail. 'But I swear before God, I swear, I never knew that he was going to assassinate poor Sarcelle. He never told me. Later, he told me, he laughed at my tears. I cried for him, for there was no harm in Sarcelle, and he was a great artist.'

'The soldiers saw . . .' Phryne bit her lip. She now knew what the soldiers had seen. They had seen René, wearing Phryne's black coat and her black hat, her stockings and shoes.

He had often joked that he could pass for a woman, had donned Phryne's night gown and danced Arabian dances in it. What they had seen was René shove the artist under the train. And under the paint they might know the face again. He had waited until Madame Sarcelle had an unbreakable alibi. And no one had even gossiped about Madame Sarcelle; it was well known that she was devoted to her husband. A good scheme, God rot him.

'Why did he kill Sarcelle?'

'To make his paintings more valuable. Me, he had me just where he wanted me. I adored him. I was his slave. I would have done anything for him. René heard Sardou, the art dealer, telling Sarcelle to die and make his work more scarce and precious.'

'The bastard,' said Phryne, horrified. Véronique nodded.

'But why now?' Phryne asked.

'You haven't heard? Now that Sarcelle's work is so valuable—there is a rage to buy his paintings which has sent the prices up to the sky—they are reopening the enquiry into his death. René said that the only people who saw him were some Australian soldiers. It was not difficult to find which soldiers had been on that train. There were only seven. The railways keep all their records. René got a friend of his to find out who they were, and the Army Office told him where they lived. It was easy.'

'You know the cream of the joke? They were all sodden drunk on Madame Printemps' methylated raki. The ones he killed didn't even see him,' said Phryne.

Madame Dubois made a sad shrugging movement which brought her bruised shoulders into view.

'The way of the world,' she said. 'And nothing to be done about it.'

'I don't agree,' said Phryne.

CHAPTER NINETEEN

'It is truly a miracle of a dress,' observed Madame Dubois. Phryne turned around and surveyed herself critically in the mirror. The night was indeed hot and would be hotter inside a crowded ballroom. The severe linen fell straight to her sandalled feet. Moving as she moved, it flowed.

'I wish Sarcelle could paint you like that,' said Véronique. 'With the sharp lines of the hair, and the smooth linen, and the roundness of the beads.'

'You shall paint me,' said Phryne. 'You were good until you devoted yourself to Sarcelle and that cochon René.'

'I haven't touched a brush in years,' protested Madame Dubois.

'Time you started. While I am gone, I suggest that you come downstairs, where I have a large policeman called Hugh Collins on guard to protect you, not to mention Dot and my gun—which you had better not mention to Hugh, if you please. You will meet my adoptive daughters and give them some painting lessons. They are nice girls, gentle and sweet. Most of the time. And that will keep everyone in one place in case there should be trouble. I do not expect it, but one must prepare. Besides, you need feeding up and it is almost dinner time. My Mrs Butler is a very good cook. Her soups are especially excellent,' Phryne cunningly informed her, knowing how much Véronique liked a good soup.

'Very well.' Véronique struggled to her feet. 'What shall I wear?'

'I have borrowed Mrs Butler's new house dress,' said Phryne. 'I remember you liked wearing colours. None of my clothes would fit you or you could rummage in my wardrobe. Soon we shall buy you some more clothes.'

'It has been ten years since I had a new dress,' said Véronique, allowing herself to be clothed in Mrs Butler's choice, a rather sprightly shade of spring green cotton with cherries on it. Madame Dubois smoothed it down as though it were silk.

Instead of the moaning, ragged figure which Hugh had carried out of that house in Fitzroy Street, she now looked like a respectable Frenchwoman of middle age. Her freshly washed hair was rolled into a chignon, her eyes were relatively calm and her hands hardly shook at all.

'It is a very nice dress,' she said bravely. 'Take me down to meet your daughters.'

'You are a courageous woman,' said Phryne, 'and it will be a pleasure.'

Lin Chung arrived as dinner was cleared away, the pad and cloth were laid over the big dining table, and watercolours, pencils and paper were laid out in preparation for the drawing lesson. Hugh Collins let Lin into the room.

Lin saw a chattering, fully-fed girl on either side of a haggard woman in green, who told them that they must draw only what they could see. She spoke Parisian French and the girls were trying very hard to understand her. With the learned sympathy of those who had also been injured and oppressed, they were sitting close to Madame Dubois, asking questions. Then a vision of such outré loveliness entered that he had no eyes for anything else. Phryne looked at once Egyptian and western, alien and familiar, and absolutely beautiful. He bowed and offered his arm.

'Silver Lady,' he said, 'you are magnificent!'

'She is,' agreed the woman in broken English. 'And always she was.'

Lin bowed to the crowd and escorted Phryne out to his car.

'We are meeting the Robinsons in the portico,' Phryne reminded him. 'And you look absolutely splendid, Lin dear. Savile Row?'

Lin in full evening dress was elegant, smooth, and a little dangerous. The suit was cut so that it fit like a glove. It was so black that light seemed to fall into it, as black as the cat Ember's sable fur.

He inclined his head at the compliment. Lin did not drive unless he had to. He had also indulged himself in the newest of the Rolls Royce cars. This one was called the Silver Ghost for the silence of its approach. His chauffeur was dressed, for this evening, in livery. Lin Chung, also, had a point to make.

Phryne leaned back against the dark grey glove leather upholstery and lit a Sobranie in a long holder.

'Lin dear,' she began, 'there may be some little unpleasantness tonight.'

'I never pay attention to people who do not like Chinks,' returned Lin easily. 'And I find that, after being ignored for a while, they go away.'

'Not that sort. You recall that I told you about René Dubois, who broke my heart in Paris ten years ago? And the soldiers who were being killed, Bert's friends?'

'I remember,' Lin lit his own cigarette. 'Tell me more.'

'That damaged woman in my parlour is René's misused wife,' Phryne told him. 'René is the murderer, and he is playing in the band at this ball. If he sees me, he may attack.'

'That,' said Lin, smiling a little, 'could be very, very unfortunate for René.'

'So I thought,' said Phryne. 'We need to catch him, Lin, or he'll keep murdering his way through those soldiers. He would love to murder me and he will definitely torture Madame Dubois until she dies, in revenge for being rescued. She didn't run away, Lin. She stayed with him because she is utterly broken. She is what I would have been if I hadn't escaped him.'

'No,' said Lin. 'You are far too strong a character to have become what Madame Dubois has become. You would have killed him or died before you were reduced to such a state. I know you, Silver Lady.'

Obscurely comforted, Phryne leaned over and gave Lin a lingering kiss. He was very beautiful, exceptionally desirable, and probably right.

The car drew up in the midst of the crowd in Carlisle Street. The Lin family livery was a tunic and trousers of heavy dark blue serge, in which the chauffeur must have been sweating, and a rather impressive laced cap with the family crest, a phoenix, in gold thread. Phryne alighted and shook her dress into place. Mr Lin was handed down. The great car glided away into the velvety St Kilda night to massed murmurs of envy which were music to Lin Chung's ears.

Among the overheated, chattering crowd, Phryne and her escort stood out as slim, elegant and strange. Lin led Phryne ceremoniously up the marble steps to the portico, where a stout lady in dark red with a magnificent orchid pinned to her shoulder and a detective inspector in his best evening suit awaited them.

'This is my wife,' said Robinson. 'Mrs Rose Robinson. Miss Phryne Fisher, Mr Lin Chung.'

After a moment of initial shock, when Mrs Robinson took in the Egyptian dress, the fact that it was made of cotton—how daring!—and the beautiful young man who was Chinese, she recovered magnificently. She held out a work-hardened hand to Phryne and said, 'How nice to meet you, Miss Fisher. Jack is always talking about you. That is a remarkable dress,' she added.

'And that is a remarkable orchid,' said Phryne. 'Is it one of yours, Jack? It goes perfectly with that wine-red of your dress, Mrs Robinson.'

'Bred it myself,' said Robinson, pleased. He was at this ball entirely on account of his dear Rosie and was now thinking that it might not be as bad as he had thought, after all. And he had always liked Lin Chung. 'Rosie likes that shade of red. She grows roses that colour. Black Boy, they're called. Grow all over the side fence and you can smell them right down the street in spring.'

'A young lady was just telling me that I ought to have a garden,' said Phryne. 'I promised to do it, if she would design it for me. I have always thought rose arbours charming. Can you tell me about them, Mrs Robinson?'

'Call me Rosie,' said Mrs Robinson, launched on her

favourite topic. 'Well, you need to make the arbour really strong. Roses are heavy, and they aren't true climbing plants, they just throw out long tendrils which can be draped and tied . . .'

Lin and Robinson exchanged a glance of masculine empathy.

'Shall we go in?' asked Lin.

'Got those invitations, Rosie?' asked Robinson.

The colour scheme of the Town Hall was exactly to Mrs Robinson's taste; dark red and gold. Gilded leaves cascaded down from the domed ceiling. Red flowers were everywhere. Scarlet and gold lanterns depended from the roof and ropes of scarlet blossoms with small electric bulbs inside were swagged along the walls. Huge gilt medallions on scarlet ropes of flowers were draped all along the balconies. No expense had been spared and it seemed, from the buzz and the scent and the passing trays of drinks, that it was going to be a night full of fashion and exertion. The band was already playing selections from the 'Student Prince' when Phryne, the Robinsons and Lin joined the mayoral party and they made their entrance to a minuet.

Phryne was delighted to see that one lady had eschewed the prevalent pink and blue and wore an ivory crepe dress with heavy silver and coral beading at the hem and a posy of shaded brown pansies. This was a woman Phryne would like to meet. Especially since she had seen that beading before. It was the piece which Julia Chivers had been working on when Phryne first encountered her.

They took their places on the dais and the debutantes came in. They formed a column of unrelieved white, stark against the opulent scarlet and gold.

Pair by pair, they made their curtsy, terribly young, good

looking in some cases only because they were young, and each smooth head dipped to the correct depth. The Mayor's daughter led the way, dressed in pink and blue, with bows.

There was a poignancy in a debutante parade, Phryne found. She had been that young once, had indeed, rather late, dressed in a suitable white gown and the regulation three white ostrich feathers and curtsied to the Queen. By then she had been twenty, on a London visit at the urgent request of her mother, and she had shucked the dress at her earliest convenience and rushed back to Paris.

But Phryne nodded and smiled as the young people came forward, the Lady Mayoress said a few suitable words and they filed aside, looking unutterably relieved not to have fallen over while curtsying or stammered while whispering 'thank you'.

Mrs Robinson, sitting beside her husband, was enthralled. Phryne thought she was a very nice woman.

The band struck up again. Where were they hidden? The sound was close but she could see no musicians. They played 'Moonlight on the Ganges' and Lin held out his hand.

'May I have this dance?' he asked.

Phryne joined him on the floor. Dancing with Lin Chung was always a pleasure. He moved like a dream and he never, never trod on toes. If he found that his partner was absent-mindedly leading, edging them across the floor, he obligingly fell into the female role and followed like a lamb.

The foxtrot was an ideal dance if one wanted to cover the floor unobtrusively. Yes, there were the musicians. It was essential to provoke René into taking some action soon, preferably tonight. If he got frightened and lay low, he would have more chance of finding Véronique and retrieving her, and more chance of murdering another soldier. One could not stay all one's life on guard against assassins.

They were the usual dance band in the usual aged-in-the-wool musicians' performance evening dress, shirts with the frayed bits trimmed off, faded patches dyed with ink. Piano, drum, guitar, trombone, trumpet, clarinet. The saxophone player must be sick. And, yes, there was René Dubois, accordion laid aside for the moment, playing a not very good double bass accompaniment. He never had trusted strings.

Phryne danced Lin Chung closer and waited to be seen. The dance was ending. She was standing right in front of the man who had broken her heart and she found that it had quite healed. He was an ordinary man. Not very tall, his dark hair pepper-and-salt now, his face as brown as a walnut and almost as wrinkled. Not an attractive proposition.

Then he glanced up and saw Phryne. For a moment he was taken aback, then he scowled with such malignancy that Lin missed a step.

Phryne stared straight into his face and then blew him a kiss. The band started on the next dance, a waltz to 'Mignonette', and Phryne floated away.

'That ought to do it,' she said. Lin swung her around.

'That was him?'

'Yes,' said Phryne. She loved waltzing.

'And you just provoked him,' said Lin.

'Yes,' said Phryne.

'Ah,' said Lin.

When they danced past again at the start of the foxtrot 'Crying for the Moon', René wasn't there. Phryne appeared unperturbed. So Lin kept dancing.

It was past ten when Molly, who had been quietly lying on Madame Dubois' feet, raised her head, pricked her ears, and gave a small, sharp bark. Hugh waved and the girls went to the front door and the back, listening. Jane at the front heard nothing. Ruth at the back heard a faint scratching at the lock. She signalled to Hugh and returned to Madame Dubois, grabbing Molly by the collar and holding her mouth shut.

'It's him, isn't it?' asked Madame through a closed throat.

'Maybe,' said Ruth. 'But he won't get in.'

'If he does, Mademoiselle,' Madame Dubois appealed to Dot, 'and if for some reason you can't shoot him, then make sure you shoot me. I'm not going back to him.'

'I don't think I'll have to shoot anyone,' said Dot calmly.

The back door slammed open. Hugh reached, grabbed, and struck. There was a yelp and someone struggled out of his grip and scrambled away over the fence. Hugh closed the door again.

'Show's over,' he said, coming back inside and sucking his knuckles.

'You 'it 'im?' asked Madame Dubois, astonished.

'A juicy one,' replied Hugh. 'And he was off like a rabbit. He'll have a black eye tomorrow. Let go of Molly, Ruth. She'll know if he's still hanging around like a bad smell. And if so, I propose to go and punch his head again,' said Hugh comfortably. Madame Dubois could not follow all the words but she knew that tone of voice.

Molly, released, wuffed a little, smelt around the door, wagged her tail and came back into the dining room. There she collapsed onto Madame Dubois' feet again and fell asleep.

'Ah, quelle mignonne!' cried Madame Dubois, stroking Molly's silky black ears. Dot poured Hugh a congratulatory glass of beer. The enemy had been driven off. With a black eye. And Dot hadn't had to use that gun, which frightened the life out of her.

She poured herself a small sherry and Madame a glass of

that harsh red wine. The disturbance had not even elicited a query from the Butler and Tobias Sole conclave, which was still going on in the Butlers' sitting room. Phryne had ordered that they be left alone until they either came out of their own will or elected Daniel Mannix Pope.

The drawing lesson resumed. Madame Dubois was really very good. Dot wondered how Phryne was doing with her evening.

Phryne was sitting the next dance out. Lin Chung had procured her an ice and she was eating it with small neat licks of her red tongue in front of his fascinated gaze.

'Why did you provoke that man?' he asked quietly.

'He's just got time to try and get into my house,' she replied, putting the spoon back into the white glass dish. 'Thank you for the ice, Lin dear. He will be repelled from there by Dot and Hugh. He hasn't got time for another try, and that will make him furious.'

'How do you know he hasn't got time for another try?' asked Lin.

Phryne produced her dance card.

'Because he has to play 'Sam, the Accordion Man' in about ten minutes, and René never missed a cue in his life. It will take about five minutes to bicycle to my house—Madame says he still bicycles—and then he only has five minutes there before he has to cycle back. He had to give his borrowed car back to his landlord. Hugh could hold him off for five minutes with one hand tied behind his back and Dot has my gun. So he will be driven away and come back here, snarling and chewing his moustache and saying, "Curses, foiled again!" In French, of course.'

'Phryne,' ventured Lin Chung.

'Mmm?' She picked a fleck of petal—the decorations were shedding—from the smooth linen over her knee.

'Remind me never, never, to make you this angry.'

'I can't imagine how you could,' she smiled. 'But I'll remind you.'

Ten minutes later a dishevelled accordionist fingered his way through 'Sam, the Accordion Man' in double time, so that the dancing crowd hurried and stumbled. Phryne smiled into René's face. It was decorated with a very impressive red patch which would be a shiner tomorrow. Someone seemed to have rubbed leaves and twigs into his thinning hair and his suit was torn across the shoulder.

But he could still play the accordion like a master. Phryne danced away, presenting him with an infuriating view of her smooth white back. She could feel his eyes boring into it. Most gratifying.

She danced a circular waltz to 'The Song Has Ended' with Robinson, who was very sure on his feet, if a little pedestrian. 'Are you having an agreeable evening?' she asked into his ear.

'The wife's real pleased,' he said, not answering the question. 'She's danced every dance. When's supper?'

'This is the last waltz,' Phryne told him. 'Soon, the hoi polloi depart, the select few move into the supper room, you get to nibble dainty things in the company of our politicians and luminaries, and then you are allowed to go home. Not too long, Jack dear. You'll be home before you turn into a pumpkin.'

'What do you . . . oh, I see. Midnight. Good. There's Rosie,' he said. 'I'll go tell her.'

The dance ended. Phryne found herself near the musicians. A voice snarled, 'You! It is you, Phryne! What have you to do with Véronique? She is mine.'

'No, she's hers,' said Phryne. 'And look what happens when you try to get into my house. Give her up, René.'

'Never,' hissed the voice. He must be standing behind a pillar, Phryne thought. 'But you, are you not tired of your Chinese? Come back to me. You always loved me. I always loved you. Véronique was just a substitute.'

One thing you could say of René Dubois, he had the sort of cheek which would stagger nations. Phryne fanned herself with her hand.

'You're an assassin,' she said calmly. 'You're a thief. And oddly enough—I know you will find it hard to believe, René— I am completely and entirely uninterested in you. Goodbye,' she said, and walked away, calmly, through the crowd until she found Lin Chung talking to a large gentleman about silk.

'Hard to find a reliable supplier, now things in China are so bad,' the large gentleman was complaining. 'And the Indian just ain't the same.'

Lin gave him a card. 'I'm sure you will find that our silk is superior,' he said. 'And we are known for our reliability.'

'I'll call on you next week,' promised the large gentleman, searching all his pockets until he found his card. Lin accepted it with the suspicion of a bow.

'Supper,' said Phryne. 'I could eat a horse.'

Lin took her arm. 'You seem very pleased,' he observed.

'Call it relieved,' she answered, as the crowd began to stream out and the select few made their way to the supper room. 'I have just let go of a long-ingrained sorrow.'

'Ah,' said Lin.

'Do you always almost bow to new customers?' she asked curiously.

'They expect a Chinese to be exotic,' he said. 'But not too exotic. Too exotic is threatening. A sketch of a bow fits the bill.

Now, we have chicken vol-au-vents, little sausagey things and more ices. Let me fetch you an assortment,' he offered.

Phryne sat down next to Mrs Robinson, whose husband was on the same errand.

'Have you had a nice time, Miss Fisher?' asked Rosie, mopping her brow.

'Yes, indeed,' Phryne replied. 'I think the Mayor is trying to catch your eye,' she told Mrs Robinson, who fluttered off to talk to His Worship. He was an affable man and liked women to be substantial and womanly. Mrs Robinson's honest pleasure in the ball had tickled him.

Supper over, the select few went to the doors to find their cars. Robinson shook Phryne's hand and Mrs Robinson kissed her. It was like being kissed by a paeony. Goodbyes were being said. Finally, only Phryne and Lin stood at the top of the marble staircase.

They walked down into the hot darkness. The wind had dropped. Lin's car stood ready at the end of the path.

Then there were voices. Sharp statements, clipped off, meant to be heard only by the destined auditor. 'Here,' said one.

'Yes,' said another.

'Here,' a third voice.

'No, you don't,' a fourth voice.

Someone—at a dig in Abbeville, was it?—had told Phryne about primitive men and their method of hunting mammoths, which were too big and dangerous to hunt up close. They had herded the huge animals to the edge of a cliff and frightened them off. That was what the soldiers were doing to René Dubois.

As arranged, Phryne had stood in the light for long enough. René had seen her and had begun to stalk her, meaning to catch and kill when she reached the bushes next to the gate.

Now he was being driven like a beast. It was working. He fired a shot which chipped a piece off the Town Hall facade.

'Lin, we must get to your car,' said Phryne. 'And get out of their way.'

'Run?' he suggested.

'Run,' she agreed.

She hauled up the Egyptian gown and raced down the footpath in a flash of bare thighs, leaping past the astounded chauffeur and into the Silver Ghost. A shot pinged past. Lin dived in beside her, and yelled to the chauffeur to drive on. The car, which he had been warming all night, started without a sound and they were off before the next shot, which whistled past and broke the decorative ball off a fence. The chauffeur took the car around in a wide circle. Phryne needed to see what happened next.

'Six shots,' said Phryne. 'He has six shots in that gun. That was the third.'

'What are they going to do?' asked Lin, who did not like being shot at.

'I don't know,' said Phryne. 'But as soon as he runs out of ammunition, I wouldn't be René for a thousand pounds.'

Two more shots in quick succession. Then one which drew forth a cry of 'Bugger!' from the darkness.

'That's six,' said Phryne.

Then they saw him, a staggering, goaded creature, half insane with rage, his coat hanging in ribbons, his useless gun thrown down. Surrounded by harassers, he stood at bay in the middle of the empty, dark road.

Then a speeding car collected him, threw him high into the air and down again, and hammered and crushed all the life out of him. He lay on the road like a broken puppet, skull cracked, pouring blood. His attackers came out of the dark, eyes still alight with purpose, shouldering each other like hunting wolves.

'Into the car,' ordered Phryne. 'Wrap something round your arm, Mr Gavin. You don't want to bleed on the new upholstery, do you? I'll be back in a tick.'

She watched them climb into Lin Chung's car. She knelt next to the fallen man and felt for his heart. It was still. He would never torture anyone again.

She turned on her heel and walked away, for the last time, from René Dubois.

CHAPTER TWENTY

The morning after the Lord Mayor's Ball, Phryne was consulting with her lawyer about a missing Mildura will and certain action to be taken in the civil court against a crooked letting agent when a policeman was shown in.

The parlour showed no signs of the hasty, joyful, strange party it had hosted the night before. The beer glasses had been cleared away, the bottles discreetly housed in the yard, the ashtrays emptied, a bloody towel soaking in salt water, the bloody bandages burned. The farewells from Johnnie Bedlow, William Gavin, Thomas Guilfoyle and Bert and Cec had not remained on the air. Neither had Madame Dubois' cry of mixed relief and horror when she heard that her husband was definitely and totally dead, though the expression on Cec's face when Véronique had kissed his hand would linger with Phryne for some time.

The taxi which had slain René was in a repair shop belonging to Johnnie Bedlow, the mechanic. The girls were at church with Dot, who felt that she had a candle to light for a departing soul and a prayer to say for a man dead in a moment. She was also terribly relieved that she had not been required to shoot him. Madame Dubois had gone too, in one of Phryne's more subdued, veiled hats.

'Hello, Jack dear, up this early on a Sunday?' Phryne asked.

He laid her photograph on the table.

'Thought I'd better tell you,' he said carefully. 'We showed that picture about. No one was really sure. Could be him, possibly he was older, not one positive identification.'

'Oh,' said Phryne. 'That's a pity.'

'However, the man in the picture was found dead in Carlisle Street early this morning. Run down by a speeding car, looks like. No one saw anything. Day men been all round the houses, everyone was either asleep or out on the town.'

'I see,' said Phryne.

'Went to his house,' continued Robinson. 'Found that Madame had gone and left a note which mentions you,' he continued.

'Quite right. She's here. She's gone to church with Dot. I knew her in France, and when I met her again and she said that she wanted to leave her husband, I said she could stay with me. She was sitting in the dining room until quite late last night, giving drawing lessons to the girls. Your own constable could tell you that,' added Phryne without a touch of smugness. 'He was here visiting Dot.'

'While we were at the Lord Mayor's Ball,' said Robinson.

'Yes,' said Phryne.

They looked directly into each other's eyes. Jilly, the solicitor, was fascinated. It was like watching a duel.

'You wouldn't know anything about this death, Miss Fisher?' he asked.

'Do you really want to ask me that, Mr Robinson?'

The policeman looked away first. 'By God, you could out-stare a cat,' he said. 'Let us look at a theoretical case, then, Miss Fisher, if you please. Suppose that we had a murder by motor car which a policeman knew about and had no way of proving. What would you advise that policeman to do?'

'In purely theoretical terms, I would advise the policeman to consider that the dead man was also a murderer. That he killed two ex-soldiers, who are mourned even now. That the police whose task it was to take on the Crown's duty of revenge did not properly investigate these murders. That the friends of the dead men, perhaps, might have taken matters into their own hands, because they believe in Justice rather than Law, and Law had failed them.'

She held up a hand to still a protest.

'And the policeman might be comforted,' she added, 'by the thought that by the death of the deceased his misused, maltreated wife has been set free.'

'Yes, but . . .'

Phryne smiled on this discomforted officer of the law. 'Do you want to ask me any questions, Jack dear?'

Robinson gave up and accepted a cup of really strong tea from Mrs Butler. No great harm had been done, he thought. And if he knew soldiers, no one would have seen a thing and no one was going to answer any queries from any cops.

'No, I don't want to ask. Two things. Landlord's creating about the empty house, wants someone to remove the deceased's effects and pay the rest of the rent. Can you arrange that? And, when she's recovered a bit, can you ask Mrs Dubois to make arrangements for the funeral? We've got all we can off the body. Few flecks of paint—common black. The driver didn't stop and leave his card and there's thousands of vehicles painted with that sort of paint. Vans, cars . . .' he paused. 'Taxis.'

'I'll break the news gently,' promised Phryne. 'And let you know about the funeral as soon as I can.'

'Thanks,' said Robinson. He put down his empty cup. 'I've been asked for an extradition order for this René Dubois by the French police,' he added. 'They're going to be disappointed.'

'Possibly,' said Phryne.

She saw Robinson and Jilly out, refusing to answer any questions. Sunday was a good time for reflection. She reflected. Paris was hers again.

She had been sitting at a white iron table in the Jardin Luxembourg, waiting for her poulet reine and sipping the first glass of her very own bottle of champagne. She was rich, for the moment. Her father had paid her a generous commission on the small Renoir, 'Berthe in a hat', which she had seduced out of Dupont, the dealer. The sun dappled down through the leaves, spring breathed scents of water and moss, the returned ducks quacked in the cascade, and Phryne was possessed of a gentle, not entirely unpleasant melancholy that none of her friends had been at leisure to share her good fortune.

Then the waiter approached with a tall young man in a loose white shirt.

'If you would be so kind, mademoiselle,' he said. 'There are no more tables. Can this person be so fortunate as to share yours?'

'Certainly,' said Phryne, her curiosity awakening. 'And a glass of wine, if you would drink with me. I am celebrating,' she told the young man. He smiled.

'It is sad to celebrate alone,' he said. He raised the glass. 'My name is Jean Lafontaine,' he said. 'My father makes this wine. Mademoiselle has excellent taste. To what shall we drink?'

He had beautiful dark blue eyes and a soft red mouth and Phryne felt the stirrings of sexual interest, which she thought had departed forever along with René. This young man might prove to be just what she needed.

'To freedom,' she said, and drank down the wine.

And Jean had been a darling. Also, he had been rich. He had even allowed Phryne to drive his racing car. The Sapphics approved of Jean Lafontaine because he was both decorative and generous and also he wrote good poetry. He had even taken her to see Miss Stein, though Phryne had ended up in the kitchen talking to Alice and drinking raspberry eau-de-vie. Thus she had recovered from René, or so she had thought. Now she was free of him forever.

Mr Butler came in, bearing a silver salver with a cup of coffee on it.

'Thank you,' said Phryne. 'Your notice is running, Mr Butler. Are you still of the same mind?'

'Well, as it happens, no, Miss Fisher. A long conversation with that young man Mr Sole has opened my eyes to a lot of things. The stories he had to tell, miss! Curl your hair. No, if it's all the same, Miss Fisher, I would like ro rescind my notice and continue in your very respectable employment.'

'That is a load off my mind,' said Phryne, breaking into a grin. 'So you have no objections to Mr Lin?'

'None whatsoever, Miss Fisher.' His impassive face softened for a moment into an expression which was almost apologetic. 'And if I delivered myself of any opinions which you might have found objectionable, Miss Fisher, I unreservedly withdraw them.'

'Done and done,' said Phryne. 'But I feel a bit sorry for Tobias Sole. I did offer him the job.'

'That's all right, Miss Fisher. I rang a friend of mine who is leaving the gentlemen's club where Mrs Butler and I used to be employed and Mr Sole said that he would accept that position with pleasure. He likes, he said, a lot of variety, and he expressed the view that your house might be too staid for him.'

'But not for you?'

Mr Butler drew himself up to his full height. His watch chain gleamed before Phryne's eyes.

'I am very happy to be staying where I am, Miss Fisher.'

'Wonderful. Tell Mrs Butler that I am so pleased. A little bonus, I think, Mr Butler? On occasions when—like last night—the company is a little noisy and late?'

'That would be very acceptable, Miss Fisher. Thank you, Miss Fisher. Will that be all, Miss Fisher?'

'Thank you, Mr Butler,' said Phryne and leaned back luxuriously. Her household was back to normal.

Monday's mail bought a crudely drawn religious tract with 'Repent!' written on it in heavy red crayon. It was postmarked Kew. Phryne grinned. Julia had commenced her campaign.

Jacob Stein arrived, with notepad, magnifying glass and pen, to value Phryne's paintings. His father had indeed been pleased with him and when Papa saw what was on this inventory, the young man reflected, his eyes would drop out of his head. Five Picassos, *five*, and seven Sarcelles, a Sisley, a definite genuine Manet, a lovely Douanier Rousseau dog . . . Yes, Papa was going to be pleased, especially since the lady had been kind enough to say that she was going to sell the big Sarcelle

'Landscape with trains', and he would have the selling of it. Phryne heard him whistling under his breath as he worked. Well, that had made someone very happy.

On Tuesday she saw Madame Dubois through the process of identifying her deceased husband, interviewing an undertaker, interviewing René's bank to release some funds, and a small but tasteful funeral on Wednesday. She was not surprised to find, following the priest with hats firmly on heads, five burly men who watched until the coffin was lowered, stuffed a pound each into the surprised hands of the widow, and went away. The remaining soldiers wanted to make absolutely sure that René Dubois was gone.

By Friday Véronique was recovered enough to buy herself some clothes. Most of her own were not even good enough for the rag-bag. She bought bright colours, purple and sky blue and yellow. René's effects she gave away immediately, except for his accordion, which she gave to the only member of that dance band who had ever spoken a kind word to her. And the bank said that René was rich, and that as soon as certain documents were lodged, they would release the funds to the widow.

Jilly lodged the documents.

Phryne came home to find the widow reading tourist leaflets.

'I think I shall go here,' she said. Phryne looked over her shoulder at the brochure. Daylesford. The spa offered mud baths, mineral water baths, massage, cold water sprays, healthy food, music in the evenings and a tranquil atmosphere.

'Excellent idea,' she agreed.

'Women who lose a husband often hurry themselves into another marriage,' said Madame Dubois. 'I do not wish to do this. I need to find out who I am and what I want, and I need to do it alone. It is unlikely that I shall find another French speaker so I shall have my thoughts to myself. I will return in two weeks,' she said. Then she wiped away a tear.

'What is it?' asked Phryne.

'That is the first thing I have decided for myself since I met René,' she said proudly.

Phryne patted her shoulder. Progress indeed.

A week later, the papers reported that Miss Elizabeth Chambers, daughter of the noted racing identity Hector Chambers, would be marrying Mr Anatole Bertrand of Café Anatole on Saturday fortnight. One percipient fashion writer noted that Miss Chambers had been indisposed since she returned from Paris but now seemed to be very well and very pleased at her approaching union.

So Daddy had paid up, Phryne thought. Elizabeth had come home a model of dutiful girlhood and Daddy's matrimonial plans were on track. Or so he thought. The mail brought her a wedding invitation from Lin Chung, a wedding invitation from Elizabeth Chambers, an invitation to a private dinner the night before at the café, and another treatise on sin, badly printed and abominably spelt, with the unusual message 'It's working!' in the same red crayon.

Phryne smiled privately and got on with her correspondence. Mr Edward Dunne wrote weekly, sending her a list of people who needed a little anonymous help. She picked one and sent a pound. It assuaged her social conscience.

Two weeks later she had a thank you letter from someone called Maisie. It was postmarked Mildura. The will had been found. Maisie was going to be an orange farmer. She was presently looking for partners for a scheme to send frozen orange juice to Europe, and the Railways Commissioner, Mr Clapp of Eat More Fruit fame, was interested.

Thus to the Café Anatole, on a warm night. There was a 'closed' sign on the door but it opened at Phryne's knock. Phryne was ushered in by a resplendent Jean-Jacques, or possibly Jean-Paul, dressed in evening costume and a large smile. A long table was laid for the party. There sat all of the Anatole family, even M'sieur himself. He jumped up and kissed Phryne on both cheeks.

'Madame, dearest Madame, do sit down and we will open the champagne.'

Jean-Paul eased the cork from a bottle wrapped in a white napkin and poured. Phryne tasted. It was superb. A mouthful of summer, yeasty, velvety. She had never tasted better champagne in her life. She said so.

'Pol Roger,' said M'sieur Anatole proudly. 'The '14. The best year of this century. You recall my family?' He introduced them all again. 'My cousin Henri, his wife Mary, my sister Berthe, my cousin Louis and his wife Janey, my nephews Jean-Jacques and Jean-Paul.'

'Of course,' said Phryne. 'Very pleasant to meet you all again.'

'This is my fiancée's friend, Julia,' said M'sieur Anatole.

Julia was still dressed in her rusty black zealot's drag, but her face was alight with joy and she held up a pair of keys.

'House?' asked Phryne.

'House,' she replied. 'You were right. They hated all that public praying and all that bible reading. But they really cracked when I threatened to join the Salvation Army and bring my band members home for supper. Then father said I could do as I liked as long as I didn't bring shame upon them and I'm moving into my own house next week. And until then I am staying with Lizzie in case they change their minds. And Mr Chambers called around to see me. After half an hour's Epistle to the Corinthians he told my father the deal was off and stormed out. I don't think I'm going to get a Christmas card from him,' she said, without any visible regret.

'Probably not,' Phryne laughed. She looked around the table. There was a notable absentee.

'M'sieur, you invited me to dinner and I see no dinner,' she said archly. 'And where is my friend, Miss Chambers?'

'She's in the kitchen,' said Henri, grinning. 'With a poor deaf-mute boy and a tramp and all of them are cooking the dinner.'

'Interesting,' said Phryne.

Before long a stream of cold dishes issued from the kitchen, starting with a cold cucumber soup, hors d'oeuvres variés, and little tartelettes with a foie gras filling. Phryne was sure that she could taste truffles, though that seemed very unlikely in view of their cost and scarcity. On the other hand, she was drinking Pol Roger '14. Truffles they were and very tasty.

Finally the cook emerged from the kitchen to accompany her pièce de résistance, a whole salmon cooked in court-bouillon, in aspic, with potato salad and petits pois and a choice of three sauces; mousseline, hollandaise and mayonnaise, to eat with it.

Elizabeth was quivering with anxiety until everyone started to applaud, and then she bowed, took off her tall hat, and chuckled. The waiter put down the huge dish without making the jelly quiver. It wasn't until he lifted his head that Phryne recognised him.

'Mr Jenkins!' she cried, 'Oh, how very nice to see you.' Phryne had felt bad about allowing Mr Jenkins to return to the tyrant Chambers, but could not see that she could do anything about it.

'Miss Fisher,' said Mr Jenkins, not stammering. 'I never would have left on my own, you know,' he confided, sitting down next to Phryne. 'Miss Lizzie just took me along with her. Told her father she needed me and I was entering her new husband's employment. He didn't even yell. He just grunted and told me to go to hell. So I went,' said Mr Jenkins, a little dazed by his good fortune.

'Jean-Paul!' ordered M'sieur Anatole. 'Open the Romaneé Conti. The 1921.'

Glass in hand, M'sieur Anatole rose to make a speech. Phryne sipped. Another astounding wine. Elizabeth stood beside M'sieur Anatole and took his unoccupied hand. She was easy with him, Phryne noticed, easy and friendly. She had clearly overlooked the moustache.

'When I consider how sad and lonely I was a month ago I am amazed at the benevolence of le Bon Dieu, although le Bon Dieu had some help in bringing us to this desirable conclusion. Our kindness to our poor kitchen boy Sam has brought a great reward. A wife who knows how to cook, a new waiter who does not drop things,'—he looked at Jean-Paul and Jean-Paul looked right back and pouted attractively—'A rich dowry and her own self, a skilled and clever and loving girl, whom we hope will be very happy with us as we will be happy with her.'

Elizabeth blushed and both wives and Berthe smiled at her.

'A lot of this we owe to our redoubtable guest, Miss Fisher. A toast!' The guests stood up. Phryne sat where she was, full of delicate food, with a feast of saumon en aspic to come, appreciated and comfortable and very pleased with the world.

'To Miss Fisher!' they chorused, and everyone applauded.

Phryne raised her own glass to them, remembering feasts past and contemplating feasts in prospect, and proposed a toast of her own.

'To happy endings,' she offered.

Everyone drank.

BIBLIOGRAPHY

Baker, Michael L., *Our Three Selves*, Hamish Hamilton, London, 1985

Barnes, Djuna, *Nightwood*, Faber and Faber, London, 1936

Barnes, Djuna, *The Book of Repulsive Women*, Bern Boyle, New York, 1989

Carpenter, Humphrey, *Geniuses Together*, George Allen & Unwin, London, 1987

Chalon, Jean, *Portrait of a Seductress*, Crown, New York, 1979

Cooper, John Butler, *The History of St Kilda 1840–1930*, Vol. II, Printer's Prop Ltd, Melbourne, 1931

Escoffier, Auguste, translated by Vyvyan Holland, *Ma Cuisine*, Mandarin, London, 1965

Field, Andrew, *Djuna*, University of Texas, Austin, 1983

Flanner, Janet, *Paris Was Yesterday*, Harvest, New York, 1972

Haitana, Hayden, *Fine Cotton and Me*, Angus and Robertson, Sydney, 1986

Hemingway, Ernest, *A Moveable Feast*, Arrow Books, London, 1996

Hobhouse, Janet, *Everybody Who Was Anybody*, Weidenfeld, London, 1975

Jay, Karla, *The Amazon and the Page*, Indiana University Press, 1988

Livia, Anna (ed.), *A Perilous Advantage*, New Victoria Press, Vermont, 1992

Longmire, Anne, *St Kilda, The Show Goes On: The History of St Kilda*, Vol. III, Hudson, Melbourne, 1985

McAlmon, Robert and Kay Boyle, *Being Geniuses Together*, Hogarth, London, 1984

Mellow, James R., *Charmed Circle: Gertrude Stein and Company*, Avon Books, New York, 1974

Ormond, Richard, *Una Troubridge*, Jonathan Cape, London, 1984

Schenkar, Joan, *Truly Wilde*, Virago, London, 2000

Simon, Linda, *The Biography of Alice B. Toklas*, Peter Owen, London, 1978

Smith, Helen Zenna, *Not So Quiet . . . Stepdaughters of War*, Albert E. Marriott, London, 1930

Souhami, Diana, *Gertrude and Alice*, Pandora, London, 1991

Spanier, Sandra W., *Kay Boyle*, Paragon House, New York, 1988

Stein, Gertrude, *The Autobiography of Alice B. Toklas*, Modern Library, NU, 1980

Stewart, Samuel M., *Murder is Murder is Murder*, Alyson Publications, Boston, 1985

Vivien, Renee, translated by Foster, *A Woman Appeared to Me*, Naiad Press, New York, 1976

Vivien, Renee, translated by Potter and Kroger, *The Muse of the Violets*, Naiad Press, New York, 1977

Wickes, George, *The Amazon of Letters*, Popular Library, New York, 1978

Papers and council records kept by the Bayside Council; the *Lonely Planet Guide to Paris*, personal visits and interviews in Paris and Melbourne.

BV 9/17
KT 05/18.